"I HAVE TO GO SEE MELANIE," HE SAID QUIETLY.

"Obviously," Casey spat out. "I couldn't help overhearing you, Dennis. We *are* lying here in bed together."

"Look," he said. "I really don't see that I have to apologize for going to her. She got a note that sounds like the one Morgan got. And she's very upset about it."

"And that's the only reason you're going," Casey demanded.

"Of course," he answered innocently.

"Fine. Then I'll come with you."

"What?"

"If that's really why you're going, Dennis, then I don't see why I can't come along, too." She knew she had gone too far. If the roles were reversed, she would be acting just as Dennis was. But she couldn't stop herself. She was hurt. Then another thought struck her. Did he have to go because *he* was the one who had written the note, and he wanted to calm Melanie down so she wouldn't go to the police with the evidence?

She looked at him again. "Okay," she said. "It's settled. I'm coming along."

A CANDLELIGHT ECSTASY SUPREME ™

WHISPER
ON THE WIND

Nell Kincaid

A CANDLELIGHT ECSTASY SUPREME ™

Published by
Dell Publishing Co., Inc.
1 Dag Hammarskjold Plaza
New York, New York 10017

Dell ® TM 681510, Dell Publishing Co., Inc.
Candlelight Ecstasy Supreme is a trademark of
Dell Publishing Co., Inc.
Candlelight Ecstasy Romance®, 1,203,540, is a registered
trademark of Dell Publishing Co., Inc.

ISBN: 0-440-19519-5

Printed in the United States of America
First printing—October 1983

To Our Readers:

Candlelight Ecstasy is delighted to announce the start of a brand-new series—Ecstasy Supremes! Now you can enjoy a romance series unlike all the others—longer and more exciting, filled with more passion, adventure, and intrigue—the stories you've been waiting for.

In months to come we look forward to presenting books by many of your favorite authors and the very finest work from new authors of romantic fiction as well. As always, we are striving to present the unique, absorbing love stories that you enjoy most—the very best love has to offer.

Breathtaking and unforgettable, Ecstasy Supremes will follow in the great romantic tradition you've come to expect *only* from Candlelight Ecstasy.

Your suggestions and comments are always welcome. Please let us hear from you.

Sincerely,

The Editors
Candlelight Romances
1 Dag Hammarskjold Plaza
New York, New York 10017

CHAPTER ONE

"This week Steele finds out that Royce has botched up the new cosmetics campaign, Veronica confronts Sissy over her theft of the diamond necklace, and Kezia returns from Mexico with a secret new boyfriend."

Casey smiled and put the newspaper down. Every week the *National Midnight Sun,* the *World Globe,* and the *Inquiring Examiner* carried summaries of the immensely popular Thursday-night TV series "The Sinners." She wondered what the tabloids would pay her if they knew she would soon be investigating on the set of "The Sinners," masquerading as a new production assistant. She could just imagine the headlines: "Hit Show Plagued by Mysterious Jinx—Actors Terrified, Production Halted, Investigator Blames . . ." But that was where the fantasy, and the humor, ended. For what had been occurring on the set of "The Sinners" was serious business indeed.

Which was where Casey Fredericks came in. As a freelance investigator, she had been called in by McCann-Fields Productions to find out what she could about a series of mishaps that had recently occurred on the set. The latest—in which part of the set had collapsed on an actress, sending her to the hospital and forcing production to shut down for days—put all the previous strange goings-on in a new light. There was word of a jinx on the set, word too of sabotage. And Casey's job was to find out whether what had happened was odd chance or malevolent purposefulness.

Casey was looking forward to the assignment. In terms of setting if nothing else, the job would be much preferable to her usual work routine, much of which took place in musty old federal buildings downtown. The East Seventieth Street town house in which most of the scenes were shot was supposed to be spectacular, grand, old, and palatial. In addition, the production company had rented the entire penthouse and health-club facilities of the new highrise next door for additional sets. Pleasantly for the cast and crew, the health-club facilities were leased exclusively to McCann-Fields Productions for several hours each day, and Casey was looking forward to working some swimming into her schedule. She had put off joining a health club for months, partly because of the expense and partly out of pure laziness. Now there was no excuse.

Casey took a last sip of her coffee, sleepily glanced at the clock—5:30 A.M.—and left for the set, which was not too far downtown from her Upper West Side apartment but all the way across town.

Once she was outside, Casey felt a bit less hostile about the series' grueling production schedule. It was a beautiful morning, a time of day Casey rarely saw, and she was beginning to enjoy it as she walked down West End Avenue in search of a taxi. The early-summer sun cast its purple glow over the dark outlines of the city, and there was a certain freshness in the air as well, a salty cool breeze coming in off the Hudson River that lifted Casey's spirits.

She hailed a taxi, and soon she was riding through Central Park toward the landmark town house where she would have her crucial first meeting with Dennis Mattson, the director of the series.

Casey sighed. It wasn't a meeting she was looking forward to. Ever since she had met Felicia Oates and Don

Atchison, co-producers of "The Sinners," she had had an instinctive uneasiness whenever Dennis Mattson's name had come up. Casey had never heard of him before, not being a viewer of the top-rated show. But the moment Felicia Oates and Don Atchison had explained that Casey would be working for Mattson without Mattson knowing who she was, her feelings were of dread mixed with suspicion.

"Does that mean you suspect Mattson in the sabotage?" Casey had asked.

"We suspect no one in particular," Don Atchison had said. "And therefore, unfortunately, we suspect everyone."

"Speak for yourself," Ms. Oates had cut in. She turned to Casey as if Atchison weren't even in the room. "And *some* of us, Ms. Fredericks, don't subscribe to any sort of sabotage theory at all. I for one don't think it's the work of one man, one woman, or a group. The misfortunes we've been hit with happen in time to every production."

"But back to this Dennis Mattson," Atchison interrupted. "He's only one of a list. But let's just say he's close to the top of that list, Miss Fredericks."

"Casey, please," she said.

He smiled. He was attractive in an indirect, quiet way, in his early forties, with dark, gray-streaked hair and a smooth, low voice. "Casey, then," he said. "And first names all around."

"Okay," Casey said. "But you have a successful show. McCann-Fields has obviously made a lot of money from 'The Sinners.' And so, presumably, has Dennis Mattson. Why would he want to do anything to jeopardize the show? Surely his salary has gone up now that the show consistently places in the top ten every week."

Don sighed. "It has indeed," he said. "But it's no secret that Mattson isn't happy in his position. He's already tried to opt out of his contract, which is for the rest of the

9

season, and we've turned him down. We're holding him to the full-season commitment."

Casey frowned. "But if he's forced to do a show he's no longer interested in, won't that affect his directing?"

Felicia smiled. "That's where your lack of experience in show business comes through, Casey. You see, vanity—that age-old destroyer—comes in when enthusiasm wanes, rescuing even the poorest of productions from failure. Sometimes one reads a review in which it's said that one actor or another apparently decided that nothing could be done to save the play and let this hopelessness overtake his performance. But more often than not, Casey, it's the opposite, isn't it?—the valiant actor struggling his best to improve the otherwise-rotten lines through his shining performance—that sort of thing. And the same certainly holds true for directors. Dennis Mattson is vain if nothing else. And no matter how much he wants to work his way out of his contract, he's not going to ruin his directing in the process." She sighed. "However, Mattson is just one of many possibilities, Casey. It's your job to find out what's really going on." She glanced at Don. "And if you're like me, you'll conclude it's a series of coincidences and sloppy mistakes, nothing more."

Don's lips tightened. "We'll see," he said. "We'll see, Felicia."

Now Casey watched the gray streets come to life as the cab left the park and began cruising down Fifth Avenue. She wondered how plausibly she would be able to pull off the role of production assistant. She knew nothing about theater, television, cameras, scripts. She rarely even watched television—the long and inconvenient hours of her job saw to that. When she had first heard about the assignment on "The Sinners" a week ago, she had watched the show for the first time in her life. And she had found it almost shockingly silly, with conflicts and pleasures so much larger than life that the show was almost comic.

But enjoyment of the show wasn't, after all, her job. Her job was to blend in successfully with the staff of the show as a production assistant, to get to know as many people as well and as quickly as she could, and to find out who, if anybody, was responsible for trying to throw a wrench into the success of the show.

Her first five minutes were not promising. Casey got out of the cab, walked past some crew members toward the town house, and immediately tripped on a wire that was lying across the steps. She heard a shout behind her and turned just as a crew member caught a falling light.

The man—about Casey's age, very good-looking in a dark, mysterious kind of way—glared at Casey and let out a stream of curses that shook her usually unshakable self.

She looked back at the man as calmly as she could and said "I'm sorry" very clearly and very evenly. She wanted to say more—that the cord had barely been visible and should have been marked off or taped down in some way, that he had no business being so rude, a hundred angry words that burned in her thoughts.

But she caught herself and simply turned toward the door; for if she was going to err, it would be far better in terms of her mission if not her pride to err in the direction of being almost timid. No one, after all, would confide in her if she seemed to take offense easily.

She let herself in, opening the huge oak and brass-fixtured door, and she was immediately in another world, somewhere between that occupied by the characters in "The Sinners" and reality. The interior of the house was immediately recognizable from the show—its oak-paneled study on the left, the parquet-floored entrance chamber, the sitting room with Louis XIV furniture immediately to the right; and directly opposite the door, the magnificent, sweeping marble staircase that was a focal point of so many of the show's scenes. But all these familiar areas were now swarming with cast and crew members, each

11

going this way or that with clipboards, wardrobe, cups of coffee, makeup cases. And they all looked so intent on what they were doing and where they were going that Casey was loath to interrupt any of them. She would simply find Dennis Mattson herself.

At the agency Felicia and Don had shown Casey a picture of the director—a glossy press-release photo, very posed and very formal. Casey had been unsettled by it, for even though it was only a black-and-white picture, she had been able to tell that those deep dark eyes were a beautiful rich brown, that his dark hair was a luxuriant near-black. His features were handsome but saved from being too perfect by a somewhat too wide jaw and high, prominent cheekbones. Casey had always steered clear of men who were too good-looking; they were almost invariably self-centered, so in love with themselves that they had little left over for others. And though Mattson had perhaps been set off from this group by his slightly unusual looks, Casey felt nevertheless that he very definitely belonged in *any* group labeled "self-centered: stay away from this type."

With the publicity picture of Mattson somewhat unwelcomely clear in her mind, Casey set out to search for the man she would be assisting. Unnoticed by all, Casey swept through the foyer, past the marble staircase and off to the right, through enormous wooden sliding doors that opened on one of the most incredible rooms Casey had ever seen. It was apparently a study, with floor-to-ceiling shelves holding beautiful leather-bound books; dark leather furniture, burnished with age; a massive old fireplace; and a beautifully intricate Persian rug. And sitting in an enormous black leather chair was Dennis Mattson, facing Casey but seemingly unaware of her presence at the door.

He was reading, with thick, black-rimmed glasses that were partially obscured by a lock of dark hair, and his feet were up on a beautiful tapestried ottoman. He was obviously deep in concentration, with the cap end of a pen in his mouth and his lips absently pursed.

Yet when Casey took one step into the room, this man who had apparently been lost to the world said "Yes?"—not looking up from what he was reading but obviously impatient for a response.

"I'm Casey Fredericks," she said, swallowing her natural impulse to comment on his rudeness. She silently observed that this was the second time in not too many minutes that she had had to stifle her natural assertiveness; and no doubt this was the second of hundreds of times she could look forward to doing the same.

"Mm?" Mattson said absently, still reading.

"The new production assistant."

That got his attention. He looked up with angry swiftness, his brown eyes sharp as they looked at her with obvious disapproval. "Felicia Oates's niece," he said, equally disapprovingly.

Casey nodded, wishing she had insisted on pretending to be a friend rather than a relative. But Felicia had pointed out that, as a producer, she'd be much more likely to tolerate ineptness and inefficiency on the part of a relative than a friend, and she had indeed had a valid if somewhat unfriendly point.

"You don't look a bit like her," Mattson observed. Casey would have been tempted to take these words as a rather oblique compliment—Felicia Oates was, unfortunately, less than attractive—had it not been for Mattson's apparently perpetual hostile tone. The observation had, in fact, come out as an accusation rather than a compliment, and Casey unconsciously responded as such.

"She's my aunt by marriage, or ex-aunt by marriage, as a matter of fact," Casey said, remembering that Felicia had been divorced for years and wishing they had spent more time together on the story.

Mattson raised a brow. "I'm surprised at Felicia. She

13

has always maintained a very firm and very public stance against nepotism."

Casey shrugged. "The rule obviously applies to everyone but Felicia. That's usually the case, isn't it? I'm sure you issue certain strict and supposedly inviolable warnings to the cast and crew that you wouldn't think of following yourself."

She thought she saw the hint of a smile, but she couldn't be sure. And then what small humor had been lurking disappeared completely as he said, "So. I gather from what Felicia told me that this is your first foray into the wonderful world of show business."

"Yes."

"No acting in college? Nothing?"

She shook her head. "No. The theater just wasn't one of my interests."

He sighed. "Even that level of experience helps, you know. Well. Nothing we can do about that."

He studied her for a few moments with intense dark eyes that made her uncomfortably self-conscious. She had a hard shell, one that couldn't easily be cracked by a too-long stare or careful gaze. In her business, blushing and self-consciousness were out of the question. But under Dennis Mattson's scrutiny, Casey felt oddly as if she *were* there because she wanted to learn about TV production and, odder still, as if she wanted to impress him with her abilities and even, she realized moments later, with her looks.

"Do you know the series, at least?" he asked.

"Well, I just began watching last week, but I'm sure I can catch on to the story line quickly enough."

He blinked, his brown eyes once again hostile. "You're not interested in the theater. You're apparently uninterested in the show. Is there a particular reason—other than economics, which from your dress and your demeanor I doubt—that you've asked your aunt to give you this job?"

14

He hesitated, and when he spoke again, his voice was softer. "And forgive me if I sound less than enthusiastic, Miss Fredericks, but this production is already plagued with so many problems that what I *don't* need at this moment is an inexperienced p.a. It doesn't have anything to do with you."

Casey studied his eyes. She had liked his last words, in which a certain kindness had come through. And in his brown eyes she saw more of the same. But then she remembered his question: Why was she here? "I'm interested in what my aunt does. She has a good, healthy share in the company she works for, and she's doing quite well for herself with this and her other shows. There's certainly room in her organization and others like it for someone like me, and I thought—and she agreed—that I'd be much more useful if I actually knew what was going on in production rather than trying to start out by seeing names and costs and items on a ledger."

He nodded. "So this job is a stepping stone of sorts, then."

"Yes, in a way, though I don't expect to return to my aunt's office until I have more than just a bit of experience."

Mattson sighed, looking thoughtful. "Well then, you'll fit right in with the rest of the company, Miss Fredericks. I'm afraid that this company, unlike other productions I've been involved with, is filled with people who wish they were elsewhere."

"Really?" she asked. "I thought acting was one of those end-of-the-rainbow things people are always happy with."

"You're right there, but only to a point. Yes, it's true that if you go into a restaurant or an office or a store, perhaps half the employees dream of being discovered by 'Hollywood.' But television is a funny thing, Miss Fredericks. It's enormously lucrative, like a great money machine that changes the lives of everyone connected with it.

15

Acting or working in TV is tremendously profitable, unbeatable in terms of exposure, often rewarding in itself. But ask the cast and crew of 'The Sinners' whether they're happy, and I'll bet half of them—once waiters and waitresses and secretaries who would have died for a part in a commercial—half of them are unhappy in their work. God knows they wouldn't give it up, but they're not happy."

"But why?" Casey asked somewhat disingenuously. For she knew that Mattson himself was a member of that unhappy half. And she wanted to know the extent of that unhappiness.

"Oh, boredom, a desire to work with great material instead of nonsense, a number of other reasons that all sound equally naive and unrealistic but that are very, very important to some of us. And also, more and more of the cast and crew are nervous about what's known as the jinx on this production. Actors are a very superstitious group, you know."

Casey nodded. "Yes. And I've heard about the jinx." She paused. "So you're one of the unhappy ones, then? Not about the jinx—but what you were talking about before."

For a moment his brown eyes shone with pride—or pleasure. But then the spirit seemed to leave him as he shrugged and said, "Only at certain moments—few and far between."

She gazed into his eyes, searching for a clue that he was lying, for she knew he was. He was very definitely displeased with his place in the production, according to "Aunt" Felicia. Yet his dark brown eyes betrayed no sign of dishonesty.

Suddenly Casey was aware that she wasn't the only one studying. Once again he was taking her in from head to toe, slowly appraising her tall, slim form. Then, when his eyes met hers, it was with a sudden heat born of hostility,

16

of conflict, and Casey had the uncomfortable sense that Mattson was about to say something very unfriendly. For one burning moment his dark gaze fought with hers. Then he said, "I think we would fare better if you were honest with me, Casey."

Her stomach jumped. "Honest?" she asked as innocently as she could.

"When I told you how almost everyone tended to use 'The Sinners' as a stepping stone, I thought I was giving you a chance—a chance to explain your true interest in acting. But you've chosen instead to stick with your story about being interested in production. And I resent that dishonesty, Miss Fredericks. I've seen it a thousand times in just this form, and it doesn't work."

Mystified but relieved that Mattson hadn't come close to the truth, Casey looked at him levelly. "I really don't know what you're talking about. I promise you I have no interest in acting. If I did, I agree it would be logical to tell you about it. But I don't."

He swung his long legs down off the ottoman and stood up. "Oh, come now," he said, standing within inches of her as his dark eyes challenged hers. "Do you really expect me to believe that?" He put his hands on her shoulders and turned her around. "Look at yourself," he said, nodding toward a mirror that was on the wall in front of them. "Just look at yourself," he said again, this time more softly.

Casey looked at a tall young woman whose appearance had always seemed uninteresting if not plain, at her athletic frame, oval face, blue eyes. She knew she was pretty in a certain way. Her eyes were wide set and clear, her hair a glossy dark auburn, her body lean and strong. But she had always wanted to be heart-stoppingly pretty, the kind of woman who turned heads the minute she walked into a room.

"You're a director's dream," he said softly, and she was

suddenly aware of his nearness, of his warm breath against her ear, his cheek brushing against her hair for a moment, the grip of his hands burning into her shoulders. "You can be anything you want," he murmured, "take any part that's written. You have one of those faces that's just—beautiful," he said quietly. "Beautiful and always changing. You could go far, you know."

She smiled, loving what he had said but also wise enough to know he had probably used those same words a thousand times before. "That's a pretty classic line," she said. "And coming from a successful director, it's even more classic." She looked into the dark eyes reflected in the mirror. "Am I supposed to swoon, as they used to say, or promise I'll do anything if you'll help me?"

For a moment his eyes darkened. "You're really not interested, are you?"

She shook her head and smiled and turned to him, loosening herself from his grasp. She was pleased when she looked into those dark eyes and felt her heart skip, pleased that she wasn't actually looking for any help from him, for she melted under his gaze, lost her strength under his touch. And now that she would be working with him, observing him, even suspecting him of perhaps sabotaging his own production, she would have to remind herself as often as possible that those deep brown eyes were not for her.

CHAPTER TWO

Dennis watched as Casey turned from him and walked across the room. He was intrigued by the smooth way she moved, with a fluid grace and ease that suggested a core of inner strength. She was dressed almost plainly, in navy-blue cotton slacks and a blue-and-white-striped man-tailored shirt, but Dennis found that this simplicity only added to the mystery, for his attention was drawn to what was underneath those plain clothes. He could well imagine the smooth thighs, the sleek hips, the narrow waist, the soft, gentle breasts beneath the blouse.

She was standing at his desk, which was piled high with papers and scripts. "This is all yours?" she asked.

He smiled. She had brought him out of thoughts that had been moving in a very pleasurable but very distracting direction.

"Yes," he said. "I've taken over this room as an office—which, unfortunately, there seems to be a dire need for. Sometimes it feels as if we do more meeting than shooting on this damn set."

Her blue eyes flickered with interest. "With Felicia and Don?"

"Just Felicia," he said. "Don Atchison has been making himself pretty scarce lately. He runs for the hills every time she has a blow-up, and lately that's been every day."

"Then I gather it's Felicia you have a problem with," she said, levelly resting her gaze on him.

19

Dennis returned the gaze, holding it long and hard as an awareness passed between them. She shifted then, and he almost smiled. She was so self-assured, with an obvious inner vitality and power. But when she was reached, touched, questioned, she reacted, and her self-assurance was replaced by something close to shyness—vulnerability, he guessed. He suspected that if Casey were aware of this tendency and knew that it was apparent to others, she would be annoyed. And he realized he had forgotten what she said. "I'm sorry," he said, smiling. "What was it that you just asked me?"

Her answering smile told him she had regained her confidence. "I asked," she said, her blue eyes sparkling, "whether Felicia was the one you are having a problem with."

He blinked. Had he discussed a problem with her? Hard to say, really, when all he was concentrating on was Casey and her blue eyes, her soft skin, her low, calm voice. "If you mean problems with the production . . ." he began.

"Well, yes," she said. "Whatever reason it is that you said you had so many meetings. I was just wondering whether my aunt was the problem."

He smiled a crooked and provocative smile. "Thinking of trying to patch things up through family pressure? It's a nice thought, but it can't be done."

"Why is that?" Casey asked.

He paused, aware suddenly that the pleasure and ease of talking with Casey Fredericks was making him forget himself. They had work to do, and in any case a diatribe on the many reasons he and her aunt didn't get along wasn't necessarily a terrific idea. "Actually," he said, looking at his watch, "we can save that for another time. If we don't get started soon, the show will be more impossible than it already is."

And together they left the study and joined the cast and crew assembled in the hallway.

20

From the moment they were out in the hall, Casey noticed that Dennis had an effect wherever he went. Glances shifted and took him in, voices faltered and slowed. Casey even saw one young woman hesitate for so long in the act of lighting her cigarette that she burned her finger.

And then Casey was distracted from Dennis when she saw an old friend from college, Ted Conroy. She smiled and waved, marveling that he had changed hardly at all in eight years. He still had the same good looks—straight blond hair, sharp blue eyes, a look of intensity that had grown stronger in the years that had passed.

"I'm surprised to see *you* here," Ted said after kissing her hello. "What are you doing? You used to avoid theater productions and people like the plague."

Casey smiled. "Well, I've changed my mind. I'm the new production assistant, actually—p.a., I guess I should say."

Ted grimaced. "First job in the business?"

"Yes. Why the look?"

"Well, you couldn't have picked a more difficult man to work with if you had tried, or a more difficult production."

"I've heard," she said. "Felicia Oates is my aunt, actually, so I already know things aren't going too well."

Ted and Casey both glanced in Dennis's direction. He was talking to a striking young woman Casey recognized from the show, but she couldn't remember what the woman's role was. She was tall and thin, with ash blond hair that was permed in loose curls that cascaded to nearly shoulder length in a calculatedly casual fashion. She was extremely pretty, with soft blue eyes, pale, freckled skin, and a full mouth, but her obvious and evidently constant awareness of this fact diminished her prettiness. Every movement, hesitation, blink of the eyes appeared self-conscious and therefore false. Casey wondered how Dennis managed to squeeze a good performance out of her.

"For instance, look at that," Ted said. "Melanie Kincannon. She plays Kezia Edwards. A starring role, right? Something an actress would kill for, right? But she's so demanding and so cranky and so just plain contrary that she slows this damn production down every day of the week. If she were some great actress from the Actors Studio or something decent, then maybe—*maybe*—I'd think she had a right to try to inject her taste and experience into this show. But she has neither taste nor experience nor ability."

At that moment Melanie widened her eyes, puckered her lips into a pout, and reached out and gently touched Dennis's cheek.

Even from the distance Casey was standing from Dennis, she could see his jaw tighten.

"It looks as if Melanie's interests lie beyond the scope of the production," Casey observed.

"Of course," Ted answered. "And she's a strange one, actually, because she's made her interest in Mattson so obvious that everyone from Mattson himself on down to the assistant grip—yours truly—knows about it. Which would be okay if Mattson were interested, but he's not, so it's just a pain in the butt and embarrassing for everybody."

Casey wanted to know more, but she knew she should be polite and ask Ted about himself. "An assistant grip," she said. "That means working with sets and props, right? That isn't all that predictable a postcollege move either, Ted."

He shrugged. "It pays well and it keeps me involved in the business, and actually I just sold a script to McCann-Fields."

"For this show?"

He nodded, and she could see that he was trying to hide

22

a smile, trying to pretend he wasn't happy about it. Casey remembered that he had always harbored a deep streak of martyrdom, seeming to feel that the world had cheated him. Now that he had been proved wrong, he apparently wasn't altogether certain he wanted to admit it.

"That's fantastic!" she said. "That's amazing. Is that the first script you've ever sold?"

"Mm."

"Well, Ted, knowing you, I can't really expect you to jump up and down for joy, but I'd think you'd be a *little* excited, anyway."

He sighed. "I was when it happened, which was months ago. But since then this whole show has gotten so chaotic and the scripts have become so mangled that I'm not so sure I'm even that glad anymore. Except for the money, of course. But really, Casey, this show . . ." His voice trailed off.

At that moment Felicia came sailing in and within seconds had pulled Dennis away from Melanie, who was left standing there looking even more petulantly pouty.

"Wonderful," Ted muttered, then blanched as he evidently remembered that Casey was related to Felicia. "Sorry," he said. "I forgot."

She shook her head. "Don't apologize. I know as well as anyone how difficult Felicia can be."

At that moment Bruce Pinkney, the assistant director, called everyone to attention. He was short, skinny, and whiny, and Casey took an immediate and active dislike to his voice. It was the kind that made you drag your feet when summoned, made you tune out when being spoken to, made you smile inwardly when being berated.

And she saw that the others shared her feelings. The reaction to Pinkney's pathetically timid request was slow and not without resentment. People came forward unwillingly, still pointedly talking and joking among themselves.

When Dennis took over, however, people speeded up

23

considerably. The scene to be shot was a simple one—a family gathering in the magnificent living room of Steele Edwards, patriarch of the Edwards clan and king of a vast cosmetics empire, and his lovely wife Veronica.

There was to be a family squabble, naturally. Melanie Kincannon, playing Kezia Edwards, daughter-in-law of Veronica and Steele, was supposed to be in the middle of something close to a breakdown—close, but not too close. At that moment, though, Dennis was warning Melanie that she was acting as if she had already been committed. "You're supposed to be frazzled, Melanie," he chided, "not certifiable. Now come on."

"She's already certifiable," muttered a low voice from behind Casey, and she turned to see Ted, working with some silver flatware that had come separated from the rest of its set.

"Why is her character 'frazzled,' as they say?" Casey whispered, bending down to where Ted was.

"Her sister-in-law, Lauren Edwards, is trying to drive her crazy—get rid of her and make sure there's no heir to the Edwards fortune in the form of a bouncing baby boy or girl. You see, Kezia is married to Royce Edwards, formerly long-lost and illegitimate son, now found and adopted son of Veronica and Steele. Royce is a failure at most everything he does, but—"

Casey laughed and waved a hand. "Forget it," she said. "I'm already lost. I'll have to pick up what I can while I watch. Thanks anyway."

Casey did learn more about the show's characters that day, and about the many duties that a production assistant performed—everything from making coffee to getting props to collating scripts to answering the phone. Unfortunately she hadn't advanced a fraction of an inch in terms of her investigation.

Not that she had expected to wrap up the case in a single day. Part of the reason she was on the set was to determine if there *was* any sabotage. And even if she discovered there was, she was not necessarily going to be investigating in any way other than what was her specialty —blending in, getting to know people's motivations and conflicts. Contrary to images put forth by television and movies, ninety percent of the job of investigating anything consisted of talking with people and doing background research on their lives if necessary. The obtaining of hard evidence—fingerprints, notes, and the like—was rare.

At the end of the day, as the crew were dismantling parts of the set and rolling cameras away, Casey caught Dennis looking at her from across the room. He was listening to Bruce but looking at her, and the moment his eyes met hers, the impact sent a tremor through her whole body.

She hadn't been able to forget the magnetic draw of his body to hers, hadn't been able to push away the memory of his nearness, his touch, his voice. When she had watched him over the course of the day—frowning with annoyance at Melanie, angrily dismissing an innocent question asked by the wardrobe mistress—she had tried to forget, for she hadn't liked him at those moments.

But now, as his dark brown eyes bore into hers, she was brought back to that moment he had told her she was beautiful, when his cheek had brushed against her hair, when his warm hands had held her tight, when his voice had been soft and incredibly warm.

Dennis said a few more words to Bruce, still looking at Casey, and then began walking toward her, coming to her without taking his gaze from hers. When he reached her and said, "Would you mind staying late for a bit?" she said, "Yes. No, I mean no, I wouldn't mind," and they laughed together. *So much for composure,* she thought, and as he walked away his thoughts were traveling a similar path. Yes, she was very self-assured; yes, she had an obvious inner strength and confidence. But when he

25

had captured her with his eyes, the strength in her gaze had come not from resistance, not from a strength that set Casey apart, but from an answering desire that knew chemistry couldn't be ignored.

Casey was aware only of her forthcoming meeting with Dennis and nothing else as she finished the last of her duties and said good-bye to the last of the cast. And then, out of the corner of her eye, she saw Dennis striding across the room toward her. He was smiling as if aware of a very pleasurable secret he wasn't about to share, and his smile reached her in a deep way that surprised her: she almost felt that it related to her.

"Do you want to get yourself some coffee before we go back into the study?" he asked. Beneath his words, his gaze, the smooth pull of his voice, there was a suggestion that nothing was really more important than being alone together; he was just going through the motions of being polite.

It was a heady feeling for Casey, something that reminded her of long, long ago, when she had had a wild crush on her boss and had lingered day after day and evening after evening in the hope that he would look at her just as Dennis was looking at her now. She had always felt there was something sexy about a situation in which two people spent the day concentrating on the job at hand but found their thoughts invaded by fantasy, dreams, hopes. The indirectness was what she liked, the idea that a man and woman could spend hours talking about something that neither was really giving any thought to, that all that subliminal communication could go on more freely, even, than in a dating situation. Since there was often no real thought of actually having an affair, the flirting and near-seduction could go further and further, uninhibited by thoughts of commitment or anything else.

Casey glanced at Dennis as she walked with him through the parquet-floored foyer into the study. In terms

26

of her theory about office relationships, Dennis was perfect in every way: extremely attractive to her but a definite "no," both because of his position and the fact that there were a lot of things she didn't like about him. She could stay close to him but remain emotionally uninvolved, while he could perhaps be a considerable help to her work on the case. Plus flirting was always fun.

Dennis motioned for Casey to sit in an easy chair facing the fireplace, and he sat down in the chair next to hers. "Well," he said, looking at her with a sparkle in his dark brown eyes. "What did you think of the day's shooting?"

She smiled. "I thought it was pretty exciting. I had thought I was inured to all that 'magic of show business' nonsense. But it *is* exciting to see the cameras roll out and the actors get their lines right and a scene come out perfectly."

He looked at her carefully. "Why did you think you were inured? What sort of work have you been involved with before?"

"Oh, this and that," she said vaguely, with a mysterious smile she hoped would cover the lie. "I've worked in dozens of fields, mostly at an assistant's or secretarial level. But all the jobs I've had have been here in the city, and I grew up here, and I guess I thought that I had seen all there is to see. Also, hearing my aunt talk all these years made me pretty much used to the idea of stars and all that. With all her complaining about all the shows she's been involved with over the years, I got a certain jaundiced view of the whole business."

He sighed. "I'm certain that none of the shows you ever heard about could have possibly rivaled 'The Sinners' in sheer . . ." His voice trailed off, and in his dark brown eyes a certain light—a light of inspiration, perhaps—seemed to die. "Oh, never mind," he said tiredly.

"No, please," she urged. "Go on."

He looked at her with a velvety gaze that seemed to

draw her closer to him. "I don't think you really want to hear the complaints of someone who's probably going through—what do they call it?—burn-out, I guess."

"I do," she said, and then hesitated. "Maybe you think I'll go running off to Felicia, though—"

He waved a dismissing hand. "I couldn't care less about that. Everyone knows how I feel about the damn show. Especially Felicia, whom I have the majority of my arguments with anyway."

"But what about, exactly?" Casey asked.

"Everything," he answered quickly. "From the no-talent Melanie Kincannon to the story line to the characterizations, the show is a bore and a pain to work on."

"Then why are you here?"

He raised a brow. "Good question. When I was hired I was totally committed to doing the series. The idea of a two-season contract didn't bother me in the least. I had directed one show, they had liked it, and they signed me up right away."

"So what went wrong?" she asked.

"What went wrong was that I went for the money and the steadiness of the work without really thinking it through." He sighed. "There's just some damn thing about show business—I don't care if you're an actor or a singer or a director—no matter how successful you become, you always remember that time when you were desperate for work; you remember those early days when it was feast or famine; and the steadiness of something like this has a very deep gut appeal." He paused. "Aside from the fact that I had wanted to do something different." He sighed. "But I had a blind spot back then. I didn't see it, and my agent didn't see it."

She frowned. "What was it?"

"That a lot of the projects I had sent out feelers on would be starting just as I was in the middle of my commitment. The contract is for twenty-six shows, Casey, but between the two seasons you're not left with enough time to do anything else." He sighed, and Casey could see that the tension within was nearly overwhelming him. "We're into the fifth week of the second half of my twenty-six-week commitment, and just yesterday I had to turn down tentatively the chance to work on something I'd really enjoy—a feature film—a major motion picture, as they say—of one of my favorite books of all time."

"What book?" Casey asked.

The Final Season," he answered quietly.

She said nothing. She had read *The Final Season.* It was a hard-hitting, action-packed story that took place during the Korean War, and it made sense that Dennis would like it. But had he also liked the underlying message of the book, which was a deeply romantic one—one that Casey herself had found a little hard to swallow?

She looked at him and said, "I can understand how you might like the adventurous aspects of the book. But I found the romantic angle a little sappy for my taste."

A corner of his mouth turned up in amusement. "Sappy? Why?"

She couldn't help smiling under his curious gaze. "Oh, the ending more than anything else, really. Here are two couples, separated not only by thousands of miles but by every obstacle on the face of the earth, and in the end we're supposed to believe that they're all going to live happily ever after. Not to mention the fact that the main character, Jason, will never change, especially now that he's going off to Hollywood to become a director. That's hardly going to make him turn faithful, which was his main problem to begin with."

"Ah. Then directors can't be true-blue husbands of the old-fashioned variety?" Dennis asked mockingly.

"Oh, sometimes, maybe, but for someone with as much of a roving eye as Jason had, I wouldn't exactly expect that kind of position to tame him." She paused, acutely conscious of the fact that Dennis was looking at her with a mixture of pleasure and curiosity.

"You don't think true love conquers all?" he asked, still baiting her.

"I—" Suddenly she couldn't think of a casual response, something appropriate to the manner in which the question had been asked.

And when Dennis saw her hesitate, his eyes grew serious. "I seem to have hit a nerve without realizing it," he said quietly.

She shook her head. "No, no," she said quickly. "I was just thinking of something else." She could tell he knew she was lying, but that was better than delving into the truth. Yes, she had had an unhappy marriage, a marriage that had shattered her trust and her love. But she wasn't fragile; she was tough and realistic, and she hated the idea that people thought she had been wounded in some way— an invariable reaction when she told the story of her ex-husband and their unhappy marriage. But she hadn't been wounded. She had simply learned, had seen the light. The only problem now was in the telling of the story. She had yet to find the right way.

Dennis apparently wasn't ready to let her denial stand, in any case. "Then you *do* believe love conquers all?" he asked, a glimmer of a smile playing on his tempting lips.

"Oh, sure, why not? Anything is possible, right?"

He laughed. "I see I'm in the presence of a true cynic. Which fits in with your chosen life-style, I suppose— jumping from job to job and field to field, perhaps man to man as well."

It was her turn to laugh. "Hardly," she said.

"Ah, then there's one special one?"

She swallowed, her mouth suddenly dry. "No, actually there's no one at the moment."

He nodded, looking at her speculatively.

The gaze held. Somehow, though Casey wasn't aware

of the shift until it had already occurred, the look was suddenly heated, intensely personal, very arousing. In a matter of moments Casey was warmed by the flush of desire, by the growing awareness that her desire was matched by his. In that one glance, in those long moments, thoughts were shared in a smoldering silence: thoughts of imagined lovemaking, embraces that were hungry and quick or slow and deeply pleasurable, whispered words of husky encouragement and fulfillment.

Suddenly Dennis looked up, past Casey, and his expression turned cold. "Yes, Melanie," he said, and Casey turned around just as Melanie came sailing into the room and past her to where Dennis sat.

Casey noticed that she was still wearing her "Kezia" clothes, and her makeup, though less exaggerated, was in the style she wore on the show. That was certainly her prerogative, Casey felt, except that she had spent half the morning complaining that she was being hounded on the street by fans. As far as Casey could see, it was no wonder: she was Kezia to a T.

"We've got to talk," she said loudly, sitting down on the ottoman with her back almost completely to Casey.

Dennis looked at his watch and then at Melanie with annoyance. "We're trying to finish something up. What is it?"

"I'm not ready to do the scene tomorrow—not the way it appears in the revisions, anyway."

Dennis raised a brow. "I see. What is it that you propose to do?"

Melanie ignored the sarcasm. "Change it, obviously."

He gave a sarcastic smile. "I see. And how do you propose to do that?"

Melanie proceeded to go into a diatribe of complaints that were not really suggestions at all but merely things she felt were wrong with Kezia's lines. Casey was fascinated. Melanie had obviously given the matter a great deal of thought, but it was equally obvious that her comments were thoroughly self-serving, based not on any interest in the quality of the show but on the number of lines her character could handle. Casey wondered how Melanie could possibly think her motives were anything other than transparent.

Yet when Melanie was through and Dennis began to speak, Casey was amazed at how he managed to sift through the barrage of complaints and find a few issues that could be dealt with reasonably and seemingly in Melanie's favor.

Melanie appeared to consider Dennis's remarks unwillingly at first, but Dennis managed to coax her smoothly and expertly, and in the end she seemed satisfied.

Almost as an afterthought she turned to Casey. "What do you think of Kezia's character?" she demanded.

"Well, she's very interesting," Casey said. "Very—" For a moment she looked past Melanie. Dennis winked. "Very strong. Certainly a focal point of the show."

Melanie paused as if testing the words to see if they had been spoken truthfully. "Really?" she finally said. "You really think so? I mean, you're not just saying that, right?"

"No, no, of course not," Casey said, not altogether truthfully. In fact she had seen the show only once, and what she had seen of Kezia's part today was, unfortunately, contaminated in her mind by her feelings about Melanie.

"Oh. Well. That's nice," Melanie said and turned back, apparently mollified, to Dennis.

He wrapped the meeting up nicely, once again strengthening the illusion that she had somehow won. He was so convincing that even Casey, to whom the whole conversation had seemed obvious, was beginning to believe the charade herself.

But the illusion was shattered the moment Melanie left.

Dennis jumped up and strode across the room, swearing under his breath.

Casey turned and watched as he roughly shoved a beautiful wooden panel of the wall inward. A large section of paneling swiveled, just as Casey had seen in countless movies, to reveal a magnificent bar.

"Drink?" he asked without turning around.

"Sure. I'll have some red wine if there is any," she said, and watched as he prepared the drinks—Scotch on the rocks for himself, wine for her. His movements were rough, impatient, brusque, and Casey could feel the tension emanating from him even at that distance.

"One thing you should get used to," he said as he walked back toward her with the drinks, "is that economy is not a word used by McCann-Fields Productions. At least not used correctly. You thought there might not be red wine," he said, handing her a glass. He smiled. "If you knew the vast quantities of everything in this house, the amount of money spent on every aspect of this production, you wouldn't have asked such a question."

"Is that so terrible?" she asked. "I would think that as a director, you would welcome all of this—really luxurious surroundings, an apparently limitless budget—it's a far cry from shooting an eight-millimeter short on the city streets, which is what most of my friends who studied filmmaking at New York University had to do."

He shook his head with impatience. "Obviously it's nice to have a high budget. But if you're producing crap, Casey, it isn't much consolation. It's almost a mockery." He took a large, hasty sip of his Scotch and set the glass down loudly on the table. "Sometimes it just makes me so damn angry," he said, his low voice husky and barely controlled. "You mentioned film students at NYU. Do you know that I would rather be teaching those kids than doing this? The salary is nothing compared to what I'm getting, but honestly, Casey, I feel as if I'm losing my

33

mind, my taste, my perspective, and whatever talent I once had working on this show." He paused, and when he spoke again his voice was heavy with irony. "And you know what? I actually find myself hoping 'The Sinners' will sin themselves into oblivion; part of me is actually disappointed when the Nielsens come in and we're so close to the top." He laughed humorlessly. "It's like being trapped in some luxury resort when your true love is to be living in a hut in the mountains. I want out no matter what it costs."

She took a sip of her wine and then looked at him carefully. "Oh, you don't really mean that," she said quietly.

He sighed. "Maybe not. I suppose that if I really didn't care what it cost, I would just walk out on my contract. And obviously I haven't done that."

He took another sip of his Scotch and drained it. The cold of the ice against his lips was jarring, and he suddenly felt as if he had been rambling, speaking with a bitterness he didn't want to reveal. He set the glass down and looked into Casey's eyes. Damnit, they were so pretty. Even though he knew what he was going to say, her eyes distracted him, made him forget everything but Casey's beauty. And he had to meet his agent in less than an hour.

"Is something wrong?" Casey asked suddenly, interrupting his thoughts.

"No, no. I was just thinking: it's getting pretty late. I had hoped we could talk about the show a bit. I wanted to hear what you thought of the changes we made today, since you're the newest person on the set at this point. But you don't even really know the show, do you?"

She shook her head. "Only what I learned today, which seemed pretty confusing."

He smiled and stood. "Maybe this will help. Follow me."

She followed him over to the desk, in a corner now

darkened by the lateness of the hour. Dennis was almost a shadow, a dark silhouette moving against a gray background, but even in the darkness Casey sensed a power and strength and masculinity that reached her in a deeply primitive and arousing way.

"It's here somewhere," he said, pushing aside stacks of papers and scripts.

"What are you looking for?" she asked.

"Our bible."

"What?"

He looked at her and smiled, his eyes catching the light from the street just outside the bay windows. "That's what the story line is called, Casey—it's that plus character sketches, all the scripts from the show's beginning, everything a writer or director or actor needs to know about the show. I thought it might help you."

He went back to searching, and a few moments later he pulled out a large, black-bound sheaf of papers. "Here," he said, setting it on the edge of the desk. "This will tell you more than you ever wanted to know about the tangled and often ill fated lives of Kezia, Royce, and Lauren Edwards."

He paused, and when he spoke again his voice was soft, like a velvet touch that made Casey's heart quicken. "I'm sure a young woman like you has little interest in whether Kezia can resist her latest boyfriend or whether she really loves Royce," he murmured, his gaze capturing hers. "But you know, sometimes things that sound awfully silly can be quite true. For instance, if I were to read that Royce had met a young woman at the office—someone he just had to take in his arms, someone he had to kiss or he would forever be thinking of her blue eyes and her soft, soft mouth—I would probably write in the script 'Damn silly' or something along those lines. Or if Steele met someone he didn't want to become involved with—his life is complicated enough at the moment—and he then took

35

her in his arms and kissed her, I would say, 'What happened here? He's decided on one course of action and he's doing the exact opposite.'" He paused, letting his eyes travel over her face. By the pale light from across the room, she could see his breath catch and then quicken. "I've been aware of you every moment of the day," he said softly, and Casey's heart skipped at his words. She had seen it, felt it, been aware of it because it had been true of her as well. "Of your eyes," he murmured, "of your voice, of your every movement."

Imperceptibly he had come closer, and now his face was inches from hers, illuminated beautifully by the outside light. His eyes were like deep dark amber, his jaw strong, his mouth decisive yet soft at the same moment, and she could feel the heat of desire emanating from his every inch. She was trapped in sudden need—his and hers both —and the silence felt heavy, ripe, as if anything could be said and anything could happen.

And when he said, so softly she almost missed it, "Casey," and put his warm hands at the curve of her waist, her eyes closed under the weight of pleasure and she lifted her head as his lips came down over hers.

A small cry of wonder mixed with need escaped from deep in her throat, and she let her hands find the silken luxury of his hair and the strong breadth of his shoulders. She felt a heat and dampness under the cloth of his shirt, could sense the strength and power beneath her fingers, and she had a quick, flashing image of what it would feel like to touch the smooth skin beneath his shirt, to feel it slide against her tingling breasts as together they moved on a path of spiraling pleasure.

His lips were gentle and warm, and when they parted hers, she felt another cry escape as she gave herself up to the delicious urgency of the kiss. She was flooded with pleasure and moaned as the tip of his tongue touched hers, as she let her body melt into his arms. In his touch, as his

36

hands roved over her back and then tantalizingly splayed over her hips and buttocks, she felt a deep suggestion of pleasure and skill and hunger and tenderness, of a need and appreciation she hadn't felt in a long, long time. Here was a man who clearly wanted her, whose desire she could feel from his fingertips to the warmth and hardness of his thighs pressing against her own, and she warmed in the heat of his obvious pleasure, urged him on in the simmering embrace.

He pulled back then, tearing his mouth from hers in a movement that left her dizzy, and he gazed into her eyes, his own stormy with pleasure and enjoyment. "I want you," he murmured, catching his breath and smiling. "My God, what you've done to me in seconds!"

She laughed. "You're not the only one."

He smiled and shook his head. "Casey," he said softly. "I knew from the moment I saw you."

She was still catching her breath, and she said nothing. *Oh, that kiss,* she thought. It had been so long—literally years since she had felt a touch that came close to being as tender, since she had felt a man's desire answered so clearly by her body and soul. Never—never had she been so swept along and away by a kiss—a mere kiss!

But it had been an interlude—brief, incredibly pleasurable, perfect because it had been so fleeting. "Well," she said, smiling lazily.

His fingers at her waist tightened, sending a ripple of warm pleasure through her. The rush of need made her lose her voice for a few moments, and he looked at her in mild challenge as she said nothing.

Then he smiled. "I think I can see a protest coming," he said dryly. "Yes, I can see it now, galloping over the hillside and coming straight for me."

She laughed. "I've never had quite that image."

"But—" he supplied.

"But yes, I suppose a protest is inevitable."

"Why?" he asked.

"It's very, very simple," she said, pulling away from his grasp and walking over to the bay window. When she turned to look at him, she was expecting to see challenge in his eyes; but she saw only tenderness. "I have absolutely no interest in getting involved with anyone at the moment. I know that's a very standard line, often offered just to hear the other person's protest, but I happen to mean it."

"I see," he said quietly.

At that moment and in that light he looked so magnificent—tanned, dark cheekbones, full mouth, eyes as if lit from within—and so full of feeling that she felt like taking it all back, pretending she hadn't said what she had.

"Well," he said. "You obviously aren't interested in standing by as I try to change your mind, so . . ." He turned away, reached across the desk, and flicked on the light. Suddenly the room was awash with brightness, the mood dissipated like mist in the sunlight.

He picked up the bible of the show and handed it to Casey. "I'll see you tomorrow," he said, and though a few moments later she said good night to him, she had his scent and the memory of his incredibly arousing touch in her mind long after she left.

When Casey got off the bus and walked up Ninetieth Street to West End Avenue, the street suddenly looked dingy and rundown. Casey liked where she lived; the neighborhood had a character and spirit that seemed to be absent on the Upper East Side. And since she spent most of her working time either downtown in grimy court-houses or traveling there and back by the subway, she usually considered the neighborhood just fine. But now, even in the darkness, it stood in stark and unfavorable contrast to East Seventieth Street, site of the town house. Garbage bags were piled up by the curb, cascading onto the sidewalk; rock music was blasting into the street from someone's apartment; a woman was yelling at her husband and he was yelling back.

Home. The apartment wasn't even Casey's. Her roommate's name was on the lease, and Casey paid what seemed like a king's ransom for a bedroom and half of the living room, kitchen, and bathroom. It had served her nicely these past six months, but now as she walked through the lobby with its chained-down chairs and tables, made her way up in the elevator with its broken buttons and flickering overhead light, and walked down the narrow tile-floored hallway filled with old cooking smells and pulsating disco music, she wondered why and how she had been oblivious to it all for so long. Yes, the apartment and the surrounding neighborhood had character—but exactly what character she wasn't sure.

When she let herself into the apartment, her roommate, Tamara, was talking on the wall phone in the kitchen. She gave a perfunctory wave to Casey and turned away, and Casey walked down the long, narrow hallway to her bedroom, thinking wistfully of the day she had spent at the town house. It had been a whole new world for her, from the furnishings to the people. And of course Dennis Mattson had been a new and unknown quantity as well.

All of which was just fine, except that she had begun the day feeling that her life was exactly as she wanted it. And now she wasn't certain this was true at all.

CHAPTER THREE

The next day, when Casey left for the town house, she was
filled with pleasurable anticipation. She had spent the evening reading the scripts of the show's first four episodes
and she had enjoyed them, but what she had enjoyed more
was thinking about the kiss she had shared with Dennis.

It had been rapturous, free of conflict until the last
moments—pure physical pleasure made up of desire and
fulfillment without thoughts, cares, or worries. As such it
had been the opposite of all her past experiences, and it
was wonderful to fantasize about and remember. She
didn't need Dennis; she didn't want him except in fantasy;
she didn't intend to have him. And so she could luxuriate
in the memory of his hands pressing the flesh of her hips,
his warm lips parting her own, the intensity of his need
filling her with flushed longing. He wanted her—on a
physical level, anyway—and because she was so sure her
answer would always be no, she felt the heady pleasure of
power as she contemplated Dennis's desire.

It had been a long time since Casey had been on top in
a relationship, since she had been the one who was in more
control than the other person. Long ago she had learned
that relationships were never equal: there was always one
who pulled the strings more than the other, one who
dominated in barely perceptible ways. Casey didn't know
if this was true of everybody or just of herself. But she
knew it had always been the case in every romantic rela-

tionship she had ever had, and that she, unfortunately, was often on the bottom.

The last time it had happened, she had decided that was it: she had had enough, it was over, and she would never let it happen again. Now she could smile—almost—at the memory. T. Mark Breckton III, whom she called Mark, had been so full of himself and of his own importance—a young stockbroker at one of the best Wall Street brokerage firms, oldest scion of one of the best Boston families, graduate of the best of the Ivy League M.B.A. programs. She had been in one of the lowest periods of her life, having just separated from her husband, Steve. She had been miserable after the breakup—lonely, rejected, certain she was destined to be alone forever. And she was feeling negative about her appearance as well. In the years she had been with Steve, she had gradually stopped paying attention to how she looked, gradually stopped wearing anything but blue jeans or whatever very plain clothes she needed for work. After the breakup she had decided to change in every way she could: the way she looked—with a new haircut, new makeup, new clothes; where she lived —she moved uptown, into an apartment with Tamara, a college friend; her attitude about dating—and this, unfortunately, was why she had met Mark.

She and Tamara had embarked on the program together. Neither one was going out with anyone, and each wanted to try a new approach—to be casual, less judgmental, and more willing to take advantage of all that New York City supposedly had to offer. Though they both knew they hated singles bars, they plunged into the scene anyway, figuring perhaps things had changed over the years. But nothing was any different. The bits of conversation they overheard—"I've never done this before, but—" "Do you come here often?" and even the ancient "What sign are you?" were the same. Tamara and Casey immediately gave up this self-inflicted punishment. There was no reason, they decided, to be so obsessive about trying to meet men; in many ways their lives were happier and easier without them.

But they were both on the lookout nonetheless. By tacit agreement they brought each other to all the parties they were invited to, and they did go out to more bars and restaurants than before. On the Upper West Side, bars were less overtly singles-oriented than on the East Side, and Tamara and Casey eventually both began meeting a variety of men.

One of these men was Mark, whom Casey had met in the classic fashion of eyeing each other across the crowded room. He had seemed brash and overly self-confident at first, but Casey felt it was an act. And later on, as she began to date him, she found she had been right. Mark was living up to an image he felt he had to have: a "bar" image that was all self-confidence and arrogance. But underneath he was fun to be with and caring, and he seemed wonderful. She had met him in a way she hadn't thought could ever bring any good—in a bar—but she was happy, and they went out together for months.

Casey didn't realize what was happening, though, until it was too late. She had been desperate for a relationship after her breakup with Steve, and when Mark began to take her out, she was so pleased that she had let her natural wariness and vigilance diminish: she slipped beneath the force of his personality as a person can slip under the wheels of an oncoming train. By the time it had happened, it was too late to change. Suddenly Mark was the one in charge. He controlled the relationship in a way that angered Casey but left her powerless as well. And at the same time he grew more and more distant. She didn't know what the problem was and couldn't fix something she didn't understand. And then one night he told her: he was seeing another woman. He had been seeing her for weeks. He wanted out.

His words were like a slap in the face, doubly stinging because they were so reminiscent of Steve, because they were so unexpected yet so obvious. Why hadn't she realized before? All the signs were there, all the symptoms.

Casey threw him out of the apartment. They hadn't been living together, but he had been spending much of his time there—perversely, Casey felt. She never spoke to him again. There were no favorite books to return, no borrowed records, not even a sweater or pair of pantyhose she had to retrieve from his apartment. There was no sign they had ever been together, in her apartment or his. And Casey realized that nothing else could have been true. The relationship had been surface only; what had seemed deep had existed only in Casey's mind. Now that it was over, there were no loose ends or frayed edges or ragged emotions. It was a clean break because there had been nothing to begin with.

Casey vowed that she wouldn't walk away from that period of her life without learning something from it. Mark had hurt her, as Steve had, and she owed it to herself to at least reap some benefit. And she decided right then and there that she would never, ever be stepped on again. She had been blind to the truth because she had been caught up in having a relationship for a relationship's sake; she had embarked with Tamara on a quest that was poorly thought out; and when she found Mark her relief had masked and bound all her other perceptions.

It would never happen again; of this she was sure. And so she could enjoy the attentions of Dennis perhaps even more than she would naturally, for she knew that she held the reins this time. And because she wasn't going to let it go any further, she could enjoy Dennis's appreciation of her even more.

When she arrived on the set, everyone was, as yesterday, running around as if the world were coming to an end. Dennis was in the foyer arguing with Felicia, Melanie

43

was preening in the doorway of the sitting room, and Morgan Ford, the actor who played her husband, Royce, on the show, was admiring her, apparently unnoticed, from a distance.

Dennis looked wonderful—even better than Casey had imagined him the night before. He was wearing a light blue short-sleeved cotton knit shirt, open at the collar and beautifully emphasizing his strong, tanned neck and thick, sun-darkened forearms. His jeans fit well without looking cheaply tight, limning the strong lines of his thighs and narrow hips in a way that was hard not to stare at.

Casey felt a tap on her shoulder and turned to see Ted Conroy standing there. He looked tired—not at all the bright young writer she had seen yesterday—with big, dark circles under his eyes and a grayish cast to his fair skin.

"You look exhausted," Casey observed.

He gave an uncaring shrug. "Yeah, I stayed up pretty late—four thirty, I guess."

"Writing?"

He laughed humorlessly. "I wish," he said. "I thought I'd write, but I ended up staring at the blank page in my typewriter for four hours."

"Oh, no. Why don't you just give up when you're feeling that way?"

"I don't think you understand," he said roughly. "You have to make sacrifices in order to get anywhere. At least that's the way I feel about my writing. And that means selling to someone you know will mangle it, that sort of thing."

"You mean to get the writing credit?"

He shrugged. "The credit, the experience, the money. There's a lot to be said for writing a show that millions of people will watch in one evening."

"I can imagine," Casey said. "And anyway, I really don't see what everyone is complaining about. I've heard

44

only negative things about this show since yesterday, but last night I took home a bunch of scripts and story lines and I couldn't put them down—I must have read till two in the morning."

The almost-hidden smile appeared. "You liked them, then?"

"Yes, a lot, although I don't know what's going on in terms of today's shooting. The scripts I'm reading took place a year or so ago."

"All right, look, this is all you need to know," he said with a spark of humor in his eyes. "The show centers around the Edwards family. There's Steele Edwards, silver-haired patriarch of the family, who years ago founded the great Edwards cosmetics empire, now a worldwide, multibillion-dollar corporation. There's his wife, Veronica, who's true blue and always supportive of him. Viewers have complained because some say she's *too* supportive—she looks the other way whenever Steele has an affair. But that's the kind of controversy that's good for the ratings."

Casey smiled. "Yes, what I read last night seemed pretty controversial. Steele was involved in a very romantic correspondence with a woman in Arizona, and he just hopped a plane to see her."

Ted smiled enigmatically. "That woman is about to tell Steele he's the father of an illegitimate son he never knew he had. A week later she dies in a freak accident, and Steele Edwards adopts the young man, Royce, as his own son." Ted gestured over at Morgan Ford, who was talking with Melanie Kincannon. Melanie looked only marginally interested in what Morgan was saying, and Casey noticed that within the space of a few moments Melanie had looked over at Dennis several times.

"Anyway," Ted continued, "the entrance of this new young man into the family doesn't sit at all well with Lauren Edwards, Steele and Veronica's daughter. Lauren had always planned to take over the Edwards empire upon

Steele's retirement, and all of a sudden she has a sibling—and a man, no less—to contend with. And no sooner does she digest this news than the second blow falls: Royce is going to marry. And worse yet, he's going to marry a young, flighty, *poor* cabaret singer/dancer/actress type from California. Lauren rather accurately sees Kezia as a gold digger, someone who's more interested in dear brother Royce's money than his charms." Ted smiled. "Are you with me so far?"

Casey smiled. "Basically, yes, although it seems to me that in a year the hostilities in the script have really grown."

Ted nodded. "Absolutely. In the past few weeks Lauren has been frightened that Kezia is pregnant. If Kezia has a baby, it will threaten Lauren's position in terms of inheritances and the cosmetics empire even further, so she's actually been trying to hurt Kezia, both physically and emotionally. And Kezia doesn't know whether there's something really going wrong—whether there's someone trying to hurt her—or if she's just imagining it. Either way, it's very unpleasant. Obviously."

Odd, Casey thought, *in certain ways the circumstances of the script fit the circumstances on the set.* Things were going wrong, and no one knew whether these things were occurring because of chance or design. "Doesn't that remind you of the show?" Casey asked suddenly.

Ted blinked. "What do you mean?"

"Well, it's the same sort of mystery, isn't it? According to what I've heard just from being here for a day—plus from my aunt, I suppose—there are people on this set who think there's some sort of subversive person running around creating havoc for the show. Then there are others who think there's a jinx, almost a curse on the show. And in the script Kezia doesn't know if she's going crazy or someone's after her."

"Which is hardly the same thing," came a dry voice

46

from off to Casey's side, and she turned to see Dennis standing not three feet away with a clipboard in one hand and a cup of coffee in the other.

For a moment his eyes rested on Casey's in a look she couldn't begin to read. Then his gaze slid angrily to Ted. "There are some props over there that need work," he said brusquely. "You'd do well to take care of them now."

"Right," Ted said, and after a glance at Casey he turned and went over to a table where several trays of costume jewelry needed sorting.

Casey looked into Dennis's eyes; she had taken such pleasure in the memory of yesterday's kiss, spent so much time fantasizing about it. Yet before her stood a man who was all anger and impatience. When he spoke, his voice was ungiving and rigid. "You really ought to check in with me or Felicia when you arrive," he said, his words edged with annoyance. "I'd rather not have to search you out."

"All right," she said evenly. "I will from now on. But when I came in you were talking with Felicia in what looked like a pretty heated exchange, and then to the lighting man, and I really didn't think I should interrupt."

He raised a brow. "That's all very admirable, but for the moment this is a studio, not an etiquette school. Please just stick to doing your job, Casey, which means finding out what your duties are as soon as you arrive."

"Fine," she flared. "I will. You asked and I said yes. There's really no reason to be angry."

His eyes darkened. "We have a show to do, Casey, and you'll soon find out that this production isn't exactly what you'd call easy going. I get angry at almost everyone on this set at least once a day. I also happen to be very fond of most of them—but this is the way I work, whether people like it or not."

She looked at him and slowly shook her head. "If that's true, it's awfully silly," she said. When she saw the flash of anger in his deep brown eyes, she realized she had

47

spoken more forcefully than she might have on a "real" job. For a moment she felt the natural apprehension that comes from saying something you wish you hadn't to a boss. But then she realized she could enjoy the freedom; indeed, she could enjoy this freedom as she had enjoyed her flirtation of the night before. Nothing that happened on the set of "The Sinners" or with anyone connected with it would ever affect her life. She went on with pleasure: "Do you really think you're making the cast and crew comfortable? As I understand it—and as you told me—this production is riddled with problems. Don't you think you might be adding to them?"

"Look," he said flatly, "that's hardly for you to worry about. Just—just go and see what Felicia needs, please, and come back to me when you're finished."

"Fine. I will." She turned on her heel and stalked off.

Dennis sighed and watched as she angrily made her way out of the room. God, what spirit. And what beautiful, beautiful form that spirit took when it was fired to anger. Casey Fredericks moved with the energy and force of rolling fire inside. She had strength and courage, a core of goodwill that allowed her to say what she really felt about his treatment of people on the set without fear of what he would say or do in return. With someone else he would have thought that at least part of her courage came from her secure position in the production. As a relative of the producer, there wasn't much chance of her being fired. But this didn't seem to be true of Casey at all. She was angry and she had said so.

And damnit, she had every right to be angry. He had treated her like a servant—which was unpleasant enough in itself, but after last night, unforgivable.

It was the damn production's fault, unfortunately. Plus no sleep, no cigarettes (eight days now), no relationship that was worth a damn. Then along comes a woman who's attractive, smart, sure of herself, sexy—and she catches him at his worst.

At that moment Melanie whined, "Morgan, stop it!" and Dennis turned just as Melanie was petulantly crossing her arms.

Dennis turned away, got a cigarette and light from a nearby cameraman, and walked out of the room.

Half an hour later Casey watched as Dennis angrily paced, a forgotten cigarette butt nearly burning his fingers and his voice ragged with anger.

They were all in what was known as the music room—a definite understatement as far as Casey was concerned. Over the years various owners of the town house had gradually changed the basement of the house into a recreation area geared to different interests, and McCann-Fields had recently added further changes for the enjoyment of Kezia Edwards, the young chanteuse played by Melanie. Now, in addition to a pool room, game room, and music room, what had once been a simple cellar boasted a stage complete with microphones, video cameras, and monitors for Kezia to use in rehearsing her cabaret numbers.

According to the day's schedule, Melanie was supposed to perform in two scenes in the music room—one in which she sang a song for Royce at the piano and one in which she rehearsed for an upcoming cabaret date. The song she sang for Royce was a love song, one she wrote while she was having her latest affair out at Lake Tahoe. Royce wasn't supposed to know about the affair or the circumstances under which the song was written, and he, in his innocence, was to be touched by the song and its words, words he thought were meant for him. And Kezia was supposed to waver and hesitate, torn between feelings of guilt and affection for Royce versus her infatuation with the subject of the song. In addition, she was supposed to be feeling fragile because of what Lauren had been doing to her.

The problem was that Melanie was apparently incapable of showing anything other than one single overwhelming emotion at a time. Dennis had run through the scene with her and Morgan five times now, and each time, as Melanie looked at Morgan while she was singing, the effect was totally unambiguous—she seemed either completely in love with him or consumed with guilt. At first, when the run-through had begun, Casey had felt Dennis was being too rough on Melanie, that he was ruining her performance rather than helping her. But she could see now why he was so deeply annoyed. Melanie just couldn't get the scene right and showed no sign that she ever would, and the subtlety was crucial to the success of the scene.

Dennis ground out a cigarette and glared daggers at Melanie. "All right." He jumped off the high stool he had been sitting on and strode over to where Melanie sat at the piano. "That's it. I've had enough. We'll come back to this, Melanie, after lunch. Do you think you *might* be able to try 'I'll Always Be Yours' and make it work? Kezia's only motivation is going to be the same as yours—to sing as well as she can for a cabaret debut she's making in a week. I really don't think that should be too difficult."

Melanie raised her head and gave him a dark look that only partially masked the hurt underneath. "All right," she said hollowly, her voice small and insecure. "I think that makes sense, Dennis, since you know that the more you yell at me, the worse I get. I really don't know how you expect me to do this scene." Her lip began to quiver as she stood up, letting thick curls of blond hair fall over her eyes.

She turned to the wall for a moment—whether wiping away genuine tears or merely pausing for effect Casey couldn't tell—and then she looked up at Dennis with defiance. "Well. We might as well begin. Luckily for both of us, nothing you say can affect my singing when it's a cappella." And she stepped up onto the lacquered stage, took the standing mike in her hands, and narrowed her eyes at Dennis. "So no matter how much you want me to look bad, Dennis Mattson, it can't work when I'm singing."

She tapped the mike, called "It's not on" to one of the crew members behind her, and then leaped into the air with a yell, hurtling back against an amplifier and crashing to the floor.

For one split second there was stunned silence. Casey had thought for a moment that Melanie's movements had been part of an act. Apparently the others had thought so too or were too astounded to move.

Then everyone swung into action—Casey, Dennis, everyone who could fit rushed to Melanie's side. She lay unmoving on her back, with her legs and arms spread, her mouth open, and her eyes completely closed.

Dennis kneeled over her and put his head against her chest. "She's breathing," he said.

A communal sigh of relief was let out, and Casey watched as Dennis gently brushed a blond curl back from Melanie's face.

"Don't move her," someone called out anxiously, and Dennis nodded.

"I know, I know. I just wanted to . . ." His voice trailed off, and Casey was surprised by the tenderness in his tone.

"Unplug that mike," someone else called to Ted, who was standing above the crowd that was kneeling around Melanie.

"What? Oh, okay," Ted said, and immediately two other crew members rose to look at the mike.

Out of the corner of her eye Casey watched and listened as the three men took apart the microphone. She heard Ted say, "Looks okay to me," and then Sam, the burliest of the three, objected. "What do you call that?" he asked. "Look at that wire!"

It was at that moment that Melanie opened her eyes. "Ohhh," she said with a sigh, looking up at Dennis.

"Don't move," he said softly, gently caressing her cheek. "Just stay quiet."

Melanie frowned, creasing her brow and pouting in confusion. "What—oh, God," she said.

"What is it?" Dennis asked.

"Everything," she moaned. "I feel as if I was just run over by a truck. Ugh. I have to—"

She strained to get up, but Dennis put a hand out and said, "Wait. Let's see if it's even safe for you to move, Melanie. Can you wiggle your toes?"

Her eyes traveled toward her feet and then her hands as Dennis asked her to move her fingers. "All right," he said. "If you feel comfortable, then." And he gently helped her to sit up. When she was sitting, Dennis rested a hand on her shoulder, gently supporting her weight. "Now tell us what happened," he said softly. "And just relax. An ambulance is on its way."

Melanie shook her head. "Oh, I'm so dizzy. And nauseous. It was horrible," she murmured. "I just—I grabbed the mike and it was off—it was dead—and then I *said* it was dead, or something, and all of a sudden there was just this awful, awful shock, like a surge of electricity going through my whole body."

"Shh," Dennis said, covering one of her hands with his. "It's all right," he said. "We'll have it all checked out, top to bottom. Now just rest," he said quietly. "And you really should lie down."

"Mm," she said drowsily. "That's . . . all I can face."

Dennis helped her down, and then he looked over his shoulder. "What'd you boys find?" he called out.

"Can't tell," Sam said. "Could be tampering, could be a simple screw-up. Wires're crossed because one's come

52

loose. With all the knocking around this equipment's gotten, it's hard to tell."

"Great," Dennis muttered. He looked at Melanie with the same surprising tenderness he had shown before. "Well, whatever it is, Melanie, you can be sure it won't happen again. And we'll just shoot around you until you're better."

She tried to shake her head. "Uh-uh. I'm not going to hold up the show. That's ridiculous. It's just—" But her lower lip began to tremble, her pitch had risen an octave, and she was obviously about to cry. She shook her head again and covered her eyes with her hands. "Oh, God," she murmured shakily. "It was just the worst, worst feeling, like missing death by a fraction of an inch."

"I know," Dennis said soothingly. "I know."

And he comforted her, oblivious to everyone still gathered around, until the ambulance attendants and Felicia came rushing in.

"Darling Melanie!" Felicia cried. "Don't move! Don't move a muscle. These men are taking you to a hospital, and they'll make everything all right. Don't worry about a thing, honey. Our insurance will take care of anything that's gone wrong."

As Felicia spoke, Melanie's eyes widened, and Casey could see that Felicia was accomplishing nothing but making Melanie twice as scared as she had been. "I don't want to go to the hospital," Melanie said, looking suddenly like a terrified young girl. She tried to sit up, propping herself on her elbows. "I feel fine," she said. "And I don't want to go," she murmured, looking desperately at Dennis. "I'm terrified of hospitals. My sister had a horrible experience in one. I can't—"

"It's all right," Dennis said. "You have to go because we want to make sure everything is perfect, Melanie."

"Oh, please," she said. "Please take me home instead, Dennis."

He looked at Melanie for a long moment and then turned to Felicia.

"Absolutely not," Felicia said. "There's no choice here, Melanie, and I'm sorry about that, but those are the conditions of *your* contract. There's been an accident on the set involving you, and we are required to do just what we're doing."

Dennis looked questioningly at Felicia. "Is that true?"

"Of course it's true," she snapped. "It's all very well for you to be so generous with your time and sympathy, Dennis, but we do have certain rules. Now if you'll let these men take Melanie as they're supposed to, perhaps we can get on with getting her to the hospital and getting whatever help she needs."

Dennis rose and stood aside as the two ambulance attendants slid Melanie onto a stretcher. Then he leaned down and looked tenderly into her eyes. "I'm sorry," he said quietly. "It—it will be all right."

Melanie bit her lip and smiled just as tears finally sprang forth. "Thanks," she said, half-crying and half-laughing. "Thanks, Dennis."

As Melanie was being carried away by the ambulance attendants, Felicia announced that she was going with them and abruptly left without saying a word to anyone else.

After Felicia was gone, Dennis vaulted up to the stage and picked up the offending microphone, which the sound technicians were still examining. "Show me what you're talking about," he said, looking from one man to the other.

As Casey watched Dennis talking with the men, and as she heard more and more questions about what had happened, she wondered: was the accident the result of sabotage? Or had it been simply an unfortunate accident, a coincidence? The technicians seemed divided. One said he had seen the same thing happen before, when no one could have possibly touched or tampered with the mike. One said he thought it had been done on purpose. Why *this* mike, when all the others were fine? And another thought it was a jinx, a pox of bad luck that had been put on the production.

Casey was amazed to hear this last remark from a man as big and strong as a bulldozer. He wouldn't have struck her as the superstitious type, but he sounded genuinely nervous. She looked around for Ted, wondering what his opinion was, but she couldn't find him; he had apparently slipped out at some point in all the confusion.

Damn. Confusion was an understatement! On the set nothing was as it seemed: accidents were incomprehensible, perhaps chance and perhaps purposeful; people had odd and unexpected, uncharacteristic views and opinions; and most confusing of all, Dennis was an enigma, at one moment angry and razor cruel, at the next tender and caring. He obviously disliked Melanie Kincannon, both personally and professionally. Yet when she had been hurt, he had acted as if his only concern in the world were her comfort and happiness and sense of calm.

The rest of the afternoon was taken up with shooting scenes that didn't involve Melanie, which was difficult because that week's show was one of Melanie's biggest in terms of the number of lines she had, but possible nonetheless.

Dennis seemed more relaxed. He announced that they'd do the best they could and would shoot overtime this week, and with Melanie gone, shooting indeed went more smoothly.

But Casey hardly paid any attention to the actors' performances; the talk between takes was much more intriguing.

Was it too much of a coincidence, everyone wondered, that what happened to Melanie was exactly what was supposed to happen to Kezia in the script? Lauren Edwards was supposed to tamper with the mike and cause a near-fatal shock to her sister-in-law. Thankfully the accident hadn't been that serious, but *it had happened*. Why? everyone asked. And how?

"You can't forget what happened to Stacy," Morgan said emotionally. "She's still in the hospital. Now Melanie's there. What does it mean?"

"It doesn't necessarily mean a thing," Dennis said. "These things do happen, painful as they are."

"But how do we know there's not someone actually trying to hurt the cast of this show?" Morgan cried. "To hurt us seriously?"

Dennis shook his head and lit a cigarette. "We don't know," he said huskily, his voice gruff from tension and all the smoking he had been doing. "But we do have a show to do."

Georgia Prideaux, the actress who played Lauren on the show, ran a hand through her long black hair and sighed. She was the opposite of the character she played— straightforward and generous where Lauren was evil and scheming, calm where Lauren was high-strung. But she looked less than relaxed at the moment. "I agree with Morgan," she said, stretching out on the red velvet *recamier* she was sitting on. "How do we really know what's going on? What happened today could hardly be chance; it's too close to our script, Dennis."

Dennis's lips tightened. "Look, I'll talk to McCann-Fields about what's been going on. That's the best I can do. But for the moment we'd do well to get on with the show. If we keep falling behind because of these screw-ups, there's not going to be a show at all."

These last words spurred everyone to action, and the run-throughs and filming continued without incident.

Unfortunately, toward the end of the day Bruce came rushing in and burst the mood of determination.

"I've got an announcement about the shooting

schedule," the assistant director called out to Dennis, picking his way over wires and between cameras as he came to where Dennis was standing behind a camera. "Felicia just called from the hospital, and—"

"What about Melanie?" several people interrupted. "How is she? What did Felicia say?"

Bruce looked disturbed by the interruption, as if the questions had broken some inner tape of announcements he had planned to play. "She'll be all right," he said grudgingly. "She has a mild concussion, and she has to be out for a couple of days."

"What about the shock?" someone called out. "Did that cause any damage?"

"No, no," Bruce said. "She'll be fine. But I'd *like* to talk about the shooting schedule."

"All right, what's the word?" Dennis said impatiently.

"We're shut down after today," Bruce said. "For two days, until Melanie's back."

There was a groan of annoyance and anger, and once work resumed the place was lethargic and desultory.

At the end of the day Casey lingered in her tasks. The crew was still arguing over whether the wires had been crossed accidentally or not, and she wanted to learn as much as she could without being too obvious about it.

But after five minutes Casey realized she had learned as much as she was going to; there was no proof. She walked out into the foyer and immediately heard Dennis's angry voice coming from the study.

"No," he growled as Casey reached the edge of the doorway. "No, damnit, no more . . . Come on! How obvious do you want to get! . . . No, absolutely not. Look, damnit, we'll talk another time. There's no point in our talking when you're being totally unreasonable. Goodbye." And he slammed down the phone.

Casey closed her eyes and sank against the wall. Dennis's words had sounded so suspicious, so damning!

"What are you doing here?"

Casey's eyes flew open, and she found herself looking directly into the stormy, dark eyes of Dennis Mattson.

CHAPTER FOUR

Dennis saw the sharp flash of answering anger in Casey's eyes and almost smiled. She wasn't easily intimidated. Not that he wanted to intimidate her—far from it—but so far the only time he had acted as he had wanted to with Casey was when he had kissed her. Since then he had been all temper and nerves, like a frayed wire.

"What I meant," he said slowly, allowing a smile to come through, "is that you really should be careful, staying so late. With the crew gone it can be dangerous walking around this house after hours—especially with all that's been going on."

She studied his face carefully. Was it concern or suspicion that had laced his initial outburst? And now he seemed so kind and soft—as he had with Melanie. Was that real or counterfeit?

"I suppose you're right," she answered. "What happened to Melanie today wasn't particularly pleasant."

He frowned. "No, it wasn't. But I do think everyone is jumping to conclusions."

"Oh, come on. You really think it was coincidence?" she asked, letting her personal disbelief mask the professional question.

"I think so, yes. Obviously we can't be sure, and there

are certainly enough nuts running around that anything is possible. But if the incidents are really a series of crimes, Casey, then they're motiveless crimes, which doesn't make any sense. Why would anyone make random problems for a show like 'The Sinners'?"

Casey was saved from saying something that would possibly reveal her professional interest in the case by Felicia's appearance. She had let herself in the front door, and because she had turned to double-lock the door behind her, she didn't see Casey and Dennis. When she turned around and saw them, she couldn't mask her surprise. Her mouth dropped open and she gaped.

For a moment Casey couldn't fathom why Felicia looked so shocked, but then she realized Felicia had probably just been startled. After all, the cast and crew members would have gone by this time.

Felicia composed herself and gave a brittle smile. "Well," she said brightly, avoiding Casey's eyes. "Dennis, I'm glad you're still here. Casey, would you mind leaving us alone for a few minutes?"

"Sure," Casey said.

"Don't leave. I want to talk to you," Dennis said, and Casey smiled and walked out of the room.

She didn't go far. She stayed near enough so that she would be able to hear at least bits of the conversation. Dennis was Don Atchison's prime suspect; Casey wanted to hear how Felicia would deal with him now that another "accident" had occurred.

"I've just taken Melanie home," Felicia said. "She'll be out until Friday, and—"

"I know," he growled. "How is she?"

"Actually, you saw her at her best. She was on the brink of hysteria at the hospital, and we had to call in her therapist."

"Therapist?"

"Analyst," she corrected. "I spoke with him over the

phone, actually, and he insisted on the delay. It seems this whole incident has upset her rather badly."

There was a silence. Then: "Well, I guess there's nothing we can do about it. I'm sorry Melanie's so upset."

"Yes, well, that's not what I wanted to talk to you about, in any case."

"Oh, really?" Casey thought she could detect an edge of wariness in Dennis's voice. Was that from guilt? Fear that Felicia was about to confront him? Or just the natural cautiousness of anyone who has been put on notice in that manner?

"I heard some interesting news today," Felicia said.

"What was that?" he asked.

"That one of the networks just bought that show you worked on last year. The whole thirteen-week package." She paused. "Interesting, isn't it? I understand Robin Smythe might direct several of the first episodes."

"I haven't heard anything about it," he said.

"And *I* hadn't heard anything about 'The Fortune' being picked up. I like to know these things, Dennis, and know them when they happen."

"Then call up one of your damn spies, Felicia. Lord knows you have enough of them. I don't have to answer to you."

"Oh, no? I think you do."

"And I think we're finished," he said, and Casey leaped back, knowing he was leaving the room.

He smiled when he saw her. "Come on," he said. "We're leaving."

She didn't ask where or why or how. She caught up with him and matched him stride for stride, saving her questions for later.

He obviously knew where they were heading. They walked quickly up Lexington for two blocks, then turned in to a small, neighborhood-type bar. It was dark, with a small bar on the left, a color TV up on the wall, and a few tables and booths on the right—a real no-frills place, but not unpleasant, Casey felt. It was certainly preferable to a singles bar with fake ferns hanging wherever you looked and people packed six deep at the bar.

Dennis gestured at a corner booth and smiled. "Why don't you sit there and I'll get us some drinks. If we wait to be served, we'll be here till tomorrow."

"Okay," she said. "I'll have a Johnnie Walker Black on the rocks."

He smiled. "I knew I liked you," he said, and turned and walked over to the bar.

After Casey was seated at the banquette, she looked at Dennis as he stood at the bar. She loved the way his pale blue shirt fit. The lines starting from his broad shoulders and tapering to his narrow hips were so clean, traveling over a back she knew would be smooth yet muscular, strong but yielding. She took a deep breath and sighed, letting herself imagine . . . and then she smiled.

How easy it was to fantasize, to make everything perfect in the imagination. Here was a man she wasn't completely sure she liked—certainly a man she had reason to suspect in connection with what could be criminal acts. But how perfect he was in her imagination as he lay on top of her, his skin warm against hers, the firmness of his body igniting her yielding flesh as he whispered, "Darling, I'm yours." How perfect he was as his coaxing fingers worked their magic on her, as his lips captured hers, as his tongue danced its pleasure with hers. She looked at his long, lean thighs and knew what it would be like to feel them part her own, knew the heat that would engulf her as his desire grew, knew the moans of lust that would bring them together in coursing ecstasy.

Dennis turned, drinks in hand, and Casey shook herself out of her thoughts. But she smiled inwardly at the luck that people couldn't read each other's minds.

Dennis had his eyes on Casey every step of the way as

he walked to the table. She was nearly but not quite smiling about something. He smiled. If he were an artist and she his subject, he'd title her portrait *Woman with a Secret*. She had become almost shy when he had turned, giving him one long, unreadable look and then glancing away.

Then, as he reached the table, her eyes met his again, and this time there was no mistaking her meaning. Pleasure surged through him as he looked at her: she wanted him.

Lord, she wanted him—at some level, anyway.

He set the drinks down and sat down on the banquette, and all he was aware of was Casey—her sky-blue eyes as she turned to him and then let her gaze slide away, the faint scent of flowers and mist and the sky, the silk-soft skin he had once brushed against his own.

Suddenly he felt twenty years younger, like a teenager who didn't know what to say to the pretty young woman sitting next to him. In many ways he hadn't encountered anyone like Casey Fredericks in that long a time.

And what was it, he wondered, that made her different? As he raised his glass in a toast and looked into those eyes, he could think only of how beautiful they were, challenging and acquiescent at one and the same time. He had seen the two qualities together before, of course, in actresses who tried to seem worldly and experienced when they were anything but, and in actresses who took the opposite approach, pretending naiveté, ingenuousness, a lack of self-consciousness that was screamingly counterfeit.

And then all at once he knew what was different about Casey. She didn't want anything from him. She wasn't an actress who wanted a part, wasn't a writer who wanted him to use her screenplay. She needed nothing from him. She couldn't use him. She couldn't do what Celeste had done.

He saw a questioning sparkle in her eyes, and he smiled.

"I'm glad you came," he said. "Considering the way I acted with you this morning, I'm surprised you did."

She raised a brow. "Yes, what about that, now that you bring it up?" She smiled. "I'm not used to being kissed one evening and then being spoken to in quite that way the next morning."

"I'm sorry—really. There's no excuse, either. The show is turning me into a monster." He took a pack of cigarettes and matches out of his shirt pocket. "And my willpower seems to be gone as well," he said, lighting up. He nodded at the matches. "I refuse to buy another lighter, since I'm hoping this won't last, but I wouldn't place any bets. In any case, my apologies. It had nothing to do with you."

She looked at him carefully. "You said those very words the first time we met," she observed, taking a sip of her Scotch. It was delicious—not too sweet, but cold and very, very warm at the same time.

He nodded. "I remember—after I was angry you had been hired."

She smiled. It seemed so long ago, yet it was only yesterday.

"I was telling the truth," he said softly. "It didn't have anything to do with you. You're just a pleasure to have around." His eyes held hers. "And you know, in my business it's very difficult to find someone who doesn't want something from you. Ninety-nine percent of the people I meet are in the business or would like to be. You're different."

"But I told you," she said. "I do want to be in the business."

"That's true," he admitted, "but you have your aunt helping you along in that area. You don't need me at all. Anyway, you're not interested in acting or writing."

She took a sip of Scotch and let it slowly spread its glow inside her before she spoke, with a tilted smile and a glint of mischief in her eyes. "I might be, you know, despite what I said before." She was surprised he didn't smile; in fact, his eyes were dark and ungiving, but she went on. "I hadn't realized how exciting the business is. There's something really magical about the atmosphere on the set. And I like the show a lot now." She raised a challenging brow. "And you were the one, if you remember, who said I could be an actress."

"It's a rough business," he said gruffly. He downed the rest of his Scotch. "It's hell on the way up when you'll do anything to get a part, and then it's hell when you get there. Your life is turned upside down and you're put on display for literally everyone in the world to see. I've seen it ruin more people's lives than I care to think of. And I wouldn't like to see that happen to you, Casey."

She looked at him skeptically. "Oh, come on. I've gotten awfully tired of seeing these stars come on 'Merv Griffin' or 'Tonight' and shows like that, saying how difficult their lives are. They shoot one movie that takes place in an awkward setting and they think they've really suffered. Yes, it's true they went down into some mine shaft or the jungles of South America or jumped out of planes, but other people do those things for a living—for a fraction of what these stars are making. It always amazes me that they're so blind and so insulated in that little community out in California that they don't even realize how foolish they sound."

He smiled, almost unwillingly, it seemed to Casey, and she went on. Something was bothering him, and she seemed to be relaxing him—aside from the fact that the actors and actresses she was thinking of really did make her angry.

"Or another thing I see and read all the time," she continued. "An actress who's making millions of dollars in movies and has an act out in Vegas goes on a talk show and discusses how for five or ten years she wanted to be in movies and worked in a restaurant or a morgue or for

64

a messenger service or whatever, and then she bats her eyelashes into the proper camera and says, 'That's when I knew I was a survivor.' As if what she went through is so difficult, as if those five or ten years of doing what most of us do for a living in some way makes her deserve the millions she's making now. When I hear things like that I keep wondering how someone who's *really* suffered feels when he hears a statement like 'I'm a survivor, Johnny.' And how do all the waiters and waitresses and messengers feel when they read that their jobs seem like fates worse than death to these people? They work for ten and twenty and thirty years, and *they* don't suddenly collect a mil plus three percent of the net, or however they put it."

"Three percent of the gross, if they're smart," Dennis said. "Net is a joke. You're getting the studio boss's limos and coke and Jacuzzi taken off the top." He smiled. "But you're right, Casey, and you're describing what Melanie is going to say in a few years if she keeps heading in the direction she's heading. 'Oh, yes, Merv,' " he mimicked. " 'It was very, very difficult—I was a singing waitress and a hostess and a secretary. But "The Sinners" was a good jumping off point for me, and now I can practice my craft—stretch myself professionally—to give pleasure to millions and millions of people.' "

There was a definite edge in Dennis's voice as he spoke, a bitter dislike that seemed to run deep. And suddenly Casey wondered: could the sabotage—if there *was* any— have been directed at Melanie in particular? And if so, were Dennis's feelings sufficiently hostile and personal to . . . She sighed. She hated thinking this way. She had been—for a few minutes, anyway—enjoying an afterwork drink with a very attractive man. Now he was a suspect again. But she had to know. And suddenly it wasn't just for professional reasons that she needed the answer.

"Did you—well, you don't have to answer me if this is

too personal a question, Dennis, but have you ever gone out with Melanie? I mean, I—"

"Are you serious?" he asked, looking at her incredulously. "You *have* been on the set these past two days, haven't you?"

"Well, yes, but—"

"I hope that's not how you think I act with women I'm involved with—or even used to be involved with, Casey."

"Well, there were some moments there today, after Melanie was hurt, when you were really nice. I couldn't have asked for anything nicer if it had happened to me."

"Thank God it didn't," he said huskily. "Actually," he added, "Melanie is a perfect example of what I was talking about earlier—and of the things I like so much about you. Even if I were interested in Melanie, at this point in my life I don't think I would ever actually get involved with someone like that."

"I don't understand. Why? Just because she's an actress?"

" 'Just' isn't quite the word, kid." He reached out and tipped her chin so she was looking directly into his smiling brown eyes. "Someone like you, for instance—you'd bleed me dry before you were done."

The comment, despite the imagery, had been made lightly. But Casey hadn't smiled; she had only half-heard it. For his touch inexorably, as always, had reached her first, dominating her thoughts and sensations and perceptions. It was the lightest of touches, but combined with the look in his eyes—of daring, humor, then sudden seriousness as his gaze melted and fused with hers—it was too much.

He inhaled slowly, and they were silent together as their fantasies simmered, burst into flame, and joined. She looked at his eyes—dark, dark-lashed, with whites so clear they were nearly blue. His skin she remembered well—too well as she tried to sleep at night and concentrate during the day. It was sandpaper rough, with smooth, silky areas she had yet to touch, soft warm lips she had touched and loved. His hair—dark, wavy, soft—was the kind you loved to run your fingers through, the kind Casey wanted to reach out and feel at that moment. But more than that she wanted the touch of his hands roving over her, of his warm skin against hers, of his body awakening her with need and desire.

"I think I should go," she said softly.

"Why?"

She sighed and looked away for a moment. When she turned her blue eyes upon him once more, he could see she was avoiding something. "It's just easier," she said quietly.

"I don't understand."

She smiled. "I just don't want to spend my evening in this bar, okay? I have things to do at home."

"Like what?" he asked, suppressing a disbelieving smile.

"Oh, things. You know."

"Mm," he said skeptically. "Well, come on, then, I'll take you home."

"No, that's okay," she said quickly.

He shook his head. "I insist," he said, smiling. "Look. It's eight and almost dark—much too late for you to go home by yourself."

She laughed. "All right," she said, deciding it was really no big deal one way or the other and enjoying his concern as well.

A few minutes later they were on Park Avenue, standing with what seemed like a hundred people waiting for taxis.

"Somehow I feel we're not alone," Dennis said. "How about walking through the park?"

"Great," she said. "I love the park."

They set out across the avenue in the purple light of the

early evening, and Casey felt a soaring of spirit that she tried to ignore. Everyone around them was dressed to go out, and there was that excitement in the air that only a summer evening can promise. And Casey realized she was happy, carefree in a way she hadn't felt in much too long a time.

"Have you lived in the city long?" Dennis asked as they headed into the park at Seventy-second Street. There were bike riders, joggers, couples walking arm in arm, men selling hot dogs and ice cream, balloons and wind-up dolls.

"All my life," she said. "Except for college. What about you?"

Dennis smiled. "I was eighteen before I ever saw a city bigger than Terre Haute. I'm from Indiana originally, the first kid in my family to go to college. And from there I went straight to Hollywood."

"Had you always been interested in movies? And known what you wanted to do?"

"From as far back as I can remember. I think that's true of a lot of people who grew up in small towns in a certain era. Our connection with what we thought of as the outside world was through movies and then later television, and Hollywood was a huge part of my life. For me it was the only place to go after college."

"But how did you start? How did you get your first job?"

He smiled. "They hired me for my legs. After that it was easy. I slept my way to the top."

She laughed. "No, seriously."

"Oh, taking any job I could, as often as I could. I did what you're doing, with as many directors as possible. I wrote a few scripts, did a little bit of acting, did lots more p.a. work, and then I was a location manager for a while. Do you know what that is?"

"No," she said. "Although I suppose I should."

He shrugged. "They're used in movies more than in television, since most series are produced on sets with no possibility of scenes taking place anywhere else. But in a movie obviously that's not the case. You're basically starting from scratch—very few people use sets these days—so for every scene, indoors and out, that's going to be shot, the location manager has to find a place where it can be done and done well, legally, often as cheaply as possible, and easily."

"Sounds as if it could be difficult in a place like New York."

He smiled. "Well, it can be, but you get to know the landlords and restaurant owners and people who are willing to let your cameras and crew in—for what's always a very handsome price, of course. But it can be difficult, because for every location you have—let's say the script calls for an old-money Park Avenue apartment—you might need one place for the interior, another building for the hallway, another for the elevator, another for the lobby, and another for the exterior shot, all because of space limitations or script requirements."

"Gee, I hadn't realized," she said. "That does sound like hard work."

"Well, I loved it," he said. "And there were easy parts, anyway. For instance, this," he said, turning up a path that led into a small, beautiful grotto of trees and benches. There was no one else around, and the spot was quiet, cool, lush. "There's only one Central Park, and when a scene calls for a love scene, say, a good-night kiss, the only question is which of a hundred beautiful spots you choose." He stopped then and turned to her, looking into her eyes with wonder. "And when someone's eyes are as beautiful as yours, Casey, no one really cares where you choose," he said softly.

He looked at her soft, moist, gently parted lips and thought, *I'll never be able to resist this woman, this incredi-*

ble combination of toughness and gentleness. He saw the resistance in her eyes—a fiery challenge that told him he could never make her do anything she didn't want to do. But in the parting of her lips, the rapid pulse at the soft, ivory-white base of her throat, the quickened breath she had taken when he had first looked into her eyes, he saw an ally.

"You've been to this spot before," she said, only half-questioningly.

He nodded, reached out, gently touched each of her cheeks with his fingertips. Her skin was unbelievably smooth and silky, and the light in her eyes told him she was enjoying his touch.

"For a movie?" she asked, knowing the answer.

He nodded again and let his warm fingers travel down along her neck to the hollows of her collarbone. His touch was warm, his fingertips slightly rough, and they heated her flesh with the promise of more pleasure to come, with the memory of his touch she had yearned for. "You planned this?" she murmured.

He smiled a beautiful, daring smile, and his eyes flashed. "You're not the only one who knows your way around this city," he said, looking at the spot where his hands were and then lower, at her breasts, at the nipples he knew were taut beneath her shirt. She warmed under his gaze, knowing what he was thinking, wanting him to go on.

"Was it a love scene?" she asked as his hands moved out over her shoulders and she felt the strength in them.

"For a love scene, yes, but it was nothing like this," he breathed. "Because the man in that movie couldn't possibly have wanted the woman who stood before him as much as I want you."

"Oh, Dennis," she murmured. But before she could say more, he lowered his mouth to hers and brought her along with him in a sudden coursing of pleasure as their lips parted in searing memory of their last kiss. His tongue was

70

sweet and urgent as it touched hers, dared hers, played a game that wove a spell over her.

And then his hands moved from her shoulders over her breasts, covering each one with a warmth that made Casey ache for a more direct touch. She knew what his warm hands would feel like on her bare skin, knew what magic his tongue would perform, mimicking the dance it was doing now. And she could imagine his lean hard form pulsating with a need that would be matched by her own as it claimed her in throbbing, rapturous passion.

God, how she wanted him. But it was impossible. She pulled away and faced him. "Oh, Dennis," she whispered. "We have to stop."

"Take me home with you," he murmured, his breath hot in her ear. He took her lobe between his teeth and gently edged it, nibbled at it, the tip of his hot, wet tongue sending smoldering waves through her.

"Dennis," she whispered, her voice caught in thickened layers of wanting. "Oh, Dennis."

"Say yes," he whispered. "Casey, I want you. I want you so much."

"We can't."

"Why not?" he murmured. "Tell me."

She pulled away, letting his hands rest at her waist but separating herself from his persuasive lips. "Dennis," she began, so uncertain as she looked into his beautiful dark eyes. "I—this is a mistake. I told you before. I really am not ready to be involved with anyone right now. I want no one in my life except friends and people I work with—and my family, of course. But no one else. Meaning no men."

"Then we'll be friends—friends who happen to share a very strong physical desire for each other." A corner of his handsome mouth turned up. "I don't see anything wrong with that. Anything else is just cutting out an experience

71

that's an unknown quantity. We hardly know each other, and you're saying no."

"What if I were an actress?"

"What?"

"You seem to have a great antipathy for actresses, or at least for becoming involved with them. What if that was what I was?"

"But you're not."

"But what if I was?"

He shook his head. "That's a ridiculous question. You can't separate aspects of people and then exchange them as if you were returning a dress to a store. You're Casey Fredericks, made up of hundreds of qualities I like and hundreds I don't know about. You're you as a whole."

She sighed and shook her head. "You're being very, very stubborn," she said, reaching up and brushing a strand of hair out of his eyes. "Which is flattering, but—"

"But what? If you're making some kind of analogy, you're missing the whole point. Don't you see that logic and reason don't have any place in what we're talking about?"

She sighed in exasperation. "That's so easy to say!" she cried. "I very logically decided that I don't want to be involved with anyone. That's no different from your deciding you don't want to be involved with people in show business." She shook her head. "It's very easy for you to say my logic doesn't apply, but it happens not to be true."

"Oh, really?" he asked. And suddenly his lips were on hers again. She felt as if hot liquid honey were flowing through her, as if this dizzying pleasure were Dennis's to create and end at will. For never before had she been so fiercely aroused by a kiss. And then he pulled away.

When he drew back his eyes were heavy lidded and dark with passion. "Tell me again," he said huskily. "Tell me more about logic and reason, Casey Fredericks."

She was still breathless from the kiss, aware in every cell

of her body of the pleasure this man could give her. "I'll see you Friday," she said and turned on her heel and headed for the road.

"Casey!"

She heard him catch against a bush and swear, and then he was there beside her, in stride as if they had never been apart.

"Look, I'm sorry you feel the way you do," he said. "But at least let me walk you home. I feel as if I've led you into a jungle by bringing you into the park."

She laughed. "Spoken like a true non–New Yorker. Look around," she said. The sun was just setting, its long rays creating beautiful purple shadows everywhere, and Casey smiled as she thought of Dennis's protectiveness. Little did he know that even in the early days of her career she had trailed men twice his size, cracked open scams at some of the toughest companies in the city, impersonating all kinds of people from clerks to corporate raiders. And then a shadow passed over her happiness, for she had completely put the fact that Dennis was a suspect—so far, her main suspect—out of her mind. She had completely forgotten his phone call of that afternoon, and to remember the deception and the possibly bleak future was dispiriting and deeply disappointing. She genuinely liked him.

She managed a smile. "I promise I'll be fine. And I'll see you Friday."

For a moment he looked as if he were weighing her words, trying to decide whether to object or not. And Casey had to admit that—foolishly—she was just a bit disappointed when he finally said, "All right, see you then," and they parted ways at the edge of the road.

CHAPTER FIVE

Casey felt thoroughly at odds with herself as she walked alone through the park. As she looked around at the couples strolling hand in hand around the lawn, the people playing Frisbee and walking dogs, Casey was saddened, both by herself and by what she felt was the inevitable and unchangeable state of the world. Here were all these people having fun, enjoying each other, being easy with each other. To be together they were compromising in some areas, she was sure, but in the end they had achieved something, and they were happier.

But she was simply unable to do this. And until now she had felt she wasn't unhappy. She was much, much too busy to be unhappy. But the stark contrast of her feelings now as opposed to when she and Dennis had entered the park and she had been so relaxed and happy was too graphic to ignore. Dennis made her feel good emotionally, physically, in ways that brought her out of herself and her problems without her noticing. And damnit, she was too mistrustful to be able to go any further, with him or with anyone.

When she got home, her roommate, Tamara, was running around the apartment in a panic. "Casey, thank God you're back. That guy I told you about is coming over, and the apartment is a wreck!"

"Calm down!" Casey cried, smiling. "You're not up for

74

the Homemaker of the Year award. He's coming to take you out, not to inspect."

"You never know," Tamara observed. "Anyway, Case, just because you're on this no-men kick doesn't mean *I* have to spend the rest of my life as a nun. Help me out a little. The living room is a mess."

"All right, all right," Casey said, and when she walked down the hall to the living room, she saw why Tamara was so upset. It really was a mess, with miscellaneous shirts, jeans, even a bathing suit on the couch, shoes everywhere, magazines and newspapers on every horizontal surface, books stacked up by the sofa and next to each chair. What annoyed Casey as she began to gather up her things was the thought that it took a man's coming over to spur her and Tamara to clean up. Living in a neat apartment was clearly preferable to living in the quagmire they were in ninety-nine percent of the time, but as long as the mess was just going to be seen by the two of them, somehow that was thought to be okay. And Casey decided it wasn't; it was masochistic to force herself to experience that little twinge of distaste every time she entered the apartment and saw dirty dishes, her unmade bed, or the chaos of the living room. She and Tamara both worked, but somehow there had to be a way to manage, and more often than when they happened to have dates. It was a matter of simple self-respect.

And perhaps it was masochistic as well to limit herself socially with abstract principles and rules, as she had for the past three years. She didn't have to go overboard as she and Tamara had once done, deciding they had to meet men no matter what pain and torture they had to endure at the bars they went to. But, as Tamara had said, they didn't have to act like nuns, either. In her thinking Casey had been as rigid as Dennis seemed to be in his. Only she hadn't seen it this afternoon.

And when Tamara's date arrived, Casey saw that her

roommate really did have the right idea. She didn't seem to be madly in love with this man, but they had only just met, so how could she tell what she might feel for him eventually? She was getting to know him, which was the normal, reasonable, and natural step Casey had somehow forgotten about.

That night, after Tamara and her date had left for the evening, the phone rang. As she ran to get it, Casey realized she was hoping it was Dennis, whom she could probably have been with at that moment if she hadn't run off.

But it was Felicia, who let her know what she already knew and unfortunately had put out of her mind: that another network had just picked up a show Dennis had worked on a year earlier, one that he cared about a great deal. And Felicia was worried that he would stop at nothing in order to be able to work on that show again.

Casey thanked Felicia for filling her in, but Felicia wanted to talk more. "I noticed you ran off with Mattson after my meeting with him," Felicia said.

Meeting! Casey thought skeptically. Felicia was being kind to herself. "Yes," Casey said simply, and then added, "That's what I'm there for, isn't it?" She bit her lip. Damn. There was no need to alienate Felicia. The woman was, indirectly, at least, one of her employers.

"I suppose so," Felicia said. "And did you learn anything I should know about?"

Only that I wish I had another job, Casey said silently to herself. "Oh, it's a bit soon for that," she said. "And unfortunately there's simply no way of telling whether the accident of this afternoon was chance or not."

"Yes, I know," Felicia said. "Well, McCann-Fields realizes you're not an electronics expert, and we did hire you because we felt you could successfully blend in and determine motives better than the other investigators Pete Winter suggested."

"We'll see," Casey said. "At this point I feel my first

priority is to determine whether there even is any sabotage."

"That sounds very logical to me," Felicia said.

And a few moments later, after Casey had hung up, she silently wished she would learn the answer soon—and that the answer would be that it all was just chance, mere happenstance. Or if it was sabotage, that it was someone else—anyone but Dennis.

Over the next two days, during the hiatus from shooting, Casey caught herself thinking about Dennis at unexpected moments. She even found that she was "by chance" on Lexington in the low Seventies; she knew he swam at the health club next door to the town house almost every day. But she didn't meet up with him.

Tamara was surprisingly negative when Casey told her about her new approach to men and about Dennis in particular.

"He sounds as if he thinks he's God's gift to women," Tamara had said. "All that 'I won't get involved with anyone who's going to use me' crap—who does he think he is?"

Casey sighed. "He isn't like that, not at all. I mean, he's very handsome and certainly in a position of power, but when he said that, it didn't come off as self-centered or conceited. I think he's being realistic," she said. "He was obviously hurt or annoyed in the past by someone who used him, and he doesn't want that to happen again. I can understand that."

"But you *are* using him," Tamara said.

Casey shook her head.

"Face it, Case, you are—by not being honest, investigating without telling him, suspecting *him* more than anyone else. Every minute you spend with him is using him."

"I don't see it that way," Casey said. "I really don't. And Tamara, I don't see why I should have to think of it

77

in those terms. We don't know if anyone is doing anything evil on the set of 'The Sinners.' "

Tamara stared. "You're fooling yourself, kid. Think of Melanie and the way she looked and felt yesterday after she got that shock. Think how cruel that was if someone did it. Would you really want to go out with the person responsible for that?"

"Of course not," Casey said. "But really, Tamara, you're jumping the gun. We don't know a thing. All I know," she added softly, "is that I like Dennis. And that's all I need to know."

Tamara knew Casey well enough to let the subject drop, but Casey wasn't particularly relieved. For she knew she wouldn't stop thinking about the subject no matter what.

Dennis spent a disconcerting amount of time during the two days off thinking about Casey. Even when he was out with Martina, he didn't hear a word she was saying. They were at Rocco's in the Village, eating his favorite veal piccata and drinking his favorite red wine, sharing the kind of time that only good, old friends can have together. They had tried romance once years ago and had recognized right away that it would never work. She was beautiful, with straight, silver-blond hair, china-blue eyes, skin that was nearly translucent. He had thought she was devastatingly attractive when he had first met her, when they had both been working on the set of an ill-fated series named "Just Call Me Max," she as a costume designer, he as assistant director. But she had revealed herself rather quickly as one of those types more often found in theatrical communities, Dennis felt, than anywhere else: unendingly, unfailingly, relentlessly masochistic and obsessed with the need for approval, with so little faith in herself and others that her attractiveness immediately vanished. At least it had for Dennis. The quality destroyed the budding romance but set the stage for a deep and enduring

78

friendship. She had needed Dennis as a friend at that time, and together they had helped each other through trials and tribulations for years.

Now, sitting across from her, he saw a twinkle in her eyes as she put down her wine. "You haven't heard one word I've said for the last five minutes," she accused.

He shook his head. "I'm sorry."

"What's her name?"

He smiled. "Casey Fredericks. New p.a. on the set."

Martina drew her head back in surprise. "Well, that's a change, Den. What happened to your rule? Which, by the way, I always found ridiculous, but—"

"I don't know why," he said, his voice edged with tension. "It's a perfectly realistic rule. I've found that people in the entertainment community—"

"Women, you mean," she interrupted.

He shrugged. "All right, that women in the entertainment community can't always be trusted. You've seen it yourself, Martina."

She shook her head. "You *know* I've never agreed with you about Celeste. You think everything was her fault; you never saw what you did to her."

Dennis sighed and lit a cigarette. "I *was* there," he said dryly.

"And *I* was very close with Celeste at the time. You have no idea what you put her through. Men never do."

He looked into her eyes—so beautiful, so filled with sadness and suffering, and defiant as well. Martina dared people to treat her badly. And somehow they always did. "Look," he said. "I think you fed each other's fantasies during that period. You were with Chris and thought he was cheating on you—"

"Which he was," she interrupted.

"All right," he conceded. "And Celeste was with me and thought I was seeing Ann."

79

Martina's lips tightened. "That you weren't actually cheating is academic, Den. Admit that you wanted to."

"I did want to," he said. "But I didn't do it, Tina. And somehow that should enter into the equation somewhere."

Martina sighed. "All right, maybe I don't know the whole story. What I do know is that she thought you were cheating on her, she was very hurt, and she did what she knew would hurt you more than anything else in the world. At that time nothing could have been worse than stealing your screenplay, and I guess she did, although she certainly never admitted it. But there's nothing you can do about that; you've decided to put that behind you.

"But what I think you should see, Den, is that you've made this big barrier to other relationships by constantly putting the onus on the other person because of Celeste. And I think you should face up to the fact that you have a real tendency to have a roving eye. You're just not willing to put any blame on yourself for what happened, and that's going to limit you for the rest of your life until you see that. Because you're going to A, cut out a lot of women who might really appeal to you because there's some odd chance they might 'use' you, and B, you're going to lose whoever you have until you realize you have a problem being faithful."

He looked at her carefully. "You've certainly done a lot of thinking about this," he said quietly.

She looked down into her drink for a moment and then turned her magnificent blue eyes on him. "I was wondering why we hadn't been able to work things out." She smiled crookedly. "You know, I had one of those you're-about-to-be-thirty-three-and-you're-all-alone panics, and I thought I'd try to settle for you."

He laughed. "Roving eye and all?"

"I don't know," she said seriously. "Maybe if you really, really cared about someone, Dennis, all the barriers and problems would slip away."

Later on, after he had taken Martina home, he thought about what she had said to him. He had never liked anyone analyzing his actions or motives. The only time he wanted people to "interpret" him was if they were interpreting something he had directed. But Martina had given careful thought to much of his life for a reason: she was his friend, and—though he was certain this was the wine talking more than anything else—she was even considering the possibility of romance once again.

The question was, was she right? Was he incapable of having a full relationship with all the trust on both sides that went with it? Did his own wariness of others stem from the fact that he knew he couldn't be trusted? He thought about Casey—her intelligent, sparkling eyes, those warm lips that could arouse him as no others could, the breathless hunger of her body against his.

And then he abandoned the analysis, the questions, the doubts. The memory of her breathless moans was much too arousing to let any other thoughts or images exist, and he let his fantasies take over as he relived and added to memories that aroused him now almost as much as Casey had then. No, he'd never get to sleep tonight, not in this achingly ready state. . . .

On the morning that shooting was due to resume, Casey took an hour to get dressed. She wanted to look attractive without looking as if she had tried really hard, sexy without being too noticeable.

"Why not go all out?" Tamara asked. "I don't understand why you don't wear that blue dress, Casey. It looks incredible. Of course, I happen to be completely against the whole idea of your getting involved with this guy, but if you're going to try, you might as well do it right."

Casey shook her head. "Uh-uh. That can't be the right approach. He's—well, first of all, p.a.s wear jeans more than anything else. But also, Dennis would be—I don't know, I can't say suspicious, exactly, but maybe wary. I think he'd wonder why the sudden turnaround."

Tamara sighed and shook her head. "He sounds like the wrong type to me, Casey. It's just what I said before. He thinks he's God's gift and that women are out to get him or something. I'd go in with a burlap sack on if I were you."

Casey looked at her roommate with affectionate annoyance. "Thanks for the advice and the confidence, Tam." And she finally selected exactly what she wanted—a deep blue cotton blouse that brought out the blue of her eyes, and a pair of black jeans, which accentuated her slim, athletic figure without looking at all like a calculated bid for attention.

When Casey arrived at the town house, all the actors were crowded around Melanie, who was holding court on a *recamier* in the downstairs sitting room. "It was worth going to the hospital for what I learned," Melanie said loudly, searching the crowd for someone who apparently wasn't there.

"About what?" Morgan asked, kneeling at her feet and looking up at her as if in worship.

She glanced at him with impatience. *He* wasn't the one she wanted to tell. Then, after one last desperate search of the crowd, she sighed theatrically and paused, waiting until the properly respectful silence had fallen. "I learned something everyone will be interested in," she said, her gaze traveling from one person to the next. "Our show is going to be in trouble soon." There were a few muffled words of agreement, but Casey guessed this tepid response was not what Melanie had had in mind. "I spoke to dozens of nurses and patients and orderlies and a couple of the doctors, and everybody I talked to felt our show didn't have enough gloss or glamour. One nurse said my and Georgia's costumes looked like uniforms compared to the

82

gowns on 'Coronado' and 'Haley's Cove.' And Georgia, we've both gotten letters, right? Saying the exact same thing."

Georgia looked as if she weren't altogether pleased to be roped into Melanie's camp. "Well, yes, Melanie, *I* certainly have. But—"

"Then why are we sitting on our butts when we could be making a fuss? This whole hospital deal really opened my eyes. I thought I was glamorous in the eyes of America." Her voice had taken on a desperate edge, and Casey suddenly realized that for once Melanie wasn't acting. "And it turns out that's not true. Now, are the rest of you happy with that?" There was an unwillingness to respond; people averted their eyes; a few shrugged. Melanie's eyes flashed. "Well, obviously I'm the only one with any sense around here," she said and stood up. She pushed her way through the already-dispersing group around her, and Casey drifted off as well, arriving out in the foyer just as Melanie found Dennis.

"I need to talk to you," Melanie said. "I've learned a lot in the hospital, and . . ." She went through the same speech she had given to the cast, augmented by whining additions that did nothing to help her case. Casey could see Dennis growing more impatient and annoyed as she went on and on. When the harangue finally stopped, Dennis winked, smiled, and said, "Well, I'm glad to see you're feeling better, anyway, Melanie. Welcome back."

Her eyes widened. "Dennis, I'm serious."

"Look," he said, no longer smiling. "We're way behind schedule as it is. I'm not going to discuss changes in costumes or anything else that isn't completely essential. And Felicia, in any case, is the one you should be talking to, Melanie. You know that."

"But you could help," Melanie said. "One word from you would make the difference, Dennis. I'm trying to make the show better, to do this for all of us."

"That's a laugh," came a soft voice from behind Casey. She turned and saw Ted Conroy. "She's never done anything for anyone else in her entire life. I don't know why she'd start now. Although she happens to be right."

"Then why don't they fix up the costumes?" Casey asked quietly. "I'm sure that sort of thing *does* make a difference in the long run."

As Melanie and Dennis continued to argue, the group that had been gathered around Melanie in the sitting room formed once again around actress and director. And Casey heard occasional quiet words of support for Melanie's position as the actress railed on.

"She *is* right, you know," Hugh Ascot, who played Steele Edwards, said to Georgia.

"Of course she is," Morgan said.

Georgia waved a dismissing hand. "You'd say she was right if she said the earth was flat, darling."

Suddenly Dennis yelled "Hold it!" and turned on the group. "In case you have all forgotten," he spat out, "we have two days of work to catch up on. End of discussion."

"But Dennis—" Melanie began.

"We're going to run through Scene Six," he said, looking beyond Melanie to the rest of the group. "Melanie and Morgan, down to the music room, please, and—"

"Oh, God," Melanie said. "I don't know if I can do the scene again. I just—"

Dennis stepped forward and put an arm around Melanie. "Just do the best you can," he said gently as he led her toward the stairs. "We'll take it slow, and all the mikes have been tested and retested. I promise—you don't have to worry."

"Well, I'll try," Melanie said quietly. And once again Casey was struck by the difference in the way Dennis acted with Melanie when the problems were personal or emotional rather than professional. He had been totally unsympathetic, uninterested in anything Melanie had had to say only moments before. But now that she was afraid —as she had been when the accident had occurred—he was all tenderness and empathy.

When Felicia came in, Morgan approached her about the question of costumes. Morgan had evidently donned the mantel as Melanie's advocate and was presenting her case much better than Melanie had to her fellow cast members and Dennis. As Morgan's eloquence attracted the attention of the other actors, support for the idea grew once again, with murmured agreements and nods of the head.

But Felicia was uninterested and abrupt. "Out of the question," she snapped.

"I don't understand," said Lisa Sykes, who played the Edwardses' maid (and secret lover of Steele Edwards). "My sister works for *Woman's Life* magazine and they don't have to pay for the clothes they photograph. Why should the costumes even affect our budget? We could probably *have* them in return for giving a credit at the end of the show."

Felicia's lips tightened. "The answer is no," she said flatly. "You should know by now that we rent most of our costumes. Now let's get on with it."

There was much grumbling as the day went on, and the shooting went worse than Casey had yet seen. Melanie was so apprehensive about the rehearsal scene that it had to be shot over a dozen times, and Dennis was clearly near the end of his rope. And oddly, though the cast members had initially been reluctant to support Melanie in her drive for new costumes, the issue had suddenly become important. Like children who have been told they can't go out to play, they were suddenly fixated on the idea, unable to let it go even in spare moments. All the dissatisfaction and uneasiness they had felt over the past several weeks were now channeled into this goal, and the feeling was simple, illogical, and strong: new costumes would make it all better.

85

Casey was plunged further and further into a foul mood as the day went on. The night before, she had decided Dennis was someone she wanted to know better. But today he was proving himself as arrogant, stubborn, and unfeeling as he had seemed on that first day. And she felt cheated.

"All right," Dennis snapped. "We've obviously gone as far as we're going to." Something caught his eye, and he turned just as Casey threw down her script. Disappointment and anger were written all over her face, and he knew with reluctant certainty that she was reacting to him—not to the show or the lines or the way the shooting had gone but to his mood and the way he had acted all afternoon. Damn. His fault.

He caught her just as she was leaving the room. "Casey," he called.

When she turned, her eyes were cold. "Yes?"

"Could you stay a few minutes, please?"

He saw a glint of defiance in her eyes. "I suppose. Yes, of course."

He nodded. "Good. I'll meet you in the study in, say, ten minutes, all right?"

"Okay," she said quietly and turned to leave quickly, clearly uninterested in prolonging her time with him.

When he walked into the study fifteen minutes later, he stopped at the threshold when he saw Casey standing near the fireplace. She was turned in profile, and he was certain she didn't see him. There was an air of complete unself-consciousness and self-containment about her as she stood, her head bent, looking at a book she had apparently found on one of the shelves. She was incredibly graceful as she stood reading, the curve of her neck as elegant and willowy as that of a wild animal at the edge of a stream. And there *was* something wild about her deep beneath the surface. He had sensed it and touched it. And he wanted more.

"Interesting?" he asked as he came in.

She jumped. "Oh. You startled me," she said. "Yes, actually. It's the novel called *The Sinners*. I hadn't known the series was based on a book."

"It's in the credits," he said. "And pretty soon your name will be, too."

"Oh, how nice," Casey said unenthusiastically. She could feel how contrary she was acting, could see the disappointment in Dennis's face. But she couldn't help it; he had disappointed her.

"So," she said flatly. "What was it you wanted to see me about?"

"I wanted to see you," he said. "Period. I *would* like to talk about the script, but that's secondary, Casey. In the two days we've been off—" His eyes searched hers, and she began to feel the inexorable pull he could exert on her at any time. "In the two days we've been off," he said again, "I've thought about what you said. And I don't want to let it go at that, Casey."

She sighed, fighting the pull. "Well," she said, "if you must know—" Something was making her continue; she had to tell the truth. "I've been thinking about it, too, Dennis." For a moment their gazes met and simmered. She went on. "But really, after today . . . I don't think I necessarily . . ." She couldn't find the words, especially when the warmth of his eyes was bringing back memories of what they had shared, of kisses she couldn't forget, embraces that had made her breathless. "You seem to be two different people, Dennis—two very different people. And today I—"

"Today I wasn't myself," he said huskily, his voice holding her in silken bonds.

She broke free by thinking of the facts she didn't want to face. Today Dennis had made it that much easier for her to believe he could be guilty of sabotaging the show. His feelings about the series were so strong that he would perhaps do anything to get out of it; his attitude toward the cast was so distant that he might be able to forget about them as individuals if he were committing sabotage; and perhaps his desire for freedom was great enough to hurt anyone in his path. "You know," she said, "it's very easy for you to say you weren't yourself. That's always easy to say, Dennis, and rarely true. But I think you were incredibly unsympathetic to what people were saying today."

His brows drew together. "What are you talking about? Look, I admit I was in a rotten frame of mind, but costumes? That's pretty unimportant, Casey, with all the other nonsense that's been going on. Morgan and the others were blowing it way out of proportion."

"No, you're wrong," she said. "You missed the point of the entire discussion, which was that they're all scared about what's been happening on the set, and they're all unhappy, and they've fastened upon something that's easy to quantify and do something about. It's a small solution to a big problem. And you completely brushed them off."

He was silent for a moment. "I hadn't thought of it that way," he said softly. "Very perceptive of you."

"Are you being sarcastic?" she asked.

"No, I mean it," he said. "And I wish I had realized earlier. I *would* have been more sympathetic."

She looked at him carefully, trying to decide whether he was speaking truthfully.

"And I did mean what I said earlier about wanting to see you. I wanted to very much."

"Oh, Dennis, I don't know." She hesitated. "What was it that you wanted to ask me about the script?"

"Well," he said, smiling. "I see we're on to that. All right." He raised a challenging brow. "You won't object to sitting on the couch, at any rate?"

"Of course not. Dennis, I—oh, never mind."

They settled onto the leather couch by the fireplace.

"Now," he said. "It's somewhere around page fifty." He turned through the script, and she watched him as he searched the pages. His profile was almost irresistibly handsome, and his beautiful lips were barely suppressing a smile. "You *would* have me reading this dross when we could be talking about all sorts of other things." He glanced at her for a moment, his eyes filled with humor. "Hm?"

"Get on with it," she teased.

He laughed and turned back to the script. "Ah. Here it is," he said. "All right, page fifty-seven, Casey."

She turned to the page, and he said, "Just read through the scene and tell me what you think." His voice was soft, sexy, distracting. But she began to read. It was a compelling scene. Royce and Kezia were in their bedroom, he dressed in a white satin robe, she just out of a shower and wrapped in a towel. She had just returned from a trip to Mexico—a trip Royce thought she had taken alone, but which was really a week-long tryst with a lover. Now, she has just found out she is pregnant—definitely with Royce's child, since she was faithful to him until last week. And she is acting very loving and amorous toward Royce.

Once again, the scene was going to call for some subtlety on Melanie's part. The audience would be divided as to whether she was acting or being sincere. Yet as Casey read it—as Kezia seduced Royce slowly and surely, drawing out their mutual pleasure, seducing the audience as well as her husband—Casey could draw only one conclusion: that Kezia meant everything she was saying and doing. She was very, very attracted to Royce at that moment, and the mood had reached Casey as well.

In something of a haze Casey looked up at Dennis with a vagueness that was too pleasurable to dissipate. "Well," she said softly. "I don't know what you could possibly find

89

wrong with this scene. I think it's very well written. Very sexy."

He smiled a rakish, crooked smile. "Oh, really? Hm. Interesting. How sexy?"

She laughed, she hoped not nervously. "Very sexy. Why? Don't you think so?"

He gazed at her assessingly, his eyes roving across her face, her breasts, her lips. "I hadn't," he said. "But now that you do, I suppose I do." He paused, and when he went on, his voice was gently caressing. "In fact—well, tell me. What I had found very unsexy was the fact that we *know* Kezia has been with her lover. What a turnoff to have a woman playing games with you after having just been with someone else. Melanie may be beautiful and sexy and America's fantasy of what a seductress should look like, but she doesn't do a thing for me as Kezia when I know she's just been in the arms of another man."

"Hm. I guess I hadn't thought of it from that perspective. But how do you know she's not being sincere with Royce?"

"After being with another man for a week? Are you serious?"

"I think it's very understandable," she said, barely suppressing a smile over his look of astonishment. "Not that I'm particularly fond of being involved with two men at once, and not that I ever would do that if I knew I was pregnant. But remember, Kezia didn't know she was pregnant when she was with the other man."

"Kezia is married," he said flatly. "Isn't that reason enough? And she's a woman."

Casey widened her eyes. "And?"

He smiled. "It's different and you know it."

"You mean you hold a double standard," she corrected.

"Intellectually, of course not. But I have to admit that at some level I find it more shocking, less easy to understand, and much less easy to accept if a woman is involved with more than one man."

"That's ridiculous!" Casey cried. "That's just completely unfair!"

He smiled. "I know. And obviously I know it's wrong. But I *am* being honest, at least. I see a difference."

"How? Why?"

He looked at her carefully. "Do you really think it's such a desirable practice?"

"No," she said. "I told you that. But it makes me go crazy when a man thinks he can see other people and the woman can't."

He shook his head. "I don't think that—at least not intellectually. But I do have to admit that emotionally I can't get past a very strong feeling that says men can do it and women can't. A man, for instance, can see another woman and not have it mean that much. It doesn't have to affect the main relationship. I don't think it's possible the other way around, though. Men—"

"Have different needs?" she interrupted.

"Maybe," he answered. "I think we handle them differently, yes."

"That's nonsense," she said. "A woman can have an affair on the side and have it mean as little as it would if a man did the same thing," she said. "Although I agree, it isn't the most desirable thing to do."

"Well, I disagree," he said. "A woman who's having an affair is making much more of an emotional commitment. It means *much* more if *she's* cheating." He paused, trying to collect his thoughts. He could hear that his voice had been rigid, could feel the tension in every pore of his body. Damnit, he was still hurting from Celeste, hurting in a way that was totally irrational. "Well," he said, managing a quick smile. "Back to the scene, then. So you think it works, Casey?"

"It depends on what you want," she answered. "When

I read it, I felt that Kezia loves Royce. No matter how she may have felt with her lover, or no matter how often she strays, she does love Royce, and she really loves him here. But I don't know if that's the effect you want. And I don't know if Melanie will be able to act out what's on paper." She looked at Dennis. "*Is* that what you want? For it to seem as if Kezia loves Royce?"

"I'm not sure," he said musingly. "And what about Royce?" he asked. "He *knows* some of the things she's done. He knows she's had affairs, he knows she's obsessed with his money, he knows she has great, great faults. He's not a masochist looking to be made miserable, Casey. So can he really love Kezia, knowing she's done all these things?"

Casey sighed and looked down at her hands in her lap, at her finger where a ring had once been, where she had set all her hopes and dreams in one tiny shining diamond that had seemed to promise everything. When it had all gone sour, she couldn't solely blame either herself or Steve. For somehow, once the magic had gone out of their marriage, neither one had tried to find it again with the other. Was it blame that stopped them from trying? Resentment over actions of the other? Guilt, perhaps? Casey had been so filled with anger and resentment that she had been blinded to the truth until very recently. And the truth was that the marriage's failure had been her fault as much as Steve's.

"What are you thinking?" Dennis asked quietly.

Casey looked up, startled. She had been so deep in thought. . . . "Oh, just—something from the past. Something that's over."

Understanding flickered in his eyes. "Have dinner with me," he said softly. Then he grinned. "And just so you don't think I'm a sexist with double standards coming out of my ears, I'll cook."

She smiled, pleased with the idea as soon as he said it. "That sounds really nice."

It was only as she and Dennis left the town house and began walking to his apartment that she realized she was incredibly nervous, whirling in a sea of apprehension she didn't understand.

CHAPTER SIX

Dennis's apartment was magnificent. In a modern high-rise on East Fifty-eighth Street, he had half the top floor of the building, a beautiful penthouse with a view that swept west from Central Park and all the way down to what looked like the edges of the city, glittering and glowing in the evening darkness. The apartment was modern in terms of both architecture and furnishings: low leather and wood furniture with solid-color rugs, abstract paintings, lots of books. But the kitchen was a complete surprise. It was large—custom built, Dennis explained—with the range built into a huge butcher-block counter in the center of the room. Mediterranean terra cotta tiles covered the floor, and beautiful burnished oak cabinets lined two walls of the room.

"This is amazing," Casey said. "You must do a lot of entertaining."

"Oh, not as much as I should," he said, "and when I do, I always call people in. I enjoy cooking only for people I really like, and unfortunately most of my entertaining is compulsory—something my agent keeps swearing is 'totally necessary,' as he puts it."

Casey smiled and watched as Dennis began preparing the meal. She hadn't had many men cook for her in her life. When Steve had done it before they were married, he had treated her like a queen, and the experience had been wonderful. But later on his reluctance and grudging unwillingness had all but erased Casey's memories of those earlier times. Now as she watched Dennis, so easy and relaxed, comfortable enough with himself that he obviously had no qualms about doing something others might consider feminine, she marveled at the contrast between the two men.

Physically they were similar to an extent Casey didn't want to dwell on. Tall, with large frames, they were both strong without being muscle bound. But Dennis looked more in shape than Steve had been the last time Casey had seen him. Dennis's hips were slimmer, his forearms thicker and more well defined, his—but Casey caught herself in the comparison and stopped. Why was she comparing the two men? It was pointless and negative, something she didn't like doing and wanted to stop.

Yet she couldn't help it. Steve was, unfortunately, the measure by which she judged all men. And, ironically, he pulled all their scores down, for in the end, no matter how promising someone looked, no matter how much better than Steve a man seemed, an unwelcome thought invariably intruded at that point. Steve had seemed wonderful; she had loved him; she had married him. And with all the romance, the passion, the seeming honesty in their relationship, the magic had disappeared.

Soon after they were married, they both had begun to feel trapped but had said nothing. Casey, hostile toward Steve for reasons she couldn't put her finger on, had begun to find fault with everything he did. All of a sudden he seemed to chew too loudly, eat too quickly, talk with his mouth full; his clothes looked out of date. What had once seemed charmingly idiosyncratic seemed merely sloppy now. Sometimes she didn't even like his voice—the voice that had made her fall in love with him years before and say yes only months before these feelings began. These were small aspects of Steve's personality. How important, after all, were one's clothes? But each day Casey could feel the relationship crumbling as she noticed one more of Steve's habits she disliked, one more trait she had never noticed.

And then, one Sunday she would never forget for the rest of her life, she had made love with him and felt nothing. It had been a typical Sunday. They had watched football together, cuddled on the couch in front of the game, eaten, and fallen into a comfortable postprandial sleep. When they awakened, he touched her, and she went along, thinking she would feel more in moments. But she didn't. It had been one of the saddest days of her life, for she had known then that it was over. Of course, there had been other times that hadn't been perfect, times that hadn't even been good for her; the same had been true of him. But she knew with the same certainty she had known she loved Steve that she would never feel the rapturous pleasure of love with him again.

Little by little, as the weeks went by, she withdrew from Steve. They lived together, talked together, acted as if nothing were wrong. And then one day, in a horrible scene that was straight out of a movie, Casey saw Steve leaving a restaurant on Broadway one afternoon. He was smiling, and Casey was about to wave from down the street. Then out came a woman from the restaurant, and the woman took Steve's arm and they turned in the opposite direction as Casey stood there with her mouth open. She watched; she couldn't stop herself. And then, her knees shaking so hard she almost dropped, she followed at a distance; again she couldn't help it. And she saw Steve take this tall, slim,

95

beautiful, blond woman into his arms and kiss her long and hard.

Oh, God, Casey had thought. Steve had always said that public displays of affection were crude. Now here he was on Seventy-ninth Street and Broadway, kissing a blonde as if there were no tomorrow.

The blow was devastating. Casey had cried for hours, had realized how much she loved Steve despite what she had thought. She had felt trapped, and she had begun to resent him; but now that she had lost him, she wanted him back.

They separated soon afterward. Casey could do nothing to stop it. It was too late. Steve had been hurt by her distance, had sought comfort and pleasure and warmth in the arms of another woman, and he had, he said, tasted a freedom he didn't want to give up.

"You're a million miles away," Dennis said.

"Sorry. I'm a little distracted—or abstracted."

"Anything you can tell me about?"

"Oh—" She hesitated and then smiled. "No, actually." She paused, her mind racing for a new subject. "I love your apartment, though," she said finally.

He grinned. "It's not too obviously a man's apartment?" He said his last words in a tone of such self-mockery that Casey laughed.

"I don't think so. Why?"

"Oh, some women feel an immediate need to domesticate me *and* the apartment the minute they come here."

For a moment Casey remembered what Tamara had said about Dennis thinking he was God's gift to women. But Tamara had heard only the words; she couldn't see the self-effacing grin or hear the humor in his voice as he spoke.

"Listen," she said. "I live with a roommate, and when there are pantyhose hanging everywhere you look and the refrigerator is filled with nothing but cottage cheese and Tab, this is wonderful."

Dennis shook his head. "This city," he said, laying out the steak and pounding it with a tenderizer. "I can never believe it when I hear men and women thirty, thirty-five years old saying they have roommates. The economy is just ridiculous. Is it terrible?"

Casey shrugged. "I've gotten used to it. But actually I'm looking for a place of my own."

"Any particular area?"

"Anything, just about."

"You sound more desperate than used to it."

"No, it's okay. I like being on my own, though."

He looked at her carefully. "Ever been married?"

She nodded. "You don't have any cold red wine, do you?"

He grinned. "I do. And we're on the same wavelength. Right behind you in the fridge there. I'm sorry I didn't offer you anything. I'm so starved I just started right in on the steak. But anyway, was that a change of subject I wasn't supposed to notice?"

Casey poured two glasses of Côtes du Rhone. "Mm," she said, looking into dark brown eyes that were half-serious, half-amused. "But I obviously failed miserably at my subtle attempt."

He laughed. "I can never do it either. But that's okay. We can talk about whatever you want."

Suddenly curiosity overpowered reticence. "Have you?" she asked. "Ever been married, I mean."

His eyes were as deep and dark and beckoning as she had ever seen. For a moment he seemed not even to breathe as his gaze melted into hers. He seemed to be saying so much, so much that couldn't be said in words. Then he shook his head. "No. No," he repeated musingly. "Although I often regret it. But that's something one can never really predict, isn't it? Along with my storybook career I thought I would have a storybook marriage and family. I come from a family of three brothers and three sisters, and having a family of my own was something I just assumed I would do. But it just didn't happen that way." He paused. "Anyway, I'm glad you're here to-night." He raised his glass in a toast. "Here's to our first evening."

They both drank, and then he went on. "You know, in many ways I wish we didn't work together. Naturally I'm glad you joined the show. I wouldn't have met you other-wise. But it's unfortunate that work becomes an issue with us. I find myself seeking you out at the worst of times instead of the best of times." He looked into her eyes. "Let's make this one of the best of times."

She smiled. "Yes, let's." And silently she told herself he was right, and that she could forget her questions about his motivations and the problems on the set for at least one evening.

They prepared the rest of the dinner together, she get-ting the lettuce and tomatoes ready, he preparing the dressing, together getting the grill ready out on the ter-race.

The terrace was breathtaking, wrapping around the south and west sides of the building, with the city sprawl-ing beyond, as in a thousand pictures Casey had seen. She had lived in this city all her life, but she had never seen this aspect of its beauty so clearly. Around the brick walk of the terrace there were small trees in tubs here and there, as well as huge, almost tropical plants that edged the terrace border along the doors to the living room. The trees and lush plants made Casey feel as if she were in a park raised high above the rest of the city, and they gave off a fragrant, heady, summery smell whenever the breeze wafted in.

After Casey and Dennis put the steak on the grill, they sat on one of the cushioned chaises at the edge of the terrace, with cool glasses of red wine in their hands. The lights of the city cast a glow down below that was mirrored by the flickering candles Dennis had set up, and there was a heaviness of expectation in the air that reached Casey deeply.

"Now is one of those moments," Dennis said quietly. "Sitting on the terrace on this kind of an evening, with the air not quite cool and not quite warm, you by my side. You know, you look very beautiful in the moonlight, Casey. Your eyes are so lovely." He paused. "But there's something about you," he murmured. "Something mysterious."

Casey looked beyond him at the lighted spires of the Empire State and Chrysler buildings, at a plane flying low overhead. When she looked back at Dennis, his eyes were shining, questioning. She smiled. "What do you mean?"

He tilted his head, almost but not quite smiling. God, she was beautiful. That mouth was enough to keep him on edge all evening. He remembered its taste, those lips, that breathless need. She was wearing a simple shirt and pants, as on the first day he had met her. But the pants hugged her in all the right places, made her movements seem pent up and wild. And the blouse made her eyes look as blue and giving and ready as any he had ever seen. Tonight, with the memories of those kisses, with the way Casey looked in the summer moonlight, she was driving him with a desire that was almost uncontrollable. But he had to remember: she wasn't ready to respond to him fully or completely. That day in the park she had been almost unbearably exciting, responding with a trembling force that aroused him whenever he thought about it. But she had backed off; she was afraid of something. He had to choose another route. If only he could know why—why this fear, this holding back, when in every other area of her life she seemed to be so straightforward.

He looked into her eyes. "You've told me so little about

99

yourself," he said, almost wincing at how corny the words sounded. But he meant them.

She smiled—nervously, he felt. "What is it that you want to know?" she asked. Then she shook her head. "Sorry. That was an obnoxious question." She took a sip of wine, darkening her ruby lips, making her smooth, ivory skin even paler in the moonlight.

"No," he objected. "What I said sounded like a question a job interviewer might ask. And I wanted this to be a relaxing evening. But it is intriguing, Casey. Most women—and men—I meet are really full of themselves. Naturally, since they're in show business. You're so much the opposite that it's very noticeable."

She took another sip of wine. "Oh, well—"

At that moment there was a sizzling from the grill, and both Casey and Dennis jumped up and ran to it.

The steak wasn't overdone; some fat had just dripped onto the coals. But Casey wouldn't have been upset even if it had burned. She was simply glad it had served as a distraction. For though she was fluent at breezily lying her way through any conversation, she had become completely tongue-tied under Dennis's scrutiny. She could tell him very little about herself without lying, and lying suddenly seemed impossible.

Dennis turned the steak, and just then the phone rang. He excused himself and stepped into the living room, and Casey heard him say hello.

"What?" he said. "No, no, I'm not. I have some company. . . . Oh, wonderful," he said sarcastically. "Right now? Okay, talk to you later." He hung up quickly, and Casey could hear him stride across the expanse of the living room. Then she heard voices—the television, she realized. "Casey?" Dennis called.

She stepped into the room. The television was on, and on the screen was the face of Celeste St. Jacques, a beautiful actress Casey happened to detest. Celeste St. Jacques seemed to be everywhere these days—on the covers of *People* and *Us, Ladies' Home Journal,* even *Time.* The year was supposed to be "the year of Celeste St. Jacques," according to *People;* and the actress was up for two Oscars for leading roles in two recent movies Casey had assiduously avoided. And there she was on the screen, with a man whose name Casey couldn't remember, apparently conducting an in-depth interview. She was sitting in a room that could well have been designed for her. Its golden walls made her wavy apricot hair look as if it had been spun out of the setting sun, and the backdrop behind her—a silly but beautiful photograph of a southern California beach—brought out the blue of her eyes.

"What show is this?" Casey asked, coming in to where Dennis was standing in front of the set.

At first he didn't answer. Then: "What? Oh, it's a special. This Bobby Barnett character interviews three different stars every month. I hadn't known this was on," he said distractedly.

"That *was* my first inkling that I wanted to be a star," Celeste St. Jacques was saying, "but there was just no way in the *world* I thought my dream would actually come true! I mean, I knew I was pretty, but I thought there were plenty of girls in my town who had to be prettier." She paused, letting her gaze rest on Barnett, obviously waiting for him to contradict her with a passionate and heartfelt avowal that she must have been the most beautiful girl in her hometown. But he merely smiled blandly—an action Casey suspected was the height of his reportorial capacity —and asked another question.

"Yes, yes," Celeste said. "Of course I had help. Doesn't everyone? One comes out to L.A. and makes friends, and help is always around the corner. But actually, Bobby, I found that there was more goodwill, more of a genuine desire to help one's friends, at the beginning. When I came out here I was like thousands of pretty girls hoping to get a big break, and I had friends. But later on I found that there was just an enormous amount of deception, an enormous amount of backbiting going on that I didn't even *know* about."

This captured Barnett's interest. He sat forward in his chair. "Really?" he breathed. "Can you tell us more, Celeste?"

Celeste St. Jacques looked demurely down at her hands as if the idea of telling more had never before occurred to her. "We-ell," she said hesitantly, "all right. I won't use any names, but actually, Bobby, I think it's important to make stories like this public if only to save other young people from making the same mistakes. You know, years ago, as I said, when we were all struggling, we all had friends—friends you could count on, friends who would help you out of a jam, friends who were sometimes lovers. My best friend was the man I intended to marry." She smiled enigmatically. "He happens to have a reputation as the greatest lover in the business, and—"

Barnett sat so far forward in his seat that Casey thought he might fall off his chair. "Tell us more," he whispered hopefully and then turned to the camera with a leer. "And perhaps we'll even learn the name of this greatest of all lovers after these messages. Stay tuned, folks."

Dennis swore under his breath, lunged forward, and flipped off the set. "I've got better things to do with my time than listen to that nonsense," he said roughly.

He stepped past Casey and headed for the terrace, and Casey followed, marveling at the anger emanating so forcefully from this man. Even his stride looked as if he were holding himself in check, holding back anger that, if unleashed, would be volcanic.

Out on the terrace Dennis lifted the steak off the grill onto a platter, picked up the platter, and then set it down and looked at Casey. "Have you ever been involved with something that seems never to end?" he asked. "I was involved with Celeste St. Jacques years ago, and she's still talking about something that happened between us as if it were only yesterday!"

"You went out with her?" Casey repeated, shocked. True, Dennis was a fairly well known director both in L.A. and in New York, but Celeste St. Jacques was now a star of international renown.

"Years ago," Dennis said as Casey followed him back into the kitchen and together they brought out salad, French bread, and dishes on beautiful brass trays. They set the trays down on one of the cast-iron tables along the edge of the terrace and set out the dishes on another table in front of a beautifully cushioned love seat that looked out over Central Park and beyond.

Casey sat down and let Dennis serve as he continued to talk. "We were planning to get married, actually," he said, his voice still low with anger. "We were both relatively new in Hollywood, definitely unknown." He shook his head. "She moved in with me the day we met. There you go," he said, setting a plate down in front of Casey. The food looked delicious: steak still sizzling from the grill, fresh lettuce and tomato salad with vinaigrette dressing, hot French bread and butter on a heavy earthenware plate.

"Thanks," Casey said, and for a few moments there was silence as she and Dennis ate. The steak was delicious— mouth-wateringly tender, perfect with the full red Côtes du Rhone.

"Anyway," Dennis continued, "I suppose you could say we were in love, to the extent that anyone that young can be. Or maybe youth wasn't the problem. Both of us were so involved with our careers and with ourselves that we had no capacity for the kind of love we thought we were experiencing. But I helped her," he said hoarsely. "I helped her in every way I could. Neither one of us could get anywhere for the longest time. I was a waiter most of the time, she was a waitress, and when she could get the work, she was a singing waitress. More wine?"

"Yes, thanks," Casey said.

After he had poured he looked into her eyes. "By the way, Casey, if you don't want to hear this story, I won't be offended. That phone call—"

"No, please," Casey said. "I'm fascinated. But let me ask you something," she added. "Was that you that Celeste St. Jacques was talking about with Bobby Barnett?"

He nodded.

"The world's greatest lover?" she asked.

He laughed. "Ah, she never granted me that," he said, eyes shining. "I was always the greatest in the *business.*"

"I see," Casey said, laughing. "Well, go on." But she was glad he paused to take a few bites of steak and some wine, for her mind was caught on what he had said, and she wouldn't have been able to concentrate on anything else. "The greatest lover in the business," Celeste St. Jacques had said. Dennis had repeated it in that self-mocking way he had. But the words had conjured up images for Casey that were impossible to set aside—of Dennis moving in the most immensely pleasing ways with her, stroking, coaxing, thrusting, moaning, rough skin against smooth, hardness giving softness ecstasy that went on forever.

In some deep inner place Casey knew that what Celeste St. Jacques had said was true; she knew it instinctively. Casey wasn't a great believer in technique as the measure of a man's sexual performance. When there was love the most inexperienced man in the world could be magnificent. That was why she felt she could tell how caring and arousing a man would be in bed, just from spending some time with him. Tenderness and caring and sensitivity were what counted. These qualities determined how giving a man would be; and Casey realized this was something she had sensed about Dennis from the beginning. He was unselfish; he could be incredibly tender; and he was obviously sensual, someone very aware of his physical presence.

And she wanted him. Suddenly she was almost unbearably aware of him and the fact that they were alone together. She had imagined making love with him so many times. There was a chance now, a real chance. Would it be wrong to take that chance?

For she realized that she desperately wanted that closeness she knew he could give, desperately needed that merging of body and soul that could sometimes—if you were lucky—occur. As she looked into his eyes she saw someone who could give her these things.

True, she hadn't known him long, and true, there were many things about him she didn't know. But somewhere deep down, deep inside, she knew he would be wonderful and kind and exactly what she needed; for he had made her aware of a need she had ignored for a long time—a need for intimacy and pleasure. And she suddenly felt lost without it.

As if reading her thoughts, Dennis turned and reached out to stroke her cheek gently. The touch sent a rolling path of warmth downward, and Casey's lips parted as she looked into Dennis's eyes.

"I just realized," he said softly, his voice a barely audible hush, "that I'm sitting here with someone I've wanted to be alone with for days. I've thought of just this scene, Case," he murmured, "and I'm spending it by talking about another woman." He moved his hand down, letting his roughened fingers ignite the smooth skin of her neck with desire. "When I could be talking about you, or us," he whispered. He looked into her eyes. "I know what you've told me, Casey, and I know what you've said. I know, too, that you've meant every word." His voice was quiet and slightly hoarse, and she loved the sound of it so close, so gentle. "I'm not the kind of person who likes to steamroll past someone's objections. I hate it when people do that sort of thing. But I don't see that kind of decisiveness in your eyes."

She gave him the full benefit of her gaze at that moment. "What do you see?" she whispered.

He inhaled deeply. "I see a woman I want to make happy in every way I know how," he said huskily. "And a woman who would make me very, very happy. Casey, I want to go slowly. Slowly this way," he whispered, moving his fingers along the smooth skin just inside her collar, "and slowly the other way, as I think you would want it. No demands, no questions, just the two of us doing as we wish with each other." As he spoke the touch of his fingers grew more exciting, sending warm paths of pleasure to her limbs.

"Oh, Dennis," she murmured. She didn't want to have a big discussion, to talk about the future or pros and cons or worries. She wanted the wonderful feeling he gave her when he held her in his arms, wanted the pleasure that only full lovemaking could bring. "I think I need you tonight," she said quietly, truthfully, amazed she could say this without thinking beyond these simple words.

"I need *you*," he rasped, and he claimed her lips with his in a deep, trembling kiss that said more than words ever could. When his tongue entered the warm, sweet recesses of her mouth, she wrapped her arms around him and then settled back as they sank together into the softness of the couch.

Dennis lay above her, with a lean thigh over hers and an elbow braced on the cushions. He looked magnificent in the moonlight, with his dark hair hanging over his face, his features shadowed but his eyes shining. She could see—and feel—that he was breathing fast, and when he reached out and began unbuttoning her shirt, she felt a sharp intake of breath. His fingers worked quickly, unbuttoning and then parting the thin fabric of her blouse, and soon she lay beneath him with her breasts bare. "Oh, Casey," he murmured. "So beautiful."

With a moan he lowered his mouth to a nipple, gently awakening it with the warm, wet tip of his tongue, and with a hand he covered her other breast, cupping its silken underside and then edging the nipple between his fingers.

"Dennis," she whispered as he brought both peaks to tingling need. "Oh, God." The pleasure spread quickly from the sharp, concentrated sensations at her nipples to a slow burning that grew deep within. Casey raked her hands along Dennis's back and over his hard buttocks.

She had looked at him, fantasized about him, thought of his lean hard body urging her on, and now it was happening, and he seemed more eager, more passionate, hungrier than he had been in her fantasy.

"I don't believe in doing things halfway," he said hoarsely, his breath hot against a hardened nipple. "If there's a woman who's right for me, I know it immediately," he whispered. "And I know, Casey, I know we're right for each other." He let his lips close over her nipple again, warming it with wet excitement, and then he raised his head and looked into her eyes. "And I want to please you every way I know how," he murmured huskily.

He raised himself above her, and she reached out for him. "Here," she said, reaching for his shirt. "Let me." And she quickly unbuttoned it, parting it to reveal a beautifully muscled chest covered with fine, dark swirls of hair. She let her fingers graze over the firm rises and valleys of his muscles, and then each hand found a dark male nipple and circled it delicately with one finger. Then she raised her head and took a nipple in her mouth.

"Oh, Casey," Dennis murmured, as his nipples peaked to hardened excitement. "Oh, Casey, your touch. You're so beautiful."

He rolled them onto their sides, and for one moment they looked into each other's eyes, saying all they couldn't quite say out loud. Then with a moan of mutual desire, together they leaned forward and joined in a deep, loving kiss.

Their tongues danced, explored, surged with the pleasure of discovery as their hands began another kind of exploration. Dennis let his warm fingers trail over her tingling breasts, over the curve of her waist, across the smooth skin of her stomach, and back to her breasts, cupping them lightly and then gently edging the nipples above with his thumb.

"Dennis," she whispered. And then his hands moved downward, playing at the edge of her waistband, tantalizing as they massaged just inside, kneading her warm flesh with an urgency that was as deep as her own. A fiery path of pleasure spread downward from his fingers, and Casey moved beneath his touch.

"Dennis, please," she whispered as he found the fastening of her jeans and quickly undid them. She shifted as he sat up and gently slid her jeans down and off and then freed her from the bonds of her blouse. She lay beneath him, clad only in her bikini underwear, and he gazed at her in obvious pleasure and desire.

"You're more beautiful than I had even imagined," he said, and he kneeled over her, lowering his mouth to each of her nipples and then with a moan letting his mouth trail downward. "And Casey, I've thought of you in my arms like this so many times—I've made love to you in my fantasies so many times." He held her, fingers splayed over her hips, as his lips roved from the peak of one hipbone to the other, searing each tender inch of flesh with a wet, urgent kiss. His lips caressing the silkiness of her thighs awakened a hunger that threatened to overpower her. Then his hand moved downward, tracing slow, coaxing circles from one thigh to the other and over the rise of flesh in between. "Dennis," Casey whispered, her fingers entwined in his hair.

And then she moaned under his touch as his fingers urged her to a fiery pitch that made her breathless.

She murmured again, and then cried out as his tongue delicately echoed the persuasive path of his fingers, sending hot pleasure coursing through her.

"Dennis, now," she urged, and he raised his head and looked at her with dark eyes filled with passion. Then he stood, scooped her up in his arms, and carried her through the living room into the bedroom. It was softly lit by moonlight slanting in the windows, and as Dennis laid Casey down on the bed, she felt as if she were on a cloud.

He stood above her and undressed quickly, tearing off his shirt and removing his pants, and then he stood before her, beautiful and strong. His legs were long and muscular, covered with the same fine dark swirls of hair that graced his chest. And he was obviously deeply aroused.

He climbed onto the bed, murmured her name, then moaned it as she touched him, wanting to give him the pleasure he had been giving her. She let her lips rove across his chest, taking one nipple and then the other between gentle teeth.

"Casey," he moaned. "Oh, Casey." And as her tongue and lips and teeth played, she explored his warm skin with questing fingers, letting them trail through the hair of his rippling chest, across the smooth skin of his stomach, over firm buttocks and lean hipbones. And then she touched him, making him tremble and clutch her closer, making him whisper her name as she had whispered his.

He reached for her then, found the honeyed core of her desire, and then moved away from her hand, looking into her eyes with a wild urgency. "I can't wait any longer," he said hoarsely. "I can't hold back."

"Then take me," she urged, writhing under his hot touch.

And he raised himself above her, gazing into her eyes

with hunger and love, and with a masterful, flaming-hot stroke he united them.

She gasped, grasping his back. And when his lips covered hers, her pleasure blazed, melting hotter and hotter as he guided her on a thrusting path of rapturous bliss.

"Oh, Casey, yes," he urged huskily as the flames burned. And then, together in a rolling blaze of passion, they were engulfed in exquisite bliss that made them one in body and soul, in the deepest and most primitive of unions.

And then they lay sated, damp, utterly quiet except for slow, satisfied breathing as they descended from the heights of contentment.

Casey felt magnificent. Though she knew it wasn't true, she felt as if she had always known Dennis was so wonderful. As he gently stroked her slowly from her shoulders down to the small of her back, she sighed and nuzzled against his shoulder, loving its smooth warmth.

"Are you happy?" he asked softly, shifting so he could face her. His hand rested in the curve of her waist, and his eyes were shining lovingly into hers.

"Oh, yes, yes," she said. "Are you?"

He smiled. "And surprised, too."

"Why?"

As he reached out and stroked her hair back from her face, she loved the look in his eyes, so warm and shining and full of affection that it was like a loving touch in itself. "Every time I was with you I was in such a rotten mood from something else. I knew we had to see each other off the set." He smiled. "I just hadn't known it would happen so quickly. You seemed so dead set against the idea of any kind of involvement."

She reached out and touched his cheek, roughened by whiskers, dampened by lovemaking. "I changed my mind," she said softly. "And I'm not sure when I did, exactly. But I'm so glad."

He smiled. "Then stay. Stay with me tonight," he whispered.

She smiled, stretching her arms lazily above her head and letting her long legs stretch toward the end of the bed.

"Don't even give it a thought," he said. "Just do it."

He laid a warm hand on her thigh, reminding her deeply and viscerally of the pleasure they had just shared. Staying sounded like a nice idea. "We can get up early and go to your place in the morning," he continued. "Shooting doesn't start till seven tomorrow."

Shooting. Tomorrow. A sickening cloud of gray descended on Casey's mood. She had put work out of her mind, completely avoiding thoughts of Dennis and the show. He was the one who had pointed out that they got along so much better when they were not discussing the show. And it would all begin again, starting tomorrow morning. The suspicions Casey had let fly from her consciousness would come thundering back with full force, and the joy of this evening would be gone forever, something that might as well have been a dream. "I think I'd better go," she said hollowly. "I have lots of things to take care of."

Dennis looked into her eyes. He could see her reluctance there as clearly as if Casey had spelled it out. Only moments earlier she had seemed filled with joy, had seemed light with carefree happiness. Now she was the wary young woman he had known before. And he had to know why, for the woman who gave him so much pleasure and made him forget all that was wrong with his life was much too precious to lose.

He reached out and stroked her soft skin, letting his hand absently explore the soft curve between her ribs and hips. "Casey," he said quietly. "I have to ask you something."

"Yes?" she said, as distantly as if they were strangers.

"You told me you lived with a roommate—a female roommate. That *is* true, isn't it?"

She looked confused. "Of course," she said. "Why?"

"And there's no one else? You're not involved with another man?"

"No," she said, this time with more feeling.

He tried to read her eyes, those china-blue eyes that could be so expressive yet so unreadable at times. And then he kissed her gently on the lips. He hoped that in time she would be able to tell him what the trouble was.

Dennis put Casey into a taxi a little while later. In a way she was sorry she had made such a fuss about leaving. When Dennis had brought up the show, she had over-reacted; the subject had been so far in the back of her mind that she had been shocked and disheartened when she was reminded of it. But now that she was on her way home and in less of a postlovemaking haze, she saw that the situation wasn't nearly as bad as the one she had painted in her mind. She had already decided quite firmly that she wasn't even close to being convinced that what had been happening on the set was sabotage. There was certainly no reason to change her opinion now—no reason, that is, except for natural fear, wariness, and mistrust that ran deep, making their inevitable rush to the surface.

Something suddenly reminded her of the story Dennis had been telling her before they had begun to make love, of Celeste St. Jacques and what had gone wrong between them. She would have to find out what that was about. She wanted to know everything about Dennis there was to know. And she would try not to think about the fact that this was a goal appropriate to her professional life as well. No, she would forget about that for now. It *wasn't* necessarily a goal; there *wasn't* necessarily sabotage. And that was all that mattered.

* * *

112

Casey was a few minutes late on the set the next morning, and when she arrived work was in full swing, with Dennis talking with Felicia and Hank Reed, the story editor, and the crew getting the sets ready.

Casey's heart soared when she saw Dennis laugh with Felicia, of all people. This was a side of him Casey had never seen; he was obviously more relaxed. And when he looked up and saw Casey, his face lit up and she felt a warm glow of happiness deep inside.

Shooting went beautifully. Dennis's mood seemed to be contagious. Everyone was making jokes, giving performances that required three, two, sometimes even only one take. Casey was so happy she felt like announcing her joy to everyone. All that had been wrong with Dennis was tension. She had made him happy; now everything could go smoothly.

As Casey was busy with her own work, she didn't have much direct contact with Dennis all day. But when they did run into each other or catch each other's eyes across the room, he was wonderfully affectionate and easy, looking as pleased as Casey felt.

At the end of the day Casey was tagging costumes for the swing girl, the costume designer's assistant, when Morgan nervously approached Dennis nearby. Most of the other cast and crew had left, and Dennis was crouched by the window, working with a lighting man. Casey was sitting about ten feet away.

Morgan, looking pale beneath his makeup, said, "Can I talk with you?" to Dennis in a voice so quiet Casey had almost not heard it.

Dennis stood up. "Sure, Morgan. What's up?"

"If we could go somewhere else," Morgan said uncertainly.

"Sure. There's a bar a couple of blocks up. I'd planned to see Casey, though, so—"

"That's fine," Morgan said and beckoned to Casey.

113

"Come along if you'd like."

Casey smiled and said she'd be done soon, and in a few minutes the three were walking up Lexington Avenue.

"So what's up?" Dennis asked.

Morgan was walking between them, and Casey saw that his profile was rigid with tension as he said, "Let's wait till we get where we're going."

They went into the bar Casey and Dennis had gone to the other day and sat at the same banquette in the corner.

While Dennis went to get the drinks, Casey tried to make conversation with Morgan, but he was clearly preoccupied and didn't seem to hear a word she said.

Finally, when Dennis returned to the table with beers for all three, Morgan reached into his jacket pocket and pulled out a white envelope. "I found this note in my pocket," he said quietly. "After the shooting was over."

As he handed the envelope to Dennis, Casey saw that his hand was shaking. Concerned, she looked into his eyes. She saw only fear.

The envelope said simply, "FOR MORGAN FORD," all in capital letters. Dennis and Casey looked at it for only a few moments, and then Dennis opened it. Inside was a folded 8½-by-11-inch piece of white paper. Typed on it was:

ROYCE AND YOU HAVE BOTH HAD IT GOOD SO FAR. BUT YOU KNOW WHAT'S GOING TO HAPPEN TO ROYCE, DON'T YOU? WATCH OUT FOR YOUR OWN SKIN. 'THE SINNERS' IS A PIECE OF GARBAGE AND DOESN'T DESERVE TO BE ON TV. MAYBE YOU DON'T EITHER. THERE ARE DEFINITELY REPLACEMENTS.

Casey looked up at Morgan in surprise. "When did you say it arrived?"

Morgan shrugged. "I don't know. I didn't notice it until I put my jacket on at the end of the day. It could have been put there at any time."

Dennis shook his head. "The number of nuts out there," he mused. "Have you shown this to Don or Felicia?"

Morgan shook his head. "No one but you two so far. It's kind of thrown me for a loop," he said. "I really don't know . . ." His voice trailed off, and he helped himself to a large gulp of beer.

"I've seen a lot of notes like this," Dennis said.

"What?" Casey and Morgan said at the same time.

"What are you talking about?" Casey asked.

"It happens with every show," Dennis explained, shaking a cigarette out of his pack and lighting it. "You must know that, Casey. You've certainly read about stars getting threats, right? Whether they're musicians or actors or actresses? Well, it happens even more with ongoing TV series. People know where to write to the actors, they get used to seeing them week in and week out, at home, and an obsession is a very easy thing to develop."

"But this is totally different," Morgan said. "Don't you see? I know Royce has been threatened. Don once sent me a whole bunch of letters my character had gotten. And after that I told him I didn't want to see any more, that he could keep all the nasty ones to himself and just give me the fan mail. But this is different, Dennis. This note was *in my pocket.*"

Dennis exhaled a long stream of smoke. "I know h￼ said quietly. "But perhaps somehow—"

"It came from someone on the set," Morgan interrupted. "There's no other way, Dennis." He looked at Casey. "Don't you see that, Casey?"

"Yes, I do," she said quietly.

"And both of you," Morgan said, "*both* of you have read enough horror stories about things like this that develop into weird obsessions. How do I know someone isn't stalking me? How do I know eight hundred pounds of camera aren't going to plow into me, like with Stacy? Or that the shock that Melanie got wasn't meant for me?

What if all those accidents were meant for me? Or what if they weren't, and everyone's going to get hurt? Dennis, I think—"

"I think you should relax," Dennis cut in. "Morgan, look. I know that getting that sort of note can be frightening, very frightening. But you're not being logical. When the dolly slipped and hurt Stacy, you weren't even in that scene. And when Melanie got the shock, there was nothing in the script that called for you to touch that mike. *If* there were any funny business going on with either of those incidents, neither could have been directed at you."

Morgan sighed and shook his head. "I don't know what to think." He paused and took a sip of beer, and when he looked up, Casey saw real desperation. "You know, I've wanted the kind of part I have for as long as I can remember. It's a plum role, the kind someone would kill for. And you know, I've even wondered about that. I know it's silly and illogical, but it was the first thought in my mind when I saw that the note wasn't the usual angry fan's note." He took another long drink of beer. "I don't want to have to leave the show. God." He sighed. "And you know, I won't, no matter what happens. It's taken me too damn long to get where I am."

Suddenly Casey didn't want to hear any more. The note Morgan had received was more important than either Morgan or Dennis knew. The note had changed everything. For now there was virtually no question that someone on the set wanted to make trouble and was causing problems, even hurting people. It wasn't chance. Chance hadn't written that note and chance wasn't making Morgan Ford turn sheet white with fear.

Casey didn't want even to consider the implications of what it meant.

She stood and picked up her purse. "I have to go," she said, avoiding Dennis's eyes. "I forgot I have something to take care of." She looked at Morgan. "Morgan, I hope the note is nothing more than a practical joke. Although whoever is doing it is sick, you know." She sighed, fury overtaking her fear. Just looking at Morgan's evident fright made her disgusted and angry with whoever had done it. "I'll see you both tomorrow," she said, and she left quickly.

She walked over to Fifth Avenue and then into the park. She avoided the paths she and Dennis had taken. She didn't want to be reminded of him until she had sorted out her feelings.

She walked west toward Bethesda Fountain, but every step of the way she was conscious of the fact that she was on a detour, that she was avoiding unwelcome thoughts that had to be addressed.

Damn. The note had ruined everything. Dennis was still the prime suspect. Her world had collapsed.

CHAPTER SEVEN

Casey was relieved to find that Tamara wasn't home. The last thing she wanted to do was discuss what had happened, since Tamara had pegged Dennis as being guilty from the beginning.

But she did have to brief Pete Winter, the man who ran Winter Investigations and who had gotten her the job, on the recent developments. With dread she picked up the phone and called him, and the conversation wasn't any better or worse than she had expected. There was no reason not to consider Dennis the prime suspect at the moment.

After she hung up Casey put the kettle on the stove for some tea and took a German chocolate cake out of the freezer. Just as she had the tea and cake ready to take into the living room, where she was going to do nothing more challenging than watch TV, the phone rang.

"Hello?"

"Casey, are you all right?" Dennis's voice was at its tenderest.

She closed her eyes. Why was this happening? Why had it happened the very day after she had made love with Dennis? She had discovered so much she liked about him last night, things she even loved about him—his smile, the way he could be self-mocking without being falsely modest, the way he showed such genuine concern for her feelings, the way he made her feel free and beautiful and desirable. She loved his voice, his eyes when they shined into hers, the way he whispered softly to her at the best of times. And now he was asking her whether she was all right, now that she had to face a fact she had avoided for days.

"I'm all right," she lied. She had to. She couldn't say, "No, I'm falling apart" or "I had convinced myself you couldn't be guilty of sabotage if there was no sabotage. Now everything is ruined." She had to lie for now. Beyond that she didn't want to think. But, unbidden, an image flashed through her mind: of Dennis entwined with her, whispering words of love only seconds before explosive ecstasy took over.

She had never thought love was possible to feel so quickly, but she felt as if she were at the edges of love, at its brink. And when she thought of the way Dennis had made her feel so deeply happy, so connected with him last night, she was certain she loved him. And she didn't want to give him up.

"Why did you leave?" he asked after a pause during which he had apparently been waiting for her to say more. "I thought I was going to see you tonight."

"I told you I have things to do," she said.

There was another silence. She heard him drawing on a cigarette, and she sank back against the wall, silently asking herself why this had to have happened now, just when she had found the kind of man she had thought didn't even exist. But, of course, maybe that was the problem. She had trusted. She had come to trust Dennis completely, given of her body and soul and taken from his, trusted though she should have known it was a mistake. And now she was paying the price.

"Casey." He sighed. He had already asked her if there was another man. She had told him there wasn't. He could hardly demand proof. If there was another man, she obviously needed time to work things out herself. By herself. He sighed again. "Okay, I'll see you tomorrow, hon. I just wanted to make sure you were all right. You looked so upset as you were leaving."

"That should come as no surprise," she said suddenly, savagely. "I don't see who *wouldn't* be upset. Poor Morgan! He's obviously completely spooked by what happened to him. And I don't blame him. If I knew someone had been in my clothes, leaving a note like that, I'd be upset, too."

"I know," Dennis said. "And one of the things I like about you is that you're able to put yourself in other people's shoes so easily, Case. But don't forget this is a rough business. Things like that do happen, and if you let yourself get wrought up every time it does, you're never going to last."

Casey said nothing. This was at least the second time that Dennis had said show business was rough. Did that mean he would feel justified doing anything to achieve what he wanted? Did he believe ruthlessness was the norm?

"Dennis," she began. She had to ask, to hear his tone of voice. "Dennis, who do you think put that note in Morgan's jacket?"

"I really don't know," he answered easily. "But I wouldn't worry that it's going to happen to you, Casey. You and Morgan are in very different positions."

"I don't understand."

"I'm not saying I do either, Case. When someone does something like that—leaves a note in a dramatic gesture straight out of some movie—you can't understand too much about the motives: the person is probably a nut to begin with. But working within whatever framework of reason might exist, I'd have to assume you won't be approached. Morgan might have the role that some crew member is secretly burning with rage for, that sort of thing. You'll be okay."

"I'm not worried about myself!" she cried and bit her lip when she heard the near-hysteria of her voice. "Look, I have to go now. I'll see you tomorrow." And she didn't even wait for him to say good-bye.

She took her cake, which was still pretty frozen, but edible, and tea into the living room, kicked off her shoes, and settled in front of the TV. There was a loud situation comedy on—canned laughter was coming at fifteen-second intervals—and Casey knew there was no way it or any other show was going to drag her thoughts away from Dennis.

No, she had gambled and she had lost. She had told herself there was no sabotage; there had been no clear evidence, and she had kept a properly open mind. Now there was still a chance—a very, very slim chance—that there was no pattern to the events, that the note was the isolated work of some unbalanced member of the cast or crew and unrelated to the accidents and mishaps on the set. But that chance was slim, which meant Casey had to face some hard, cold facts.

She heard the door slam and Tamara call, "Hey, I'm home!" and she swore under her breath. Even though she knew it was petty and unimportant, at that moment she couldn't stand the thought of telling Tamara she had been right.

She stood up just as Tamara came bouncing into the room. "Hi, Tam. How'd it go?"

Tamara was having an ongoing fight with her boss, the features editor at *Today* magazine, and it had been getting worse for weeks. "The worst," Tamara said. "Hey, save me some of that cake." Casey put it back on the coffee table. "How about you, Case? Did you catch your masked man yet?"

Case. Casey suddenly remembered that Dennis had called her Case in that last phone call. She loved it when someone she was fond of called her that. But that pleasure wasn't hers to enjoy anymore.

"Hm?" Tamara prodded.

"No, I didn't catch any masked man," Casey muttered. "And listen, you know it's more important than ever that you don't talk about my work to anyone—like that new boyfriend, for instance."

"Ken? What does he care what you do?"

"*I* don't know," Casey said. "It's natural to ask about someone's roommates."

"Well, he didn't ask about you, all right? We had more interesting things to talk about," Tamara said, curling the icing off the cake. "Mm. This icing is great."

"I know." Casey laughed. "They shouldn't even bother putting the cake in. But really, Tamara, be sure you don't break down on this issue."

Tamara looked quizzical. "What's the matter with you, Casey? No one's going to put out cigarettes on my wrists trying to get me to tell them what you do. If anyone asks, you're an administrative assistant—no, production assistant—with your aunt at McCann-Fields Productions. What's the matter with you, anyway?"

Casey sighed. "Oh, I don't know. I'm sorry. I don't want to talk about it, but let's just say it's not going quite as well as I had hoped."

Tamara looked concerned. "Well, if you want to talk about it, Case, I'm here."

"Thanks," Casey said. But she knew she was bearing a sorrow she wanted to keep to herself, for she had been a fool, a blind fool.

The next morning, when Dennis saw Casey standing and chatting with Ted Conroy, he suppressed his natural impulse to go up to her. Thank God he wasn't in the kind of mood he had been in when Casey first arrived, when he had interrupted her and Ted as if he were some sort of angry administrator. His instinct was to go up to her at some point when she was alone and ask her again what the matter was. But another instinct told him to give her room.

And she *was* independent in every way; he had to remember that. Other p.a.s were often annoyingly dependent, needing to be told what to do at every moment of the day. But Casey had managed to make herself useful to everyone who needed her and did much of her work before anyone even told her what to do.

He sighed. Who was he kidding? He didn't care that she was independent on the job, that she could work well without direction. All he was doing was trying to distract himself from the fact that she just wasn't interested. They had spent an incredibly great evening together, the kind he hadn't had in years. Once he had gotten out of the foul mood that had been dogging him lately, he had given himself over to the pure pleasure of being with Casey. And there was no question about it—she had had a good time.

Sure, in the sexual sense he was pretty sure that was true, but he meant emotionally as well. They had touched more than just physically. Hell, they had really been together. But she had cooled off damn quickly after that.

Dennis tried not to let his mood affect the production, and his determination worked for a while. But when one of the production secretaries came up during a break to tell him he had a call from Parker Claypool, his agent, his calm went out the window. He went into the study to take the call.

"Yeah, Parker."

"Signed, sealed, and delivered," his agent said. "KBC wants you to direct at least six of the season's shows."

Dennis's heart tightened. "What did you say about it?"

"I said no way—like you said—no way unless you got out of 'The Sinners.' "

"Right," Dennis said sourly. "Damnit." Just then Felicia sailed past the doorway, clacking her absurdly high heels across the parquet floor. She was a stubborn, stubborn woman. And Don, for all his outward charm, was worse. What right did they have to interfere with his career in this way? There were half a dozen directors he could send their way who would give anything to direct the show. Hell, his own assistant would be happy to take over, and Bruce would be fine. Dennis had the chance to direct something he loved—a drama that was serious and caring without being sanctimonious, funny without being crude or crass. *His* shows had been the ones that KBC had bought; *his* shows had been the ones that had turned the network around from no to yes. And now someone else would get to take over, while he was stuck with "The Sinners."

"You've spoken to Atchison, too?" Claypool asked.

"I've spoken to everybody," Dennis said. "Everybody here, everybody at McCann-Fields." He laughed humorlessly. "The only one who will listen to me at McCann-

123

Fields is the cleaning woman. She said she'd release me from my contract. 'It's only right,' she said. I swear the company would do better if she were in charge."

"Look," Claypool said. "I'll see what leverage I can get in terms of the network and the sponsors, and you do what you can at your end."

"Right," Dennis said and hung up.

At that moment Felicia walked past the door again, in the opposite direction, followed by Don. Dennis vaulted off the desk and caught up with Don in the hall.

Don was walking quickly, though not with the neurotic rapidity of Felicia's gait, and he barely looked at Dennis as he followed Felicia into the sitting room, where most of the cast and crew were assembled. His graying hair looked even grayer, Dennis noticed, and he wondered if Don was sick. Perhaps that was the reason he had spent so little time on the set lately.

Don didn't sit down. He stood with Felicia at his side, and Dennis felt they looked poised to make some sort of negative announcement. For a moment of wild hope he thought they were perhaps going to announce cancellation of the show. But Don's next words dashed Dennis's hopes.

"I understand there's been some concern on the set about the various accidents we've had."

There was a murmur of agreement, and then Melanie spoke out. "Not just accidents, Don," she said, looking at Morgan. "Morgan got a pretty strange note." She bit her lip. "And whatever problems we all may have with each other, Don, none of us wants to see any harm done to the others. We—we want this stopped."

Don's lips tightened. "Do you still have the note?" he asked, looking at Morgan.

Morgan nodded and went off to the dressing room to get it. While he was gone, Melanie tried to repeat the contents of the note to Don. But she was shouted down every few seconds, having gotten so many words wrong that the message was virtually unrecognizable. Finally Morgan came back and handed the note to Don, who read it slowly and then handed it to Felicia.

"What about the police?" Morgan asked. "Couldn't they do something?"

"Are you kidding?" Ted said loudly. "There's a burglary every three seconds in this city. The police are hardly going to care about some note you got. Why should they?"

Morgan looked away as if he hadn't heard, and Casey's heart went out to him. He was very vulnerable; that had been obvious from the moment she had first seen him, pining away for the uncaring Melanie. He didn't seem to have the veneer of self-confidence the other cast members had. They were all able to put on a carefree act at a moment's notice. But Morgan seemed to behave from the heart at all times, and now that he had received this threatening note, he seemed more vulnerable still.

"Look," Morgan said quietly to no one in particular. "When it happens to you, maybe you'll feel differently." And with shaking hands he took a pack of cigarettes from his vest pocket and lit one.

"Unfortunately," Don said, "I'm afraid Ted is right. We're not going to interest anyone but the *World Globe* or the *Inquiring Examiner* in our story. And I'm sure you'll all agree that we don't want *them* on the set. For now I suggest we all be extracareful, extrawatchful, and above all, calm. You have my assurance that when the time is right—*if* that time ever comes, and let's hope it doesn't—the proper authorities will be called in. Until then let's do the best job we can." He turned to Felicia. "Would you like to add anything, Felicia?"

She abruptly shook her head, and for a moment she looked extremely odd, as if she were going to burst into tears or start laughing uncontrollably. Casey was shocked. Felicia was usually under such firm control. But conditions on the set *had* become tense, and perhaps the woman had problems outside work as well.

"By the way," Don said suddenly. "We went up a point in the ratings last week."

Felicia turned and left the room just as a cry of joy swept the crowd. Casey was amazed at how quickly the mood of gloom could dissipate. Even Ted, who was if possible less likely to crack a smile than he had been in college, was almost, if not quite, smiling. She went over to him and asked what exactly a point meant.

"It's the percentage of all the households with TVs in them that watch us. Each point is worth over eight hundred thousand people, Casey, so you can imagine how pleased the sponsors are when this kind of thing happens, and the producers and the network, too. More people means they can charge more for each commercial."

"You mean the rates are based on the audience figures?"

Ted nodded. "Although they won't be based on, say, last week's audience, the one Don just mentioned. Haven't you ever heard of sweeps week?"

Casey shook her head.

"Well, I'm not sure if there's more than one—I think there's one each season. But anyway, I know there's one in February. That's when each network sets the cost of advertising for its shows, and naturally each one wants really high audience figures, to be able to say, Look, you advertise your toothpaste on our network, and we're delivering x million households. So they inflate the figures any way they can, usually by showing as many shows with as much sex and violence as they can get away with." Ted smiled. "Those two bring 'em in every time."

Casey smiled, but she was only half paying attention to Ted's explanation. For she had noticed as he was talking that Dennis was the only person in the room who wasn't overjoyed or even pleased over Don's news.

She turned her gaze on Ted again, but she couldn't get the image of Dennis's cold, unsmiling face out of her mind. How was she going to live like this, in this never-ending guessing game? How long could she go on not knowing, not understanding? Ted was going on about ratings and points and Nielsens, and he might as well have been talking in a foreign language. It was Dennis she wanted to be listening to, Dennis she wanted to be with.

And she didn't even have the comfort of knowing she was doing the right thing by staying away from him. Memories of the night they had spent together kept returning—of their laughing in bed, hugging each other, whispering, speaking volumes with their eyes. She had come closer to him in that one night than—

"Casey?"

Ted was looking at her questioningly.

"Oh, yes, sorry," she said.

"Well?"

She shook her head. "I'm sorry, Ted. I was thinking of something else for a second. What did you say?"

"Will you read my script? I really need some advice. Every night I go to sleep and I feel as if I'm going insane. I'm so angry at what they did to it that I . . ." His voice trailed off. "I just don't know what to do," he finished weakly. "Maybe if you could read both versions—the one I wrote and the one they're going to shoot next week—maybe if *you* felt the changes were justified, I could accept it a little more easily."

"I'm flattered," Casey said. "But I don't know why you're leaving it up to me. I—"

"I'm not leaving it *up* to you," he interrupted. "I just want another opinion. Anyway, remember Freshman Comp? Who was the only person who got that nut of a professor to give her an A?"

Casey laughed. "But you just said it. He was a nut. But

127

okay, give it to me today and I'll read it over the week-end."

"Great," he said. "And Casey, if you think the rewrite was justified, I'll—I'll change my plans."

Casey looked mystified, but Ted said no more. He smiled enigmatically, turned, and walked away, and Casey was left standing there in confusion. Ted had seemed upset, very upset. Did *he* have sufficient motivation to try to sabotage "The Sinners"? And what had his last remark meant?

Casey's heart raced as she thought of the implications of the questions and their answers. Maybe Dennis *wasn't* the most likely suspect. Maybe Ted was equally likely, or even more so.

She sighed. What a choice—friend or lover. But lord, if she did have a choice, there was no question, no question at all.

For the rest of the day Casey was distracted by inner questions and hypotheses. The ray of hope that Ted's behavior had created was threatening to burst forth into a full, glorious corona of sunlight. But Casey couldn't let it. How could she decide Ted was guilty and Dennis wasn't, as if she were choosing a dance partner? For deep down wouldn't she still distrust Dennis? No, the only way she could operate without driving herself to distraction would be to keep an open mind somehow and to try not to think of how much she cared for Dennis. That simply got her nowhere at all.

Casey left at the end of the day without saying good-bye to anyone. Her resolve hadn't been working. The scripts Ted had given her were like burning hopes. She knew that if she found the rewrite as terrible as he evidently found it, she would seize upon this to try to throw guilt upon her friend. She felt torn apart, pulled in different directions, none of which she wanted to go in. And she wondered if she'd ever find a way out.

She walked down the steps of the town house and turned west and began walking down Seventieth Street. Suddenly someone caught her by the arm, and she jumped and whipped around, her body instantaneously energized for action.

But she was looking into Dennis's eyes.

Her heart was racing, galvanized by the surprise of his touch, and for a moment she just stood there staring with her mouth open. Then she caught her breath. "You nearly scared me to death!" she said.

He smiled. "I thought you said you were a born and bred New Yorker, inured to that sort of thing."

"Inured!" She laughed. "I'm *ready* for it, not inured! You're lucky you didn't get a swift kick in the shins. Or worse!"

"Worse? Then I am lucky indeed. But most of all I'm lucky to catch you. You know that I had to huff and puff my cigarette-ruined lungs for half a block to catch you?"

"Oh, come on. You're in great shape and you know it." She raised a brow. "I thought you were above fishing for compliments."

"Not when they come from you," he said softly. "Some of the things you said to me that night, Casey, I'll treasure forever."

She said nothing, looking into his eyes and seeing only their deep softness that seemed to pull her closer. "Oh, Dennis," she said quietly. "You make it so difficult."

He frowned. "But why? What's difficult, Case? You've told me one thing with your eyes—a very clear and seductive message coming from the most beautiful blue eyes I've ever seen—and something completely different every time I come close to you."

"I told you when we first met, when you first kissed me, that I didn't want to get involved—not with anyone. It didn't have anything to do with you."

"But it does," he said. "Don't you see? We've gone too

129

far for you to say that. Once you've come as far as we have, when you pull away, that action *does* apply to the person you're withdrawing from. It's not abstract anymore. If you don't want to be involved, Casey, that statement is about me." He paused, looking into her eyes, and when he spoke again, his voice was soft, gentle. "Is that true, Casey? If it's me you don't want, then tell me. We'll drop it right here."

"Oh, Dennis, it's not you."

"Then come," he said, slinging an arm around her waist. "Are you busy tonight?"

"No."

"You don't have 'things to do,' as you always put it?" he asked.

She smiled and shook her head.

"All right, then." He smiled. "You're always talking about being a born-and-bred New Yorker. Tonight you're going to be squired around town by a born-and-bred Hoosier, and I'll bet I take you at least three places you've never been."

She laughed. "You're on," she said. "But what are the stakes?"

His eyes darkened. "The stakes are the rest of the night, Casey. If I win, you spend the rest of the night with me, as I choose."

She smiled. "Interesting," she said. "And if I win, same deal?"

He nodded. "Together or apart, in whatever way you'd like."

She wondered at the power of this man who could make her throw away all her resolve, all her logic and reason. She wanted to be with him; she warmed at the thought of the bet, but would she pay later on, with a broken heart?

You'll never know, an inner voice said, *unless you try, and you'll never know love or affection or the simplest of pleasures if you keep fighting.*

She smiled. "Let's go," she said. "But I'd like to stop off at my apartment to change, and I should drop these scripts off, anyway."

"What scripts?" he asked.

"Oh, Ted's, actually. He wanted me to look at something."

"Look at what?" he asked as they walked toward Madison Avenue.

"Uh, the script he wrote and the shooting script."

Dennis shook his head. "We really did a job on it," he said. "But Ted's going to have to get used to that if he's going to write for television. I've seen how tense he's been looking these past few days, and I've been meaning to talk with him."

"Maybe that would help," Casey said. "Oh, there's a cab!" she cried just as Dennis launched into a magnificent run. He caught it, and a few moments later Casey and Dennis were heading across town.

Dennis reached over and covered her hand. "I'm glad I caught you," he said tenderly.

She whispered back, "I'm glad, too," but silently she wondered. How much longer would she be able to go on like this, not knowing and feeling powerless? She had resolved not to cheat herself. She wasn't going to give up a very promising relationship because of a suspicion, a hypothesis. That wouldn't be fair; not at all fair. Yet how long could she endure the uncertainty? She had coddled herself by telling herself that there was no proof of any sabotage. Then, when Morgan received the note, she had had to change that belief system. Clearly someone was trying to undermine production of the series. And now all she could say was that she didn't know it was Dennis.

But how long would she be able to feel this way? And did she believe her own words, deep down?

As she looked at Dennis's handsome profile, thought of the blissful night they had spent together, she knew she loved him. She truly loved him. But how deep did that love run? Would it blind her from the truth? Or would distrust blind her from a deeper love?

The ride in the taxi was short, and when Casey opened the door to her apartment, she was relieved to find that Tamara wasn't home. Right now she had so many conflicting feelings that she just wanted to be alone with Dennis, without further complications. And she knew that if Tamara were here, she'd look at Dennis with such outright suspicion and keen concentration that he would have to notice.

"Very nice," Dennis said as Casey led him into the living room.

"Thanks," she said. "Why don't you sit down while I change?"

"Why don't you come here?" he said softly. And he held out his arms—those magnificent, strong arms she knew so well—and she came toward him.

The moment she touched him she was filled with a deep and powerful memory of their lovemaking, filled with a warm desire for what she had loved so much. His hands, reassuring and strong, pulled her close and held her at the small of her back so she was aware of every inch of his male frame. The warmth spread through her limbs as she remembered, as her body remembered, and when Dennis looked at her with deep brown eyes heavy with desire and dark with need, she melted inside.

"I've missed you," he whispered. "I've missed you and wanted you today." His lips were so close to hers they were almost touching.

"I've missed you, too," she said quietly, her hands on their own quest for pleasure as they moved around to Dennis's chest and searched his muscled form. Her fingers raced over the thin fabric of his shirt, searching for the male nipples beneath, and when she found them, they were already hardened, and Dennis moaned her name.

132

"Let's make love," he whispered.

She looked up at him, tempted. And then she remembered it was impossible. Tamara would be home at any minute. "Later," she murmured. "My roommate will be home soon."

He sighed and shook his head. "I forgot. Then get dressed," he said, giving her a playful slap on the behind. "And don't forget I've got a bet to win."

"What kind of thing should I wear?" she asked.

"Oh, well—I don't want to give anything away. Just wear a dress, Casey, or a skirt."

She changed into a deep blue silk wraparound dress she loved because all she had to wear with it was a pair of panties and sandals, and she came out to the living room a few minutes later.

Dennis looked pleased. "Well, that was fast. And you look beautiful, Casey. You'll be the center of attention at each of the mysterious places we're visiting."

She glanced at him in challenge. "You've picked yourself a tough bet, you know. There are very few places in this city I haven't been."

He smiled. "We'll see."

A few minutes later, as they sat in a taxi headed for East Thirty-fourth Street, Casey looked questioningly at Dennis. "Thirty-fourth Street," she mused. "Hm. There's Gimbel's and Macy's, but they're on the West Side," she said.

"I knew it." He laughed.

"Knew what?"

"You'll see," he said cryptically, and a few minutes later, when they got out of the taxi at the corner of Thirty-fourth and Fifth Avenue, Casey really was mystified.

"You *might* win this leg of the bet," she said.

"I might." He laughed as he led her from the curb. "Welcome to the Empire State Building."

"What?" she cried. "Do you really think I haven't been here?"

"Have you?" he asked.

"Well no, actually, but—"

"You didn't even know what it was," he said as he took her arm and led her in. "Nobody who's grown up in New York ever visits it. But I thought it might be nice to show you a little of your city, aside from having a very keen interest in winning this bet."

And it *was* nice. From the observation deck they could see magnificent vistas of the city and its surrounding suburbs from every direction, and when Dennis drew her into his arms for a long, deep kiss, she was swept up in the romance of the city once again, just as she had been on Dennis's terrace.

Casey loved the way Dennis acted in public—not at all like Steve, who had always been loath even to hold hands. Dennis was completely the opposite, sweeping her into a deep embrace on the observation deck, holding her hand as they left, drawing her close as they rode in a taxi uptown to their next destination.

Once again Casey was mystified as the cab pulled up on Fifth Avenue and Fiftieth Street at Rockefeller Center, and Dennis said they would walk the rest of the way. They passed the skating rink—an outdoor restaurant in the summer—and walked to 30 Rockefeller Plaza, which was a very familiar looking building to Casey. But she knew Dennis wasn't going to take her on a tour of a high-rise office building.

He smiled as he led her into the lobby. "Still don't know, hm?"

She laughed and shook her head.

"And you say you know this town."

He took her to the sixty-fifth floor, to the Rainbow Room, a mesmerizing Art Deco palace that had lovely music, delicious food, beautiful dancing.

Casey and Dennis danced cheek to cheek, holding each other close as they glided to the music, nestling against each other and treasuring the closeness.

"Well, you seem to be winning," she said, "through some weird fluke I really don't understand."

"The weird fluke is that everyone I know who's from this city has missed most of its most famous and really wonderful spots." He smiled. "Are you ready for the third?"

"One more dance," she said, and as he took her in his arms and swept her along to the gentle rhythms of the orchestra, she felt as if she were in paradise.

When Casey and Dennis got out of a cab in front of the Plaza Hotel and Casey told Dennis she had been there dozens of times, he shook his head.

"But that's not where we're going," he said, and she followed as he walked up to one of the top-hatted hansom-cab drivers lined up at the edge of Central Park. And soon she and Dennis were riding in a flower-bedecked carriage, with a very discreet driver in his seat up ahead playing soft, romantic music on the radio. The carriage was hooded at its front, and Casey and Dennis sat facing the rear of the carriage, nestled under its canopy as if in their own private and wonderful world.

Casey smiled into Dennis's eyes as the horse and carriage headed into Central Park with a clip-clop gait she had loved for as long as she could remember. "Well, you win," she said. "And I love this, Dennis, I love it!"

"I'm glad," he said softly and drew her close in a tender kiss that made her tremble with the memory of all he had given her. Every time he touched her, every time she looked into his eyes, she was awash with memories that warmed her to the core: of Dennis's nibbling wet kisses along her inner thighs, of coaxing fingers that had drowned her in desire, of his moans of pure male pleasure,

135

of the way his hot strength could fill her with honeyed rapture.

And now as she sank back into the seat and wrapped her arms around Dennis, feeling his wonderful strong back and inhaling his male scent with deep pleasure, she wanted the overwhelming fulfillment he could give her again. His tongue made promises as it danced with hers, his warm hands branded her as his for the rest of the night as they stroked her back, claimed her hips, seared a thigh beneath her dress. And a low moan that came from somewhere deep inside him sealed those promises with arousing certainty.

Dennis tore his lips from hers, and his eyes were dark, and by the lights of the park and the light of the moon, he looked like a mysterious dark stranger. But by the taste of his lips and the tenderness of his touch, she knew he was the man she loved.

"So I've won," he said, the huskiness of his voice reaching a place deep inside her.

"So I see," she said, "although you cheated just a little."

"How is that?"

"Oh, this beautiful ride—it's lovely, Dennis," she said slowly, enjoying herself as she saw the surprise and daring flicker across his face.

"But—" he supplied.

"But it's not really a place. So it doesn't count."

"Is that so?" he murmured, fighting a smile. "Does that mean this is going to be a contested victory?"

"You could say that," she said. "Depending, of course, on what your idea of victory was going to be."

"I see," he said quietly, a hand suddenly on her knee. The touch was instantly arousing as his hand moved to her thigh. "It all depends, really," he said, letting his fingers trace a lazy circle beneath the hem of her dress. "Well, maybe I'll take you home, and we can have some wine out on the terrace, do a little more dancing, make love."

The thought of lovemaking so near, so close, made her awash with desire. "That could be nice," she said thickly, gazing at Dennis's beautiful moon-shadowed face. She wanted that rough skin of his cheeks raking the tenderness along her cheeks, beneath her breasts, along her inner thighs. And she wanted those lips to work their magic on her in the million ways they knew how.

"But maybe I'll just take you home," he said. "And go home myself."

"You're a bastard. You know that?"

He laughed, his eyes glittering. "I know I said I won, Casey, but I wouldn't want you to do anything you didn't want to do. Maybe we should split up."

He was ruling her. In the deepest of ways, with the lightest of touches, she had fallen under his coaxing spell. But two could play that game.

She splayed her fingers over his lean, hard thigh. The response was immediate, and she flushed as his eyes grew heavy with instant need. "I don't know," she said lightly. "If you think we should split up, just say the word."

"Casey," he moaned and pulled her into his arms, covered her lips with hungry lips of his own, entwined her tongue with his in a kiss that touched the core of her being.

When the hansom cab pulled up at the Plaza again, Dennis, a mischievous smile on his handsome lips, asked Casey if she wanted to go in for a drink.

"I—don't think so," she said, still hazy with pleasure from that last kiss. "We could have a drink at your place, you know."

"We could, but remember, tonight you spend as I wish," he teased.

"Don't be too sure," she answered, suppressing her amusement. "I've always had tricks up my sleeve."

"I'll bet you have," he answered pointedly.

They walked hand in hand back to Dennis's apartment. It was a lovely summer evening, with that certain smell of

June Casey had always loved, and they walked a leisurely path, both knowing they would be together for as long as they wanted that night once they got back to the penthouse.

But the moment they stepped in the door, Casey was achingly aware that they could finally come together fully and deeply and hungrily, and when Dennis caught her at the waist and spun her around, she looked up and saw the same fierce passion reflected in his eyes.

"Thank God you're here," he said hoarsely, letting his hands splay over the curve of her hips, sending deep waves of fire through Casey's limbs. "What made you come?" he asked. "What made you say yes when I found you tonight?"

She looked into his eyes, remembering how they had looked when he had asked her, remembering how they looked when he was stroking her deeply and urgently at the crest of passion. It was those clear brown eyes and that tenderness, as well as a thousand other qualities she couldn't resist. And she didn't want to be reminded of why she was resisting—that being with Dennis was a mistake, that making love with him was a mistake, that loving him could only end in unhappiness.

"Just kiss me," she murmured, and, groaning, he did as she asked, with a soul-touching kiss that sent rolling fire through Casey from head to toe.

He swept her into his arms and she clung to him, loving his scent, his strength as he carried her into the bedroom and laid her down gently on the bed.

She glanced at him mischievously. "Even if I hadn't planned on coming here, I guess I would have had to since I lost the bet."

"That's right," he said quietly. He kneeled above her, one knee on either side of her hips, and looked at her hungrily. "You're mine for tonight," he whispered, and he reached down and parted the silk of her dress. It fell away easily, and his hands covered her breasts. "My God, how I've wanted to do that all night," he whispered. "Do you know what that does to a man, Casey? Knowing that at any moment a woman's dress could fall away with one pull of a sash?"

"Tell me," she whispered. "Show me."

His fingers were exquisitely delicate as they trailed over her breasts, catching each nipple and then tantalizingly moving away. He awakened each silken underside with slow circles, made each nipple tingle with sparking need that spread like fire.

"Dennis," she whispered as her hands found the hardness of his thighs.

"Oh, Casey," he moaned as she kneaded the firmness beneath the fabric of his pants, the long sinewy thighs that could urge her on with such hunger.

"I want you to know something," she murmured.

"Know what?" he whispered.

"There's nothing you could ever ask me to do—nothing—that I wouldn't want to do," she said as the touch of her fingers grew more intimate.

"Casey," he whispered.

"Here. Come," she said, guiding him off her and onto the bed. "Let me." She began to undress him slowly, parting his shirt and letting her lips awaken each nipple, letting her fingers rove over his beautifully rippled chest. He lay back then, and as he cupped her breasts in his hands, she unfastened his belt and then unfastened and slowly unzipped his pants. She drew out the pleasure, stopping when her own grew too great to do anything but whisper her rapture, and as each new inch of his thighs was exposed as she stripped him of his pants, she leaned and kissed their hard strength.

His hands moved from her breasts to the soft curve of her buttocks, and he slid her dress off just as she slid his pants over his ankles. The touch of his hands on her hips,

139

on the backs of her thighs, branded her, and she lowered her mouth to the waistband of his briefs and licked along the edge, wanting to tantalize him as he was her. His skin was incredibly smooth, and when the tip of her tongue touched the line of hair at the center of his stomach, he moaned. "Oh, yes, Casey," he whispered, grasping her more urgently as his touch and hers grew more intimate.

She could barely find her voice when she spoke again. "But Dennis," she whispered, "even though I never welsh on bets, I have been known to turn the tables," she murmured as her fingers crept inside the band of his briefs. "And unprecedented shifts of power do sometimes occur," she murmured as she found the strength of his desire and he cried out in pleasure.

"Oh, God, Casey," he breathed. "Oh, yes."

She tore off his last garment, exposing him in all his masculine beauty, and she let her lips and hands work wondrous magic. He reached for her, grasping for her panties, but she swung away. She thrilled as he whispered, trembled beneath her touch, and then he caught her, whisking her bikinis off in one swift movement. And he shifted to his side, whispered, "Darling, you must let me," and soon she was flooded with warmth and need as his fingers, tongue, rough cheek, wet lips roved a burning path along her inner thighs and then quickly brought her to a fierce pitch of trembling longing.

He pulled his lower body away from her and she lost all concentration, all thoughts except the deep pulsating knowledge of growing, coursing pleasure. "Dennis," she groaned. "Dennis, please."

"Do you still think the tables are so easily turned?" he muttered, his breath hot against her inner thigh.

"Dennis, I need you," she gasped as the tip of his tongue brought her to the brink of blazing wanting and words left her.

Letting his hand stay at the softness of her fiery need,

he shifted around so his eyes were looking into hers with dark passion. "Tell me again," he demanded, his voice low but impelling.

She wrapped herself around him, her body yielding, shifting, fitting with his out of deep, primitive knowledge, and she whispered, "I need you, Dennis."

For a moment he looked into her eyes, his expression wild and unreadable. "Then no games," he said hoarsely. "No bets, no power, no words of challenge. Just the two of us, Casey, together."

For a glowing moment his hand stoked the fires deep inside her, and Casey clutched at him. And then, with a piercing cry of pleasure and triumph, Dennis made them one, masterfully taking her body and soul higher and higher, to the heights of glowing rapture with wild, stroking, fiery movements and cries of blazing arousal. She was flowing with love, possessed by a glow inside that was growing, a glow of hunger that seemed endless. And then in a burst of explosive passion, they cried out and rose in a shimmering course of ecstasy that took them beyond the heights of pleasure into pure, raging fire. And they were joined as if forever, in timeless suspension of everything but rapturous bliss.

Afterward, sighing with small sounds of satisfaction, they held each other.

"You're so wonderful," he murmured. "So beautiful and responsive and giving at the same time." He stroked her hair as she settled against his chest. "And we don't need any games, Casey. Not ever again." He shifted to look at her, his eyes shining into hers. "You're magnificent," he whispered.

"So are you," she answered, smiling. And together they drifted off into contented, dreamless sleep.

The ringing of the phone brought them both out of hazy

sleep, and Dennis sighed and looked at her with a mixture of anger and amusement.

The phone had rung once and then stopped, but Casey heard a voice coming from the answering machine next to the bed—Dennis's voice, in fact, saying ". . . after you hear the tone." There was a pause, a tone, and then: "Dennis, Jerry. Just wondered if you caught Celeste on the tube the other night. A real beaut. If you missed it, I've got it on tape. Catch you later." There was a click, then a dial tone.

Casey glanced at Dennis. He was looking up at the ceiling.

"Was that what we saw the other night?" she asked.

"What we didn't see, yes."

"If you didn't want to see it, why did that Jerry call to tell you about it?"

He sighed and turned back on his side and faced her. "What are friends for?" he said and smiled. "Actually I probably would have watched if you hadn't been here. I *did* have a few other things on my mind, though." He reached out and let his finger travel a smooth path from her cheek down along her neck, up over the silk of her shoulder, over the rise of her breast.

"You never finished that story," she said softly.

"I know."

"Are you going to?"

"If you'd like," he said softly, easily. "Although I don't often like to reveal my dark side," he murmured.

"Everybody has one," she answered. "Anyway, I'll be the judge of whether you have one or not," she added, smiling, realizing only afterward the irony of what she had said.

He pulled her close and then rolled over onto his back, settling her against him so her head rested on his shoulder. "It's a long story," he said softly. "It took place over many months, many years ago, out on the Coast. Anyway, as I think I told you, Celeste and I were living together, in love

142

in some way I can't quite remember now. Maybe I don't want to remember. And we were both struggling." Casey loved the sound of his voice, soft, vibrant, warm in the darkness, comforting and fascinating at the same time.

"Neither one of us could get anywhere, but there were enough signs of encouragement that neither one of us would have considered giving up. Celeste would get callbacks—sometimes one, sometimes two, sometimes three for a part. She knew she was on the right track, and at that time she wasn't so vain that she didn't admit luck played a huge part in everyone's success. She knew it did, and she was waiting for her turn."

He paused. "Now she's forgotten that luck, I'm sure." He looked at Casey and smiled. "Just listen to the stars you see on the talk shows. If they mention luck, they haven't forgotten. If they mention hard work and talent and perseverance, watch out. Anyway, I had bit parts, bit jobs, bit chances, and I was writing back then as well."

"Writing what?" Casey asked, not wanting to interrupt but not wanting Dennis to skip any details.

"Oh, screenplays. There was one I had finished, and I had written several treatments. Anyway, I was trying and writing, and she was trying and waitressing, and one day she packed up and walked out."

"Just suddenly? With no warning?"

"Oh, we had fought," he said. "We had fought about everything. You know, when you're eating scrambled eggs and toast every night and every single penny counts and you never know where the rent money is going to come from, you fight a lot. She was jealous, too. She thought I was having an affair with her best friend."

"Were you?"

He grinned. "Good question. No, I wasn't. I wanted to, but I didn't. Celeste didn't believe me. At first she wasn't sure, and we'd fight and make up, and she'd believe me for a while. Then one day she thought she knew—"

"Any particular reason?" Casey asked, getting the impression, though she couldn't be certain, that she was hearing only one side of the story.

"Well, yes," Dennis said. "Actually, Ann and I had gone off for a long drive. I had taken her to an audition, and it had gone badly. They told her in less than a minute that she was wrong for the part, and afterward we drove along the coast, went for a picnic, that sort of thing."

Casey looked at him skeptically. "I'm sure the 'that sort of thing' part was what bothered Celeste. I think it would have bothered me."

"We were friends, Ann and I," he said. "We could have been more but we weren't. And I do believe in men and women being friends. Don't you?"

"Yes," she said guardedly, "as long as one acknowledges the undercurrents and doesn't pretend. Yes, of course. But anyway, go on with the story." She smiled. "We can argue later."

He raised a brow. "I can imagine," he said. "Well, anyway, Celeste was gone when we got back. A friend of ours had told her I had taken Ann to an audition, and Celeste had assumed the worst, decided enough was enough, and left. To this day she believes Ann and I had an affair."

"Well, I can understand, then, why she'd be upset. If I thought you were having an affair with *my* best friend, I'd be damn upset."

He shook his head. "She knew it wasn't true. She had to convince herself it was because of what she did. Do you want some wine, by the way?"

"Sure."

He sat up and swung his long legs down to the floor, and a few moments later came back with a bottle of red wine and two glasses. After he poured and got back into bed, he continued. "Anyway, I didn't realize it at the time," he said, his voice low with new anger, "but along with her clothes, her knickknacks, all the stuff she probably still has, she packed my script." He shrugged. "I had shelved it. I hadn't looked at it in months. She knew I wouldn't notice it was gone." He paused, taking a sip of wine, lost in thought, back in a time that was obviously unpleasant for him. "She moved in with a producer," he said hoarsely. "I was angry, sorry, hurt. But if I had known what was going on," he said huskily, "I would have done something about it."

He put the wineglass down on the night table and then turned to Casey. He looked into her eyes with dark intensity. "She used my script," he said quietly. "She rewrote it here and there, mostly to give the part she wanted a little more meat. I'd say she added thirty pages to it. Then she put her name on it, told her boyfriend the producer she had written it, and they made it into a movie starring Celeste St. Jacques, produced by Dave Cruise."

Casey's eyes widened. "Are you serious? What was it called?"

"An Eye for Pleasure," he said.

"My God," Casey said. "I saw that!"

"It was a big box-office hit—skewered by most of the critics, but the public loved it. And it put Celeste on the map."

"I don't believe it," Casey said. "Why didn't you sue? Didn't you do anything?"

He sighed. "Yes, I did a few things when I heard— consulted a lawyer, talked to Cruise, talked to Celeste . . ."

"What did the lawyer say?"

"That it would be a difficult case. I hadn't ever shown the script to anyone but Celeste. I had shelved it when I thought it needed too much work. I hadn't registered it with the Writers Guild, the Copyright Office, with anybody. And unfortunately, more important than anything else at the time was the price. I was an out-of-work actor-

145

director, and it was difficult even getting an attorney to talk to me, let alone to take on the case. And it was too risky, they all said, to take on contingency."

"But still, a whole script!"

Dennis shrugged. "I was called to New York then, too—my first commercial—acting, not directing. That was the most important thing in my life at the time. It was work—with a real paycheck attached." He sighed. "Anyway, the incident did become very well known out in L.A. A lot of people believed me, a lot of people avoided Celeste and Cruise. For a while, anyway. But Celeste's career had been made. And you know how it works out there, anyway. Their crime wasn't that they had done it, it was that they had gotten caught."

"That's amazing," Casey said. "Just awful. But Celeste is such a big star now! Do people still talk about it? Hasn't she been censured in any way?"

"Nobody cares," Dennis said. "It was a long time ago. And I've forced myself to forget it, too. I think it's important to move forward, to put the past behind you, no matter how corny that sounds. What gets me, though, is that Celeste has not only always denied it, but she's changed the story. To her friends, I'm someone who had an affair with her best friend, and then, hurt because she had left me, turned on her and claimed I wrote a script she in fact penned herself. Although she would never mention my name on the air or be specific enough to create any sort of libel situation, she still gets a tremendous amount of mileage out of this 'poor little me at the beginning of my career' speech she gives. That's what bothers me almost as much as the original action does."

"My God," Casey said with a sigh. "That's so awful, Dennis."

"Well, it's over," he said quietly. "And as I said, I like to put things like that behind me. As far as I'm concerned, the only present reminder I have of that past is what I told you before—perhaps an unreasonable rule, but one I can't shake."

"You mean you're not going out with actresses or people who could use you."

"I'm a pretty self-contained person, Case. I have a lot of work, not much spare time on my hands, and I'm not one of those people who mind spending time alone. So when I do get involved with someone, I want to know she's someone I trust. If that trust isn't there, I'd just as soon be on my own."

Casey smiled—an inappropriate response, she knew, but the only one that would mask her real feelings. Dennis had unwittingly just spoken the saddest words he could have uttered. For the trust he had based their relationship on was nothing but an illusion.

CHAPTER EIGHT

On Sunday night Casey left Dennis's and went back to her apartment to get ready for work and read Ted's scripts. To her surprise, Ted had been right. What had begun as an interesting, fast-paced script had been turned into a much less coherent hodgepodge of very short scenes and unnecessary inclusions of cheap stock footage. What originality Ted had managed to introduce had been steamrolled, so that only the barest outlines of plot remained to show the relationship between his original script and the final revision they were due to begin shooting.

The next morning when Casey got to work, Dennis, Felicia, and Hank Reed, the story editor, were already locked away in conference over the script. A few minutes after Casey came in, Ted arrived, and Casey went up to him immediately. They walked to the edge of the hallway, Ted looked around, and Casey told him she had just heard that shooting was going to be delayed while more revisions were made.

Ted looked at her. "So what did you think?"

"I think you wrote a great script. And I think they did mess it up. Tell me why."

"What do you mean?"

"They obviously had reasons for making the changes they made. Why didn't you take the job on yourself and make the requested changes?"

"I did," he said in a carefully controlled voice. "Under the terms of the Writers Guild contract, Casey, once McCann-Fields bought my script, I had to provide them with a first draft, a second draft, and a polish. Which I did. And no matter how good you are, the story editor is always going to have to go over it again and again and again to make sure that it all works out in terms of the conditions—what the producers inevitably want in terms of plot changes, what the director wants in the way of line changes, what the set calls for that the writer might not have realized. But Casey, I've been with this show long enough to know all of that. What they did to my script was a massacre!"

She sighed. "I know," she said quietly, and silently she wondered if she perhaps was fanning the flames of Ted's anger, unconsciously hoping he was the one. Was she seeing his situation as worse than it really was, trying to convince herself that he had greater motivation than Dennis did?

"And look," Ted seethed, nodding at Georgia, who was pacing the floor with Hugh Ascot and trying, apparently, to learn her lines. "I'm not the only one who's angry about this episode."

Indeed, as Casey and Ted drifted into the sitting room —the cast's unofficial gathering place while on breaks— there was ample evidence that Ted was right. Everybody was unhappy with the script.

They were soon followed into the sitting room by Georgia and Hugh, arguing at the top of their lungs. "I don't *know* how to say it, damnit, Hugh. No one would know how to read such an absurd line. No one would ever *say* such an absurd line."

"Then I don't know how in hell you expect to run through this," Hugh growled, and Casey was shocked. She had never before heard Hugh so much as raise his voice.

At that moment Casey heard Felicia, Dennis, Hank, and the production secretary, Joanie, emerge from the study and come down the hall. Felicia entered the sitting room followed by the others, and she looked drained and haggard, as if she were held together by the most tenuous of threads. Dennis looked furious, though when he saw Casey from across the room, his face lit up and he gave her a quick wink.

She smiled, but Felicia's next words made the smile disappear. "We're going with the script as is—minor changes only." There was a roar of anger and disappointment.

Finally Georgia's clear contralto came through. She addressed Dennis rather than Felicia. "Then Dennis, you're going to have to help me with these lines."

Shocked silence fell upon the room. Georgia was unanimously considered the most professional of all the cast members. She was extremely talented but extremely quiet as well, almost invisible except when the cameras were actually rolling. She involved herself in none of the petty jealousies that plagued every cast, inserted herself in none

149

of the childish quarrels. She normally needed no help, little direction, and could always be counted on. But for the first time in two years, she was asking for help.

Dennis looked as surprised as the rest of the onlookers, and Georgia supplied him with the answer to his unspoken question. "You see, I really don't have the slightest idea what to do—what Lauren is being asked to do is completely out of character."

"Why?" Dennis asked.

Georgia shook her head. "Lauren is a very direct person, Dennis. She's nasty, but she's direct. She rarely does anything behind the scenes, and when she does she's so incapable of keeping a secret that she lets her victim know right away what she's done. What you and Felicia and Hank have changed the script to simply doesn't make any sense. The *original* script—Ted's script—called for Lauren to have a physical confrontation with Kezia. She's no longer acting behind the scenes. The two of us were going to have a good old down-home, low-down cat fight. I would have hurt Kezia, she would have lost her baby, and on to the next episode. Now I'm supposed to poison her food. The average person doesn't have poison around her house!"

"Lauren is hardly the average person," Hank broke in. "And the poison isn't fatal. It's there to scare Kezia. As an added benefit, she'll lose the baby. But Lauren couldn't have predicted this at the time."

Casey shivered involuntarily. Though she was often exposed to life at its worst, she couldn't help being unnerved by the discussion. These people—"The Sinners"—were ruthless. Had their characters inspired someone in the room to be equally so?

"But poisoning is so—so *passive*," Georgia complained.

"I disagree," Morgan cut in, and everyone turned, looking as surprised as when Georgia had first spoken. Morgan was quiet and had been quieter still since receiving the note; he was not usually one to contradict anyone else—especially Georgia.

"What did you say?" Georgia asked.

He reached for a cigarette and lit it before speaking. Then he rose from the beige Queen Anne's chair he had been sitting in, and Casey watched as he took on the role of someone more outspoken than he himself was. He wore an enigmatic smile as he spoke.

"You see, I've been giving this sort of thing a good deal of thought lately—ever since I got my not-very-cheering note." He paused, taking another long drag on his cigarette. Casey could see he wasn't quite as pulled together as the persona he was playing; the vulnerable and shaken Morgan Ford was still visible beneath. "Anyway, I've always been a great mystery fan, thrillers, that sort of thing. And as any of you who share my interests will agree, poisoning—whether it's fatal or merely intimidating—is the number-one female form of treachery. These—"

"That's silly," Melanie interrupted. "Are you saying they divide crimes by sex? That's just ridiculous," she said harshly, looking at Morgan with contempt.

Casey sighed. How could Morgan stand the abuse Melanie heaped on him? She seemed to have more contempt for him the more people were around to witness it.

"That's exactly what I'm saying," Morgan said, undiscouraged by Melanie's ridicule. And, as on another occasion when he had spoken before a group, his confidence seemed to take a sudden leap as he warmed to his subject. "Haven't you ever thought of the suicides you've read about?" he asked, looking not at Melanie now but from person to person in the group. "Men tend to shoot themselves; women tend to poison themselves—overdoses and that sort of thing. The reason, they say, is vanity, how one would look afterward. I could go on, but the point is this: I think the new version of the script is dreadful. But I *do*

151

think changing Lauren's harassment of Kezia to poisoning from pushing is an improvement. And I hope that stays, no matter what other changes are made."

"There won't *be* any more changes," Felicia said in a clipped voice.

"Then McCann-Fields will deserve anything they get," came a low voice from nearby. It was Ted, livid with anger.

When the production secretary had finished typing up the script changes, Casey collated and distributed them and helped cue Morgan with his lines while Melanie sulked over some undivined slight. Dennis, Felicia, Hank, and Joanie had already gone back into the study for another round of revisions, Felicia's announcement notwithstanding, and by the time lunch, served downstairs, was over, the four still hadn't emerged.

Finally Melanie, apparently irked that no one was paying any attention to her, threw down her script. "Why are we even learning these lines?" she exploded. "They say this scene is okay, but why believe them? They'll just change the lines again and again and again. What's the damn point?"

"We've never had this kind of script trouble before," someone said. "What the hell is going on?"

"Maybe it's the new story editor," someone else said.

"No," Georgia objected. "I've worked with Hank before and he's the best."

"Well, all I know," came a small, high voice from the corner, "is that someone is trying to kill this show every way they know how, and I'm getting out."

These words had been spoken by Lisa Sykes, the young woman who played the Edwardses' maid and Steele Edwards's secret lover. She was a beautiful, quiet young woman, the least theatrical of all the cast members. Casey had heard she was engaged to a lawyer, that she had fallen

152

into acting almost by accident. And as Lisa went on, Casey could see that there was a fear in her eyes that was perhaps inappropriate to the circumstances but very real nevertheless.

"I've told my fiancé about what's been going on," she said, tucking a wisp of delicate blond hair behind her ear. "And he doesn't like me being here."

Hugh nodded approvingly. "He's being properly protective of you, my dear," he said, smiling at her as if she really were both his paramour and his maid.

Lisa frowned, looking uncertain. "I don't want to sound meek," she said. "I mean, I can make decisions on my own and all that. But Carl brought it up and I really don't disagree with him. This production could be headed for lots of bad things. It happens, you know."

Melanie looked at Lisa with disdain. "I can't *believe* you're letting a man make that kind of decision for you," she said, her voice seething with anger. Casey stared. Melanie had never struck her as particularly liberated or concerned with that sort of issue. Perhaps she was just annoyed that Lisa was, if only for a few minutes, the center of attention. "Don't you know you're never going to get a chance like this again?" Melanie demanded, echoing the sentiment Morgan had expressed to Casey the other day. And it was an important one: for an actor the series was much, much too important to harm in any way. Everyone on the show had been, until recently, relatively unknown. Their careers had been launched with the show, and perhaps some of their careers could end if they left the show or the show ended. Which meant that, sadly, once again Casey had to draw the conclusion that someone on the nonacting end of the show—Dennis or Ted, for example—was a much, much likelier candidate as the saboteur.

"You're a fool," Melanie continued, apparently not noticing that Dennis had just stepped into the room. "And someone who takes a step like yours deserves everything she gets."

"And what step are you taking, Lisa?"

Casey felt a flash of jealousy go through her.

Lisa looked down for a moment, looking more uncertain than ever. "I, um, I'm not coming back to the show," she said quietly. "My contract runs out in a few weeks, and my fian—I've decided not to come back."

Dennis looked at her in disbelief. "Does Felicia know?" he demanded roughly.

Lisa nodded. "My agent has already talked to McCann-Fields. Nothing's final yet, but—"

"Wonderful," Dennis interrupted. "This is all we need. May I ask why you're leaving?"

She looked up at him with watery blue eyes. "I—the show—it's not what I want."

"It was before," he said forcefully.

"That was before Stacy got hurt," she said quietly. "And then Melanie, and Morgan's note, and . . . I just don't like it. I'm about to get married."

Dennis's voice rose in anger. "Have you learned nothing from all these months?" he demanded. " 'The Sinners' is nonsense in many ways, Lisa, but there *is* a reason the American public is addicted to it. The characters touch the pulse of the viewers, Lisa, because they do what they want—whatever they have to—in order to achieve their goals. They each go beyond the limits of what's right, beyond the limits of the law and where ordinary people go. *But they get what they want.* Now, do you want to be an actress?"

"I don't know," she said quietly.

He threw up his hands, and she quickly said, "Yes, yes, I do."

"Well then," he countered. "Do you think it's all going to be easy? As easy as your getting this part apparently was? You're already close to the top, kid. If you give up now, everyone will think you're crazy. But more important, Lisa, you'll be throwing away the best chance you'll ever get to do what you want. Look at Lauren Edwards— is she going to let Kezia worm her way into what she thinks is rightfully hers? Is she going to let Kezia cut a chunk out of the Edwards family fortune? No, she'll do anything she has to in order to prevent it. The show's characters often go too far by society's standards, they're 'The Sinners,' after all. But we could all learn from them."

Lisa sighed and looked down at her hands again. "I just don't know," she said in a small voice.

"Well, I suggest you think about it," Dennis said gruffly. "And shooting's off today," he added, looking at the rest of the group. "We have more problems with the script than we anticipated."

There was a groan of disappointment, and Casey felt it was ironic that, right after delivering a speech that had inspired much of the cast, Dennis was announcing another postponement. Casey hadn't found the speech one bit inspiring, though. Given the unwelcome thoughts she had about Dennis's motivations, she didn't like hearing that he felt the ends justified the means, that sometimes one had to cross the borders of justice or proper behavior to achieve what one wanted.

When she spoke to Dennis a few minutes later, he was much more soft-spoken than he had been in front of the group.

"I have to meet with Felicia for a while," he said, his tone velvety. "Will you stay until I'm finished?"

"That depends on how long you're going to be here, Den. Don't you think it would look a little odd if I sat out in the foyer for hours? Not that I would want to anyway, but . . ."

He shrugged. "I'm not going to argue. And we might run late, anyway. Meet me at my apartment, then?"

"I'm not going to argue with *that,*" she said softly. And

155

when he gave her his keys and his hand brushed hers, he ignited a spark of heat that swept through her and made her warm with the promise of pleasure.

A few minutes later Casey left the town house and headed down Lexington Avenue with a spring in her step and a smile inside. There was something exciting about her clandestine meetings with Dennis, as if there were something forbidden going on.

But then as Casey passed a newsstand and saw the cast of "The Sinners" on the cover of *Modern Screen and TV Highlights,* she realized she was fooling herself, trying to make herself believe something that wasn't true. She had a fleeting mental image of Melanie fingering Dennis's tie, looking into his eyes with the promise of all he could desire. Melanie probably thought she would seduce Dennis one of these days. For her, it probably seemed just a matter of time. But it wasn't; he wanted Casey, not Melanie. And somewhere, at some level, no matter how immature it was, Casey wished Melanie—and the others—knew she was seeing Dennis.

Oh, well. Perhaps that would come with time. She certainly couldn't blame it on Dennis, in any case. He didn't seem to have any qualms about showing his feelings for her in public. He was subtle, but he seemed to be following her lead more than anything else.

No, what was really bothering her was the reason for the secrecy, the one element that never disappeared. She was more aware of it because she was going to Dennis's apartment without him for the first time. She was spying on him; it was as simple as that.

She introduced herself to the doorman—not something she would normally have done, but he stopped her and asked her to announce herself. After explaining that she had Dennis's key and his permission to go upstairs, and learning to her surprise that Dennis had called ahead to be sure Casey would be let through, Casey was finally released into the elegant lobby, which was beautifully lit with high crystal chandeliers and accent lighting over lush, dramatic plants. She was painfully conscious of her role all of a sudden. Would she someday be leaving this lobby in tears, banished from Dennis's apartment as Celeste St. Jacques had been banished from his life? If she solved the case and discovered the culprit hadn't been Dennis, would he ever trust her again? And what if the unthinkable happened—what if Dennis was the saboteur?

The elevator gates shut with a clang, and Casey let her mind silence her thoughts for now. She knew nothing more than she had earlier, when she had agreed to meet Dennis at his apartment. Was she going to let her thoughts ruin all their moments together? For she truly felt she had chosen a course that was fair to herself—seeing Dennis as long as she didn't *know* he was doing anything wrong— and wavering just made her feel worse.

The moment she walked into Dennis's apartment, Casey let her fears and questions slide away. She loved it here. This was where she had made love with a man too wonderful to suspect. This was where she had given herself up to an experience she had to admit she was afraid of after all her mistakes of the past. And she had loved it. And loved him.

She walked through the foyer and into the living room, turning on a light here and there so the room was softly lit, and then she opened the doors of the terrace and let the summery breeze waft in.

When Dennis came in not much later, Casey was out on the terrace, and she turned and watched with pleasure as he came striding out to meet her. He was smiling as he took her into his arms, and she looked at him questioningly. "You look ecstatic," she observed. "Did something good happen at the script conference?"

He shook his head, still smiling.

"Did something good happen on your way home?"

He shook his head. "The something good I'm smiling about happened the day you walked into my life," he said. "Do you know how wonderful it is to leave an awful script conference and *know* that when you come home the person you most want to see in the world will be waiting for you?"

"Oh, Dennis," she said happily, "what a great thing to say." She reached up and pulled her to him in a kiss that was gentle, affectionate, playful. She smiled into his eyes.

"Very nice," he uttered passionately. "But Casey, I did have something a little different in mind."

A corner of her mouth lifted.

"Make love to me," he said huskily. "The way you did the other night. The way I'll never forget as long as I live." His breathing quickened as his hands grasped her hips and held her against him. "I want you more than I've ever wanted any woman in my life. And I'm going to take every chance as quickly and as often as I can to have you." His lips were close, warming her own with their nearness, and the heaviness of his eyes spoke of the passion she ached to experience. "And I want to give you pleasure, Casey, as much pleasure as you give me every single time."

"Then take me," she whispered.

And in moments they were undressing quickly, hungrily, by the soft light of the bedside lamp.

"I love to see you," he whispered as he lay facing her on the bed, "in all your beauty, in your most perfect state. You were made to be this way," he said, reaching out and touching the curve of her hip with his hand.

Her eyes closed under the hot touch, and she whispered, "I was made for you, Dennis."

"Oh, darling," he murmured, exciting her as his hands roved upward, cupping her breasts and sending shimmers through her.

From somewhere inside Casey felt a small moment of fear. What she had just said to Dennis was the kind of thing that she felt was okay to say during lovemaking, when passion took over and reason left off, but tonight she had been freed the moment he had touched her. When he had, branding her with need as he was now doing, she *did* feel she had been made for him. She felt she was his, that she belonged to him and with him, body and soul forever.

And Dennis's hands and lips and tongue made her forget all her fears and questions. He worked magic on her from head to toe, whispering words of encouragement and affection that deepened each touch, each kiss, each caress.

"You're so beautiful, so giving." He groaned as his fingers etched a tingling path over her back, around to her breasts, over her hips and buttocks, awakening her to the yearning he and he alone could create in her. "Your skin is so soft," he whispered. He looked into her eyes and inhaled slowly. "And do you know what?" he murmured as his hand moved up and down her thigh slowly, urgently, making her arch toward him. "You *were* made for me," he said, and she trembled, murmuring his name.

Looking into his eyes and seeing the love and excitement there made her pleasure even greater. "But why? Why us, together? So special?" She could barely get the words out, could barely speak under the onslaught of his fingers filling her with sheer delight, but she had to know, wanted to ask, wanted to know what he thought.

"Because, darling, we *were* made for each other. We were." And he covered her lips with his and they moaned together, and with a cry of joy he thrust his hard strength into her softness. She held him tightly, his back damp and warm under her fingers, his rough cheek grazing her own, and she was engulfed by a burning ache that grew and grew until she thought it couldn't possibly grow anymore, and she was breathless with wonder and joy.

She was filled with deep love for this man who was filling her with his self, his pleasure, his passion, and all

159

that she could think of, cry out, and whisper was her love for him.

And then the love and pleasure and feverish need exploded into a glowing, undulating, ecstatic blaze that sent them together into a universe made only of passion, of rapturous sensation that united them, melted them, into one being.

Gradually, slowly, Casey came back to consciousness and awareness of the wonderful man who held her in his arms, his breathing gently slowing.

"I don't think I've ever felt quite like that," Casey said, her voice quiet in the darkness. She let her fingers find his chest and then let a hand slide around to his back.

He pulled her close, swung a lean thigh over hers, and whispered, "I'm so glad."

She smiled in the darkness, but there were also tears in her eyes. She didn't think he understood the depth of her feelings, the true difference between now and what she had previously felt. She was no blushing virgin, no just-kissed princess awakened from years of chastity, but each time she made love with Dennis, she felt almost as if it were the first time. The experience was so, so different from anything she had ever felt.

It wasn't even that his movements, his touch, his techniques were different. There was love in every touch—a warm, deep love she felt at every moment more deeply and fully, that she was sure he felt as well. And she had never experienced this before.

It wasn't that lovemaking with her ex-husband or with Mark had been terrible. At times she had been happy—very happy. But she had never felt the deep connection she felt with Dennis, the feeling that they were one, they were together. And afterward, with both Steve and Mark, Casey had often felt a hollowness that grew inside, an empty loneliness made all the deeper by the physical closeness of the man lying at her side. She had just made love

160

with the man, and she felt emptier than she had ever felt before.

But now every breath of Dennis's was her breath, every heartbeat of hers was his. They knew each other as intimately as it was possible for two people to know each other.

"Tell me about your marriage," he said softly, bringing her closer. "I want to know, Case."

She sighed, gearing herself up, and he took her silence for reluctance. "I want to know because I care so much about you, Casey. I want to know everything about you."

"Well, I don't know where to start. It—it wasn't the greatest marriage on earth. I guess it didn't even start out that way."

"Why did you marry him?" he asked gently.

"Oh, I thought I loved him. And I suppose—no, I know—I thought it was the right thing to do."

"How old were you?"

"Twenty-four."

"That's not that young," he said. "For jumping into marriage, I mean."

"Well, no." She sighed. "I think that in a lot of large cities like New York, people do tend to get married a little bit later. But no matter where you're from, there's always some pressure there, even if you're not that conscious of it. You don't know what it's like because you're a man, and luckily it's really changing these days, but the fact is that no matter where you're from, when you're a woman and you reach a certain age, you're expected to get married." She paused. "I don't know. Maybe that's true more of my family than it is of most families. But I felt that pressure."

"And that's why you married Steve?"

"No, no, but it was partly that. You know that feeling you get when you wonder whether you'll ever find your Mr. Right—or Ms. Right, in your case."

161

She felt him shift away from her, and he turned on the bedside lamp. "Do you mind the lamp?" he asked, his eyes shining with affection. "I like to see my Ms. Right while she's talking."

"Oh, Dennis," she murmured.

He stroked a lock of dark hair behind her ear. "Beautiful as your hair is," he said, smiling, "I do prefer your eyes. And I like to see them when you talk." He leaned over then and gently kissed each one, then lay back and faced her. "And please go on," he said quietly. "I shouldn't have interrupted."

"Well," she began. But her mind wasn't on her marriage to Steve, on the problems of the past she had put way, way behind. No, she was thinking of what Dennis had just called her. Ms. Right. She smiled. It was so corny and so wonderful.

"What are you smiling about?" he asked, smiling himself.

"Oh, nothing," she answered. She couldn't help being evasive. For even though he had just said something very affectionate, very direct, she couldn't cross that last gap that separated them. She couldn't acknowledge what he had said. For underneath, as always, there was the fear that he would turn on her, turn and say, "You misunderstood; that isn't what I meant at all." Or, "I wasn't being serious; don't tell me you thought . . ."

She looked at him. Dennis was too kind to say that sort of thing, too caring. But even so she couldn't shake the fear.

Better not to think about it, she decided, and she picked up the thread of their conversation. "Actually," she said, "what happened with the marriage is something I've always feared would happen again if I remarried."

"What was that?" he asked with concern.

"I guess the romance just went out of it—just disappeared. And it was a lot worse than that sounds. We closed off from each other, Dennis." She sighed. "At the end, when—when I discovered that Steve was having an affair, I really blamed him one hundred percent. I thought everything was his fault, and that it had all fallen apart because of *his* personality flaws and *his* failures. But that wasn't true. I had withdrawn from him completely." She shrugged. "And in a way, I can understand why he needed someone else."

As she looked into Dennis's eyes she tried to see inside, to see how he felt about what she was saying. Part of her wondered whether she had gone too far, whether she had said too much. What she was admitting to Dennis, after all, wasn't very attractive or alluring; she was telling him about a painful period of her life in which she had been less than perfect.

But part of her knew that to do anything less would be cheating herself. She had learned from her earlier relationships that they hadn't gone deep enough; she hadn't given enough of herself, just as the men hadn't given enough of themselves; and that the only way a true relationship could exist and flourish securely and for more than a brief interlude was if you went more deeply than your courage necessarily allowed.

At least she hoped this was true.

"That must have been very hard for you," he said quietly. "But what's interesting—and sad—to me is that you were both in a very unpleasant, very unpromising situation—in a marriage that clearly wasn't working—and yet you each reacted very, very differently."

"What do you mean?"

"Well, you apparently kept your distance. Maybe you withdrew even more. But Steve went out and found someone else."

She swallowed, suddenly less relaxed than before. "What are you saying?"

He blinked. "What do you mean?"

163

"Just what I said," she answered. "Just what I asked. What are you saying?" She could hear the tension in her voice, although she hadn't meant for it to come through. But it had edged her words and raised her voice to brittle-thin sharpness.

"It goes back to what I once said to you before—that I think men and women are essentially different in that respect. That in the same situation most men will do one thing and most women will do another. Men basically are not monogamous creatures."

"Oh, great!" she exploded. "God, I thought that's what you might be leading up to. You men are all alike. I knew that you thought that to some extent, Dennis. But how dare you interpret something that happened to me—that happened in *my* life—so that it fits your theory? A very self-serving theory, I might add."

"Self-serving?" he repeated. "How can you say that, Casey? It's not exactly complimentary to say that half of the human race is incapable of sustaining monogamous relationships."

"That's not what I mean and you know it," she answered, sitting up against the cushioned headboard. "You don't care about giving yourself or the rest of your sex a gold star; that's not what I'm talking about. What you do care about is stating what supposedly is a fact and then acting upon it, using the theory that 'this is the way we men are' as justification. That's just such nonsense. It's like saying sorry, that's just the way I am. I can't change. That's a load of baloney."

"You may very well feel that way," he said evenly, reaching for a cigarette and matches. He lit his cigarette and exhaled before speaking again. "Obviously you do feel that way. And you certainly have a right to your opinion. But we apparently disagree on what you just said as well. I've said those very words you think are so awful. I've said

164

I'm a certain way and that I can't change. But I don't see anything terrible about that."

She looked at him and shook her head. "I don't believe it," she said, her voice low with anger. "I just don't believe it."

"Casey, it's not as if—"

The phone at Dennis's side rang and jarred them both. For a moment they stared at each other. Casey felt completely alienated from him, horribly different from the way she had felt only minutes before.

And then after he said hello, when his voice went velvet soft and he said, "Oh, hi, Melanie," Casey felt as if a cold hand had just clutched at her heart.

CHAPTER NINE

Casey was sickened by Dennis's tone. It was so caring, so smooth, not at all appropriate for Melanie if what he had said about his feelings for her was true. When Casey had asked him if he had ever gone out with Melanie, his reaction had been one of astonishment, and he had seemed to wonder how she could have even entertained such a thought.

Yet now his voice was tender, soothing, reassuring, and Casey remembered why she had asked Dennis that question in the first place: he was consistently tender, soothing and caring with Melanie when she needed such treatment.

Casey listened carefully—anxiously—to the conversation.

"Yes, Melanie . . . Really? What did it say? . . . Look, honey, calm down . . . No, calm down, you don't have anything to worry about." He paused and looked at his watch. "All right, I'll be right over."

Casey felt as if she had just been punched in the stomach. She looked at Dennis, but he was avoiding her gaze.

"Right," he said to Melanie. "I remember. Good-bye." And he hung up.

Seconds went by as Casey continued to level her gaze at him—wishing it were more than a gaze—and he continued to avoid it.

Finally he turned and faced her, and even then he wasn't looking into her eyes. "I have to go see Melanie," he said quietly.

"Obviously," she spat out. "I'm not going to bother saying I couldn't help overhearing, Dennis, because we *are* lying here in bed together."

"Look," he said. "I really don't see that I have to apologize for what I'm about to do."

Her heart was thudding, ready to pound out of her chest in a moment. "Are you kidding?" she asked. She shook her head. "I don't know why not!"

"Melanie is very upset," he said slowly. "She got a note that sounds very much like the one Morgan got. She just found it in her purse." He paused and then sighed. "And she's very upset about it."

"As you just said," Casey snapped. "And that's the only reason you're going."

He blinked, and this time he did look at her. "Of course," he said.

"Fine. Then I'll come with you."

"What?"

She shrugged. "If that's really why you're going, Dennis, then I don't see why I can't come along, too." She knew she had gone too far. She knew there were situations in which, if the roles were reversed, she would be acting just as Dennis was. But she couldn't stop herself. She was hurt, damnit.

And then another thought hit. She had completely set aside the reason Dennis was running off to Melanie's. Melanie had received a note just like Morgan's.

Oh, God, she thought. Did Dennis *have* to go to Melanie's? Did he have to because he was the one who had written the note, and he wanted to calm her down so she wouldn't go too far—to the police, for example—with the evidence?

She looked at him again. "All right?" she asked. "It's settled. I'm coming along."

He narrowed his eyes, studied her for a few moments, then turned and swung his legs out of bed. "You're being irrational," he said as he walked to the bureau.

"Am I?" she asked, her voice high with tension. She watched as he pulled a pair of briefs from his top drawer, watched as he put them on. "Of course, I suppose that's another female thing to do, isn't it. We monogamous females are pretty high-strung, aren't we?"

"Maybe you are," he said without turning around.

Casey jumped out of bed and stormed out of the room. The sight of her clothes strewn across the living room carpet was infinitely depressing. As she walked about picking up socks here and jeans there, she could feel tears rising, her throat closing with tension and impending sobs. Damnit, she wouldn't cry. That he would expect. But as she looked at her clothes and began to pull on her jeans, buttoned a shirt that didn't do all that much for her after all, she could just imagine Melanie and how she would greet Dennis in half an hour.

Melanie, Casey had heard, had managed to keep endless clothes from the show, diaphanous gowns that showed off her tall, slim form to perfection, even a shortie nightgown Casey was shocked had even been allowed on TV. And

167

Melanie would be sure to look her best for Dennis. Of that Casey was certain.

The sound of Dennis's footsteps on the carpet made Casey look up. He was dressed in jeans and a pale blue button-down shirt, and he was opening the coat closet near the front door. He brought out a sports jacket, slung it on, checked himself in the mirror on the inside of the door, and closed it.

He turned to the breakfront behind him, scooped up the keys Casey had thrown there when she had come in, and then finally he looked at Casey.

The look in his eyes made her wish he had already left, for she saw only distance there, no love at all. "Good night," he said simply, and he turned, opened the door, and left.

The door closed, and Casey closed her eyes against tears she absolutely refused to shed.

A few minutes later Casey was on the street, desperately searching for a cab. There wasn't one anywhere in sight. Finally she walked down to Fifty-seventh Street to a bus stop, but again she saw nothing coming.

The tension inside her was almost unbearable. She was so angry, so hurt, so wildly furious she could hardly think. All she could concentrate on was not breaking down in public.

But her thoughts dragged her back over the evening, over and over and over again. How had it turned so horrible? Dennis had seemed so happy; she had been so happy. They had shared their love in the most magnificent of ways, melded their souls in the most glorious way that existed on earth. And then something had twisted, wringing all the goodness out of the experience until there was—what? Only bitterness, suspicion, jealousy, mistrust. Not even an ounce of affection.

She remembered his tone of voice, the sight of his back,

the flatness of his words as he had said, "You're being irrational."

Her heart raced at the memory, reacting as strongly as if he were saying them once again.

But had she been irrational? She remembered how unhinged she had felt. Coming straight after Dennis's questions and speculations about her and Steve's marriage, his decision to see Melanie was too much, and she remembered feeling very out of control.

But where was his sensitivity? She had just told him of a very private part of her life, told him things she had never told a man before because she had been afraid of getting this close, afraid of scaring him off, perhaps. And Dennis had reacted by alienating her completely, first by drawing conclusions he had no right to make, next by running off to another woman.

And she had become so unsettled by his words and that horrible tone of voice that she hadn't even thought of her job or the implications of Dennis's actions until the questions had come unbidden into her mind. And then she had put them aside, caring much, much more about what Dennis was doing on a personal level, what he was doing to her.

She had been blinded once again, and she didn't even know in which area she was more blind—personal or professional. All she knew was that the trust she had begun to build up had been shattered.

Dennis got out of the taxi at Spring Street and walked over to Greene, where Melanie's building was. From the outside the building looked like what it had once been—a clothing factory with a grimy exterior and high-ceilinged floors that could hold heavy manufacturing equipment. On the inside, though, the building had been converted into luxury cooperative lofts, one to a floor, each with perfect parquet floors, modern kitchens with butcher-

169

block counters and tabletops, all modern conveniences, and wood-burning fireplaces.

Dennis didn't particularly like Melanie's loft. When he had gone last year to the cast "picnic" she had held, he had disliked the trendiness of the place, with the kind of carefully chosen flower arrangement—a glass globe with three tiger lilies in it—that was de rigueur at the time, and Melanie's obviously slavish devotion to whatever was current and accepted.

But right now he wasn't thinking about Melanie's loft, inside or out. He was thinking about the woman he had just left back in his apartment.

Damn. It always screwed up, one way or the other. Casey had been wild, irrational, the opposite of the cool, almost detached young woman he had first met, when she had seemed to need nothing, had seemed totally self-possessed. Where had her sudden streak of jealousy and possessiveness come from? She had never struck him as a Celeste St. Jacques type. Never.

He climbed the stone steps to Melanie's building and rang the buzzer marked Kincannon outside the front door. It was ridiculous, really, that the woman paid a fortune for a place you still had to walk down from to answer in person, but he supposed that was the price you paid for living in Soho.

After what seemed like an hour Melanie came down. "Oh, Dennis," she said in a quavering voice. "I'm so glad you came."

"That's okay. You were scared," he said, looking down into her eyes. Funny, he had never noticed how blue they were. Or how smooth her skin was.

She smiled. "Come on. I just opened up a bottle of wine," she said and turned and began walking up the stairs.

She walked ahead of him slowly, sensuously, with a grace that was almost hypnotic. She was wearing—he didn't even know what it was; maybe they called it an at-home gown. Satin, deep purple, incredibly soft-looking, feminine.

When she reached the landing she turned and smiled before opening the door. "I've changed it a lot since you were here last," she said, hesitating so that when he reached the landing he was touching her, thigh against thigh for one brief but charged moment.

He looked into her eyes. They were asking him to come closer. Her parted lips were beckoning; he felt the heat of her nearness. And then she turned and walked on, opening the door of the loft and letting her scent waft back to Dennis in the breeze from the windows.

When he followed her in and saw what she had done, he was stunned. He would never have recognized it as the same place. Gone were what had essentially been turnoffs to him—the trendy posters, the high-tech furniture, the photographs of Melanie wherever you looked. In their place was airy space, vast reaches of it, with bare, white-painted brick walls, low couches and platform beds covered in pale cotton fabrics, woven rugs on a plain, wide-board floor. The whole place instantly made Dennis feel relaxed. As he followed Melanie into the airy center of the room, where there were white Haitian cotton love seats and a sofa and a low marble-top table with wine and cheese, he realized his entire body had until that moment been tensed as if in preparation for a physical fight. But now his shoulders relaxed, his breathing slowed, and as he sank back into the sofa and watched Melanie pour the wine, he felt calmer than he had in ages.

"This is great wine," she said, turning and handing him his glass. "It's a red that a friend of mine has bottled for her out in the Napa Valley, and I think it's just incredible." She sat down next to him and turned so she was facing him, her blue eyes looking into his with a softness

171

and strength he found fascinating. "I think *you're* incredible, too," she said softly. "Really, Dennis."

For a moment he looked at her and saw only beauty, only a sultry loveliness he wanted to make belong to him. Her skin was pale and smooth, her mouth soft and ready to be kissed, her voice breathy and young. There was something very vulnerable about Melanie, utterly different from the way she usually was. She seemed giving and ready and his.

Then he thought of Casey—the way he loved her when she smiled, laughed, made love with him, but then angry, as he had left her. She didn't trust him, and she didn't own him.

"Dennis?" Melanie asked softly. "You know, I've wanted to ask you here before. I mean I've tried in a lot of different ways. What made you come tonight?"

What had made him come? The note, of course. But had it been another evening, with a different sort of Casey, wouldn't he have let the note business play itself out on its own?

"You're always so nice to me when something bad happens," she said in a little-girl voice, widening her eyes. "I mean when something bad happens to *me*. Maybe I should get hurt more often." She leveled her gaze on him. "If that's what you like," she said quietly.

"No, that isn't what I like," he said softly. Suddenly she was unappealing again, her former softness and vulnerability now something merely designed to please rather than genuine.

"I don't—all right," she said. "Look. I realize—"

He held a finger to his lips. "Don't," he said softly, wanting to save her from going on.

"I don't understand," she murmured.

"Let's—let's leave it as it's always been, Melanie. A minute ago I forgot myself. It was very easy with you. But there is someone else."

172

She widened her eyes. "It's that Casey Fredericks, isn't it?" she demanded, her voice suddenly strident.

"Look, that isn't really the point, whether it is or isn't."

Melanie shook her head. "Really, Dennis. She's just a *p.a.*!" She studied his eyes, trying to rekindle the heat that had been there, but then she sighed. "Why did you come, then?"

"You *did* call."

She pouted. "Oh, I see. You know, I could have called anybody. I mean, normally I wouldn't have even turned to you. But you were so nice when I got hurt."

"Melanie, don't misunderstand. This isn't about that. I'm not saying I don't like you or anything of the kind. But I am saying that nothing has changed between us or is going to change. I shouldn't have come if that's what you were going to think. I had my own—never mind. Anyway, I'm sorry, but that's the way it is."

Her pout grew more pronounced. "Oh, great. So now that I'm really scared, you're going to leave me in the lurch. How do I know some nut—the nut who wrote it—isn't going to come in my window tonight? Thanks a lot for the help, Dennis, because when they find me dead in the morning, you can say, 'Maybe I could have helped, but I didn't.' "

"Oh, come on, Melanie. Aren't you being just a little melodramatic?"

"You haven't seen the note!" she cried. "How do you know?"

He hesitated. "Then show it to me," he said.

"Fine, I will," she answered, and she walked angrily to the other end of the loft. She picked up a piece of paper from the night table by the bed, glanced at it—although he doubted she was actually reading it; the gesture had been too theatrical—and then came toward him with her arm outstretched as if she wanted to keep as much distance between herself and the note as possible. Another studied movement, he felt.

The note was much like the one Morgan had received:

> YOU AREN'T IN TROUBLE JUST ON THE SHOW. HOW ABOUT REAL LIFE? THE SHOW IS GARBAGE. HOW LONG DO YOU THINK IT CAN LAST? IT'S GARBAGE AND SO ARE YOU, MELANIE KINCANNON, FOR STARRING IN IT.

After Dennis read it, he set it down on the table. But before he could say a word, Melanie started anew. "*Now* do you see? *Now* do you see what I mean? I'll be afraid to walk on the street, Dennis."

He sighed. "You've gotten a lot of mail from this show, Melanie, more than anyone else."

"This was from someone on the set, Dennis. Don't you see?"

"All right. I agree something should be done. We'll bring it up with McCann-Fields in the morning."

"And that's it? That's all?"

"Look, Melanie, I don't know what else I can do. *You* know the problems—the same ones that existed when Morgan got his note. This is New York City, not some small town in the Midwest. The police, justifiably, wouldn't be interested. I don't know what else we can do."

"What about a private place? Like a detective agency?"

He shrugged. "We'll just have to see tomorrow morning," he said.

"Thanks so much," she said sarcastically. "You know, I think you'd be a lot less blasé about this whole thing if it were your precious Casey Fredericks it was happening to. I see the way you two look at each other. Everyone sees it."

He stood up, suddenly tired, wanting to be alone more

than anything else. "Good night, Melanie," he said tiredly.

"What? But you can't leave! What am I going to do? How am I going to sleep?" she asked shrilly.

He hesitated. It was so difficult to tell if Melanie was sincerely afraid or merely making another play for attention. He was pretty sure she wasn't genuinely scared. She had been on her own for years, both in New York and L.A., and she had had a pretty rough time of it over the years. "I'll take you to a friend's house if you want," he said. He looked at his watch. "It's late, but I'm sure if you called someone—"

"I called *you*," she said.

If she *was* frightened, she wasn't too frightened to still try this one-note song she was singing. And he was tired of it. "I'll see you tomorrow," he said, and without looking at her again, he left.

It was difficult to get a cab. It was late, and the streets around Melanie's loft were empty. Dennis was glad, though, for it gave him a chance to think as he walked uptown along Sullivan Street. He had almost made a mistake, a big mistake. He had been so angry at Casey when he got to Melanie's that his anger had almost propelled him right into Melanie's arms. He could have slept with Melanie in a moment—would have if something she'd said hadn't put him out of the mood.

But Casey—what about Casey? What had nearly driven him into Melanie's arms still existed as a problem, as a rift between them, as something that had to be solved. Sure, his temper had been up and he had gone to Melanie's more out of spite than because he really wanted to. But as he thought about Casey now, he became agitated all over again.

She wasn't what he had thought—very self-contained, perhaps even a little cool, certainly not the jealous or possessive type. And she had flown wildly off the handle.

175

Had she been right? Had he been wrong? He didn't want to be with Melanie, but didn't he still want that freedom?

A cab whizzed by and stopped at a red light ten yards away, and Dennis launched into a sprint and caught it. The driver was talkative—a man from Brooklyn whose daughter had just had twins, whose wife had just had all her teeth out, and whose cab had just gotten a new transmission—and Dennis found himself acting rude and uninterested, answering monosyllabically or not at all. Damn this man and his problems, when he had problems of his own.

Of course there wasn't a chance that Casey would be there when he got back. He had barely looked at her or said good-bye when he left. And he didn't even know if he wanted her there. All he knew was that he felt like hell.

The apartment felt emptier than ever when he got home. Casey had left all the lights on, and everything was just as it had been—except that her clothes were gone, and she was gone; nothing remained except memories.

He poured himself a drink and brought it into the bedroom, feeling maudlin and angry at the same time. He had screwed up, and the most depressing part was that he couldn't even fix it because he didn't know what had gone wrong, who had been right and who had been out of line.

He got undressed and into bed, and immediately felt worse. The sheets, the pillowcases, the comforter were all laced with Casey's scent. Dennis drained his drink, turned out the light, and tried to blot the evening from his mind.

Casey felt horribly uncertain when she saw Dennis the next morning. He was late—everyone was already on the set when he arrived—and when he came striding into the sitting room, he barely looked at her.

"All right, we've got a lot of work to do," he said, looking at no one. "The dailies yesterday were atrocious, and we're reshooting the cocktails and dinner scenes."

"*Again?*" Lisa complained.

Georgia shot her a black look. "You're leaving in three weeks anyway, Lisa, so give it a rest, all right? The rest of us have a show to do."

It was the first time Casey had heard Georgia sound so testy. Obviously the most professional of performers was feeling the strains of the production.

Dennis went on about the day's schedule, and Casey could see he was tired. Melanie looked tired, too. What did that mean?

Casey had barely slept all night, tormented by visions of Dennis with Melanie. The fact that it had been Melanie who had called, Melanie whom Dennis had gone to see, had only made the hurt that much harder to take. Melanie was someone Dennis had sworn he found unappealing; and he had run to her, run from Casey and their evening together.

The thought of their shared passion was very, very painful in a sharp, immediate way. But Casey also felt a duller kind of sadness, one she knew was more important and something she had to give thought to. Whatever had happened between Dennis and Melanie last night was only a symptom of an even greater problem, which ironically had come up right before Melanie called. Dennis didn't think it was possible for a man to be faithful—speaking from experience, obviously. And she couldn't have picked a more unfortunate flaw if she had tried. Infidelity seemed to be the downfall of every single one of her relationships. Why and how could it have happened again?

It was hard to imagine that the Dennis she had loved last night, the one who had been so caring, so loving, so tender, was the same man who later on had been so defensive, so withdrawn, so hostile. Or that he was the man tiredly going over scene changes with one of the cameramen at the moment. For it seemed to Casey that he was conspicuously making a point of pretending she wasn't

177

there. And the wonderful Dennis of last night would never have done such a thing.

Dennis broke away from the cameraman for a moment and announced the next scene that was to be shot, and Casey was asked by the wardrobe mistress to buy a new sweater for Melanie for the upcoming scene.

When Casey heard her assignment a wave of anger passed through her. A sweater for Melanie! For the woman *her* lover might have spent the night with. All because someone had made a mistake and sent over one that was two sizes too small. Casey could feel the flush of anger rise on her cheeks as she left the house. Why did it have to be Melanie?

As she walked up Lexington Avenue she realized that the chance of finding a store open at that early hour were next to nil. Finally she got up to Eighty-sixth Street and was half-sorry to see that Gimbels was open. Now she'd be able to get what Melanie needed.

Childish images of revenge dominated her thoughts as she combed the first floor. She'd get something hideous, and it would be too late to take it back and get another. She'd leave the pins in it, in strategic places. She'd . . . But what was the point? If something *had* happened between Melanie and Dennis last night—she could hardly bear to think about it—then making Melanie look less attractive or trying to hurt her in some way wouldn't help. And knowing Dennis and the streak of tenderness he had shown for Melanie the other day, it would probably bring them even closer!

But where did that tenderness come from? Why was there so much about Dennis she didn't understand? With her, he was all tenderness, all love, all kindness when things were going right. But with Melanie? Had he been lying when he said he didn't like her? How could he have so many sides? He had been a stranger last night, a hostile stranger. Did that mean there were still darker sides to his personality?

At one level Casey half-hoped Dennis would turn out to be guilty of all the goings-on on the set. Maybe he *was* a stranger; maybe he wasn't the wonderful person she loved. She'd find out he was guilty and move on, putting the present back into the past. It would be a painful but brief episode. And in a sense she wouldn't have lost someone she had really loved. She would have lost only a memory, an illusion. She would have misjudged.

But living with this mystery, this uncertainty about a man who was constantly changing, was too difficult.

Casey took a quick cab ride back to the town house, ran up the steps, opened the door, and ran straight into Dennis.

"Where have you been?" he demanded.

"Out getting this sweater Melanie needed. And don't look at me like that. It's not easy finding a clothes store that's open before ten."

"If I'm looking at you in any particular way, Casey, it has nothing to do with the sweater. I don't give a crap about that."

"Then what?" she asked. "Go pick on someone else if you're looking for a fight, Dennis. I'm not in the mood." She tried to walk past him, but he grabbed her by the arm. "Let go of me," she said, turning away from him.

"Casey, look at me," he said quietly.

She did, but looking into his eyes hurt her deeply, for she was looking into eyes she still loved. All those unanswered questions meant nothing when she was face to face with him.

"Casey, I'm sorry about last night. I just wanted you to know that." He paused. "You were right about—about certain things." He looked past her then, down the hall. "About Melanie, for example. It wasn't really the note she was concerned about."

179

"I could have told you that," Casey said flatly. "And actually, Dennis, that really wasn't the problem."

"I don't understand," he said.

She looked into his eyes. He really didn't understand. He didn't see that his running off to Melanie was only part of a larger problem, a deeply held belief of his that was a complete and total barrier to their ever being together. Melanie and what had happened last night were of almost no importance. "Look," she said, "I'll talk to you some other time about all this, Dennis. We can't discuss it now, with people popping in and out of the hallway every two seconds."

"Dennis!" came an angry voice.

Then Melanie stuck her head out of the living room, and Casey looked at Dennis with renewed anger. "You have a show to do," Casey hissed, "in case you've forgotten."

And she stalked off down the hallway. Melanie was looking at her curiously, and Casey suddenly regretted that she had stormed off while Melanie was watching.

But what difference did it really make? Dennis still didn't understand. It was obvious in his whole approach. Clearly he thought he had made a mistake by leaving last night. That was just fine, and it sounded as if nothing had happened between him and Melanie. But it was equally clear that it was because of chance alone.

Casey brought the sweater to the swing girl, who found Melanie and gave it to her while Casey was still nearby.

"You got this?" Melanie asked, looking at Casey with a cold, almost clinical curiosity.

"Yes. And whatever you think of it, you're going to have to wear it or wait until the rest of the stores around here open."

Casey turned before she could get the full effect of Melanie's expression, but when she heard Melanie say a

180

few moments later, "But she's just a p.a.!" she smiled her first smile of the day.

While Casey was helping Joanie get the script changes in order and Melanie was apparently off trying the sweater on, Casey overheard a few of the cast members talking in a corner.

"I can't believe Melanie's not more nervous," Lisa said. "She showed me that note, and it's supercreepy."

Ted laughed. "Supercreepy. Where are you from, Lisa?"

Casey smiled as Lisa narrowed her eyes at Ted. "What's it to you, Conroy?"

"Ohh, we have a tough-talking broad here all of a sudden," Ted said, and everyone else laughed.

"Oh, come on," Lisa objected. "You don't have to call it supercreepy if you don't want, but it *is* scary. And my boyfriend said I . . . well, I don't know if I should say this." She swallowed nervously, looking like a young girl waiting to see the principal.

"Come on, what?" Ted prodded. "Don't start turning into Melanie-Miss-Pregnant-Pauses-of-All-Time," he said. "Your boyfriend said what?"

"Well, that we should all be real careful about not being alone on the set after hours, and that we should even be careful who we talk to—people who may be our friends, even—because I . . . Well, he doesn't think we should let each other know what we're doing, like in our time away from the studio or on breaks. It might be dangerous. Because it's got to be one of us."

"Oh, really," Georgia broke in with a disdain that made Lisa's eyes widen. "Now, I must admit I was unnerved by Melanie's accident—and certainly Stacy's—and the note that poor Morgan received. But I wouldn't necessarily put them all together." She shook her head. "Not necessarily at all."

181

"But how can you say that?" Lisa objected tremulously. "The notes talk about the accidents."

"Well, darling, a *news*paper could talk about the accidents. That wouldn't mean the reporters had caused them. Any lunatic can write a note and pretend he's done something he hasn't had a thing to do with. And that's my theory. There were two unfortunate accidents on the set. A few mishaps, too, of the sort that can happen in any production. And someone, admittedly unbalanced, among us is playing a very unpleasant practical joke." She smiled at Hugh and raised a beautifully sculpted brow. "And if it's you, Hugh darling, I wish you'd stop."

Everyone laughed. There couldn't have been a less likely possibility than quiet, reserved Hugh. But the laughter died quickly, and as the discussion went on Casey could see that there was a genuine, deep fear felt by most of the cast.

Shooting went extremely badly when it finally got underway. Dennis was angry, Felicia interrupted with changes every five minutes, and finally she and Dennis called a break that would last until after lunch.

While Dennis, Felicia, Hank, and Joanie retired into the study to rework the script once again, the cast and crew did what they always did during these seemingly interminable breaks. Georgia knit, Hugh and Morgan read mysteries, Lisa wrote letters, Melanie read the paper or tried to find someone to talk to. There were half-finished crossword puzzles, half-empty coffee cups, and old newspapers everywhere, and though the studio manager, a frazzled young woman named Charly Keats, kept running through picking things up, the clutter began to pile up. People were impatient, bored, and apathetic, and when lunch finally was brought in and laid out on the long table in the pantry—which was never used in the show—the cast was furious when Felicia called them in for a quick meeting.

"We've got the new shooting schedule," she said, clapping her hands for attention. "And several new pages of rewrites."

There was a groan of annoyance. "Come on!" someone cried. "How many times?"

Casey turned to see who had spoken—it was a voice she hadn't recognized, probably a crew member—but she couldn't see. However, when she turned back to Felicia, she saw that Felicia was quite annoyed. "There will be *more* changes," she spat out, "which we'll work on through lunch. Now Dennis has a few more things to go over with you, and then you can get back to your break."

Dennis went over several conceptual changes that hadn't yet been worked out on paper. "I'm telling you this so that you can think about it while we're working," he said. "Get into character if you want. Melanie, this one's a big change for you. You're going to show that you really do love Royce, despite what you may do on the outside." He flashed a look at Casey and immediately looked away.

Her heart skipped when he looked into her eyes, and now, as he went on, she wondered if he had looked at her by chance or not. He was talking about something they had discussed together on their own—whether someone could love two people at the same time, or love one and be involved with someone else. Was Dennis remembering that discussion from a time that seemed so long ago? Was he trying to make an analogy with last night, perhaps saying, I went to her, but it's you I love?

Casey realized she was probably reading much too much into his look, which could have been just random. Still, it made her think. She had totally forgotten about that discussion, in which she had said it was possible to be involved with two people at the same time; he was the one who had said the idea of a woman doing so was a turnoff to him, and that had been when she had discovered his double standard. But maybe it was time for her to look at her own feelings: not doing so had contributed to the breakup of her marriage, and she had the feeling she was purposely not seeing something again. But it would have to wait. Dennis left, Hank took over for a few moments, and then the cast rushed off to lunch. And Casey, starved herself, was among the first to grab something to eat.

The food, as usual, was decent without being exciting— a wide selection of cold cuts, salads, sodas, coffee, tea, fruit, and dessert. There was some griping from time to time because Felicia and Dennis sometimes went out to lunch, often with Hank, and today someone joked about the fact that no one but Joanie had emerged from the script conference to get something to eat. Felicia, Dennis, and Hank had probably sent out for something better.

"Don't kid yourself," Ted objected. "A woman like Felicia doesn't need to eat. She's not human like us."

The comment didn't get much of a laugh. Ted had said it sourly, with so much obvious passion seething under the surface that Casey guessed people had been put off.

But Casey did understand Ted's feelings. She had seen what had happened to his script and had understood the frustration he must have felt. Now, when she went to him, she saw the old light of humor in his eyes so faintly that she wondered whether she was only imagining it.

"How're you doing?" she asked, sitting down next to him with a plate of food. "I haven't talked to you in a while." And there had been good reason, though she couldn't say this. Her investigation had bogged down. She wasn't doing as well as she might have, and she knew this was because she felt awful considering either of the most likely possibilities: Dennis or Ted. And every time she looked at Ted, she felt guilty.

He shook his head and heaped some potato salad on his fork. "The worst," he said. "And I know I've been quite a pain around here, complaining and bitching all the time. I just can't help it." He looked over at Morgan, happily

184

eating with Melanie, and then shook his head. "And those two. Can you believe it? Today he finally got his wish."

"What do you mean?" Casey asked.

"I guess it happened while you were out this morning, when Melanie broke the big news about that crazy note she got. I'm sure you can imagine how it went. She was the center of attention for a cast of dozens, but for her nothing is ever enough. So she finally fastened on Morgan, saying they had to stick together now that they were both 'in danger,' as she put it."

"Really?" Casey asked. "I wonder if that will last." She certainly hoped it would; but whether it did or not, it certainly gave credence to the idea that nothing had happened between Melanie and Dennis last night. "He seems like a really nice guy," Casey continued. "I never really understood why Melanie wasn't interested in him in the first place."

Ted shrugged. "Who knows? One thing I do know, though, is that I could do without him these days."

Casey didn't like the choice of words. "Why?" she asked.

"All that nonsense yesterday about poisoning being better than cat fighting. He may be right, technically speaking, but do they want to write a textbook on criminal behavior or get ratings?"

"I don't understand," Casey said.

"Look. When you write a show like 'The Sinners,' the point isn't to be technically correct in every detail. The point is to make it believable and, above all, exciting. And a cat fight between two women is a hell of a lot more exciting than seeing someone slip powder into someone else's food. I'm really surprised Felicia didn't see that."

"Well, I guess everybody makes mistakes," Casey said.

"Yeah, well, they're not going to make any mistakes with any more of my scripts."

"What do you mean?"

185

"I'm not writing any more for them. I'm sticking to my own screenplays for now. I've got to reevaluate my life, Casey, figure out what I'm doing wrong. Because what I'm doing now is making me bitter. It's making me do things I don't want to do."

At that moment Joanie came in and began frantically passing out script revisions, and Casey and Ted split apart in the confusion.

At the end of the day, when Dennis, Felicia, and Hank were going over the dailies, Casey left. She felt very much as she had when she had gone out that morning for Melanie's sweater: flushed, uneasy, queasy. She hadn't had a personal word with Dennis since that morning. Their exchanges had been limited to toneless requests and responses, and she knew, feeling strangely weak as she did, that she couldn't face him at that moment. Also she had had yet another depressing conversation about the case with Pete Winter, and all she wanted was to be alone.

When she got back to her apartment, Tamara was at the door with a suitcase and her purse. "Are you leaving already?" Casey asked. "I thought the trip wasn't until tomorrow."

Tamara shook her head. "My crazy boss decided we should go tonight—get a fresh start tomorrow morning and all that."

"Well, have a great time," Casey said, feeling suddenly much queasier and much vaguer. She stumbled past Tamara down the hallway toward the living room, then stopped and swung into the bathroom.

"Hey, are you all right?" Tamara called, coming quickly down the hallway. "You know, you look a little weird."

"I feel more than a little weird," Casey murmured, feeling as if she were speaking from underwater. Suddenly Tamara seemed to sway in front of her, and she closed her eyes.

"Hey, come on," Tamara said. "Sit down."

Casey turned and slumped down along the wall, landing in a heap on the tile floor. "I'll be all right," she said weakly. Tamara looked far, far away.

She came and sat down on the edge of the bathtub in front of Casey. "Listen, I don't know what to do. I should stay, but I really have to catch that plane."

"Are you crazy?" Casey asked. "Get out of here. I just feel a little strange, that's all. I must have caught something."

Tamara hesitated. "Maybe I should call your family."

"Will you stop? I've been sick before, Tam."

"You? You're never sick. I've never seen you miss work."

Casey tried to smile. "Well, this is a first, okay? And it may not even be that. Go ahead, don't miss your plane, and I promise that if I feel really lousy, I'll call someone."

"Well, okay."

Five minutes later Casey was leaning over the toilet, vomiting so hard she nearly blacked out.

When it was over, she was so weak that all she could do was crawl back from the toilet and lie on the floor.

As if from far away she could feel that her body was on the bath mat but her face was on the cold tiles, and she knew it would be better to be completely on the rug. But she couldn't move a muscle, and she fell into a deep sleep, waking up only hours later.

CHAPTER TEN

Casey spent most of the night throwing up in violent bouts that ended with periods of sleep she was desperately grateful for.

At six A.M., the time she was usually on the set, Casey awakened with a start. She crawled and then shakily walked to the wall phone in the kitchen and dialed the number of the town house. Standing was difficult, waiting as the phone rang even more so, but finally there was an answer.

"Sinners Office." Felicia's voice. That was odd.

"Felicia. Casey." Her voice felt creaky, as if she hadn't used it in years. "I'm not going to be able to make it in today. I must have some kind of twenty-four-hour bug or something."

"Intestinal?" Felicia asked.

"Yes. I know a lot of it has been going around lately," she said, irrationally feeling she had to make her story more believable.

"Casey, you're not the only one from the set who's called in. I've gotten eight calls so far this morning."

"What?"

"Yes, it appears that it might not be a virus. No virus could be caught by so many people at the same time." She paused. "There's talk of food poisoning."

Oh, no, Casey thought. *Poison!* That was the means Lauren Edwards had used to hurt her sister-in-law Kezia.

Good lord! Could this be another instance of life imitating the show's scripts?

She voiced her speculations to Felicia, but Felicia was unconvinced. "Really, Casey. I agree it's a rather appalling and certainly unfortunate coincidence, but it's hardly likely. I would imagine the procedure would be rather intricate, wouldn't you? No, I'm afraid I'm partially to blame for what happened."

"You? Why you?"

"Oh, you know what they say about heat and that sort of food—all that mayonnaise in the potato and chicken salads. The tuna salad, too. It wasn't a cold day yesterday, and that food sat on those tables while we held that meeting."

"That's true," Casey said hesitantly.

"In any case, I'm afraid there's no way we can test it," Felicia added. "The porter cleaned all yesterday's garbage out last night, and I called the deli this morning—they had just opened—and they have nothing on hand from yesterday."

"Maybe they're just saying that," Casey said. "To avoid liability."

"Well, if they *did* have anything left from yesterday, they certainly don't anymore. I'm afraid they would have thrown all of it out the minute they got my call."

"That's true," Casey said. "But you should have let me handle that, Felicia. It would have been better to go there without warning them."

"I suppose you're right," Felicia said.

"By the way," Casey said, reluctant to ask the next question. "Did Dennis call in sick?"

"No, he's here," Felicia answered. "And unfortunate as it is that we have to lose a day or more of shooting, this will give us a chance to get the script tightened up even more. But anyway, Casey, to answer the question you haven't yet asked me, Dennis didn't eat any lunch yester-

189

day." She paused, waiting for the information to sink in. "Naturally, Casey, I assume you would want to know such a thing, though from what I've heard about the—relationship the two of you have developed, I must admit I have some doubts. In any case, I'm informing you."

Casey was hit with a violent wave of nausea at that moment and just managed to say good-bye and stumble into the bathroom in time.

Afterward she crawled into bed, took the phone off the hook so no one, especially Felicia, could call, and fell into a deep and dreamless sleep.

Somewhere there was a ringing again and again, somewhere in the dream. But it wasn't a dream, Casey realized as she opened her eyes and saw where she was: in her bedroom, at night, after a day she couldn't remember at all.

And the ringing came from down the hall: her doorbell.

Casey dragged herself out of bed and pulled on a robe, then walked slowly down the hall to where someone was now pounding on the door. It was a circumstance that might have alarmed her at some other time, but she was too worn out to be anything other than mildly, tiredly curious.

She looked through the peephole and immediately let the cover fall closed. It was Dennis! "Just a minute," she called.

"Casey, are you all right?" he called.

"Yes, yes, just wait a second and I'll be right there." She turned away and shakily walked the few steps to the bathroom, where she washed her face and brushed her teeth. Looking in the mirror, she saw an exhausted-looking young woman staring vaguely back at her with glazed eyes, hair that was a mess, and skin as pale as a sheet.

She stumbled back to the door and opened it.

Dennis stood there with deep dark eyes full of concern

and affection, and for a moment Casey forgot everything —that she was sick, that she had fought with him, that there were a thousand unanswered questions.

"Are you all right?" he asked. "Case, I tried to call you all day."

"I'm better now," she said quietly as she turned and he followed her inside. "I took the phone off the hook, though," she said as they walked down the hall and into the living room.

"Why?" he asked as she turned on a light and settled onto the couch. He sat next to her, and she curled up so she could look at him and rest her head against the cushioned arm at the same time.

"I didn't want to talk to anyone. Felicia was going on and on about I don't know what. I just didn't want to hear anymore. And you." She smiled. "I was so sick I almost forgot our fight."

"Look, Casey, we've got to talk. You don't know how worried I was today, out of my mind that I couldn't be with you, knowing what you were going through."

"You came pretty late if that's true," she said, mistrust winning out over love.

"You had said you didn't want to talk. You made that clear over and over and over again yesterday in your tone of voice, and your eyes, in everything you did."

"Then why did you come?" she asked flatly.

"Because I'm not willing to let some silly misunderstanding or argument get in the way of something that's very, very important to me. And in this case I don't care how you feel. *I'm* not letting it drop."

"That's hardly your prerogative," she said dryly. "I didn't even have to let you in." She closed her eyes, sorry she was acting so childish. "Sorry," she said, opening her eyes. "But Dennis, I just don't know. . . . Don't you see, we're still operating on two different levels. With different understandings and different problems. *You* see what hap-

191

pened yesterday as some 'misunderstanding.' But it goes much, much deeper than that."

"Then explain," he said. "Look, Casey, all I know is that I met you, I fell for you, things happened quickly, and then they fell apart. I'm not willing to let it go. You tell me the problems and we'll fix them together."

He leaned forward and ran a hand along her cheek. "And tell me, too, darling, if you're too tired to talk. I came blasting in here demanding all sorts of explanations and resolutions, and I don't even know if you need anything. Do you want something from the kitchen? Or from outside? I can make soup, I'll have you know."

"Could you? Do you, I mean?"

"Sure. I'm not afraid to roll up my sleeves and make a little broth for a good friend." He winked. "And I think I'm going to have to begin reminding you of my good points all over again. You're supposed to *know* that I cook. Remember? My house? The other night?"

She laughed. "I remember. But it doesn't really count. All men cook steak. I want real evidence."

"Then tell me your heart's desire," he said quietly.

She looked into his velvety brown eyes, at his strong, handsome jaw, at the lips that had whispered such tender words of love to her. *He* was her heart's desire. She wanted him to be the way he had been before, when they had been together and loved each other as if the rest of the world hadn't existed. He was right that they hadn't spent much time together: they had shared ecstasy, and then the trouble had begun. But how sweet that time had been.

"Oh, Dennis," she murmured. What could she say? She couldn't even tell him half of what was bothering her.

"Come here," he said, holding out his hand.

She sat up and leaned against him, and he wrapped an arm around her and held her close.

"You've always been a mystery to me," he said quietly. "No matter how close we've gotten, no matter what I've asked you, there's always been something you've held back," he said. "Except when we're making love." His hand stroked her arm, warming her with its comforting movements, making her feel safe and relaxed and secure. He knew this wasn't the time to make love, even to make any kind of overture. "I know we hit a bump in the road, that I did the worst thing I could have done last night by walking out on you. But you can't give up now, Case. We have something we can talk about—what happened last night at Melanie's—and we can work it out."

"Well, what did happen?" she asked softly.

"I turned around and I walked away from Melanie, Case. But I did more than walk out. I made a decision to try to make something work with you. And you can't walk out now."

She sighed, filled with questions she didn't want to ask.

"I know how angry you were," he continued. "*I* was angry at you. I didn't know what I felt, what I thought, even what had gone wrong. But I knew I couldn't let this thing we have end. And I realized that what I did was really a big step for me."

"Why?" she asked.

He shook his head. "I didn't know I was taking it at the time. But Casey, I've never done what I did that night. Even with Ann—remember, Celeste's best friend?"

She nodded.

"It's true I wasn't having an affair with her when Celeste thought we were. But afterward, after Celeste walked out, Ann and I took up together. It was inevitable for many, many reasons, not all of them good. But last night I did something I had never done before. I had never walked out on a woman like Melanie."

A woman like Melanie. Casey hated the sound of those words. "By 'a woman like Melanie' I gather you mean beautiful?" she asked, her voice less strong than she would have liked.

"Yes," he said. "And don't look at me like that, Casey. I'm including you in the definition. You *are* the definition. But don't you see? I had never done that before. And afterward I saw that I was ready to change, that I wanted to change. For you. But you have to do something now for me."

"What's that?" she asked.

"You have to trust me."

She smiled, taking the leap as she looked into his beautiful eyes. But the pleasure lasted only a moment. He was asking her to trust him, something she wasn't certain she could ever do. And how could she answer honestly either way when she was being so dishonest with him?

"It's the only way," he said softly. "And I know that's hard for you, Casey. I know that I couldn't have picked a worse night to do what I did—after you told me about your husband and your marriage. But there are parts of you that seem very tough. That makes it easy for me to forget—"

She shook her head. "I don't want you to think I'm fragile, Dennis, in any way. If I ask for something, it's because I want it, not because I'll fall apart like some delicate flower if I don't have it. I'm just realistic. And you're a perfect example of why."

He shook his head. "You've lost me."

"I was married to Steve. It wasn't one of the world's great marriages—partly my fault, partly his. Neither one of us was to blame—or both of us were. I swore off relationships for a while. But then I decided that was just silly. Life is too short and all that. I decided there was no reason to go for the brass ring—just to try to have a simple, uncomplicated relationship and enjoy myself. And the guy I picked—Mark—started seeing other women without bothering to break up with me. Now maybe that's coincidence, maybe not. Some people would say I had gone out and picked those two men knowing subconsciously that they would do that. I don't know; I don't consider myself particularly masochistic, but you never know—"

"And you put me in that category? With Steve and the cheater? Casey, I told you, nothing happened."

She sighed. Why couldn't she be more flexible? Why couldn't she give at least an inch? But her heart was caught. "I just—maybe we could wait—hold up a bit." *That* was it. Why hadn't she thought of it before? They could wait until her investigation was over. If he was innocent, fine. If he was guilty . . . She sighed. He just couldn't be. How could he be, when she loved him? Was it possible to love someone who had done what the saboteur had done? Was it possible to love someone and not know if he was guilty or not?

"Wait for what?" he asked. "Casey, you're forgetting *me* in all this. I need someone like you. I want you. I'm going through one of the most awful periods of my life professionally, and you make me happy every time I see you, every time I'm with you. Why should we wait?" He hesitated. "Are you sure there's no one else?"

"Are you crazy?" she asked. "After all we've said? After all I've *complained* about?"

He laughed. "Okay, you're right. But look, you're the one who said you could see how Kezia could love Royce and still have an affair with some other man. I've never forgotten that."

"That was—well, that was . . . I don't know. Maybe I was trying to impress you, trying to seem sophisticated."

His eyes softened, and he smiled. "I can't tell you how I love to think of your trying to impress me. All you had to do was look my way—let me see those eyes—let me see you laugh."

She remembered the beginning and how easy it had been then. He had seemed so wrong for her: arrogant, almost too handsome, an easy prime suspect in her case. And then he had caught her unawares. Now she could look back and know she had been trying to impress him, trying to make him notice her. But then she hadn't even known it was happening. And now he was being so wonderful—now that she was beginning to see the reasons she should stay away from him, and the certainty of getting hurt in the end.

She wished he weren't being so nice. It was easier to turn away from him and shield herself, let her suspicions take over, when he was being rotten. At those times she almost hoped he was guilty, then she could be rid of him. But now every emotion she felt was painful, for when she loved something he said or did, she was reminded that she should give him up, that inevitably the happiness would end.

"You make things so difficult by being nice," she said quietly. She turned and looked into his eyes. "You really do."

He reached out and touched a finger to her lips. "Don't," he murmured. "I won't hear that kind of talk. Now, you're worn out. You've had a rough night and a rough day, and I probably didn't help by nearly pounding your door down." He gently brought her head to his shoulder and stroked her hair. "Just rest," he said. "And we'll talk when you're better."

She closed her eyes, inhaling the scent from his shirt, loving the feel of his shoulder and his hand gently stroking her hair. If only things could be as peaceful as they seemed at that moment! Suddenly she hated her job, which was keeping her from the man she loved. For years now her work had been her whole life, and she realized she had been hiding behind it the whole time. She could always feel safe, always feel secure knowing that she was Casey Fredericks, private investigator. No one could touch her, no one could approach her, and she was great at her job because she was playing a role a hundred percent of the time. Suddenly she didn't want to play a role any longer.

She wanted to be herself, to show herself. And that was impossible.

She remembered the story Dennis had told her about Celeste St. Jacques and she wondered whether he would be able to trust her again when she finally told him that she was a private investigator and had even been investigating him.

She reached out and let her hand rest on his thigh—all muscle and sinew and strength. "Dennis?"

"Mm."

She took her hand away. Now was not the time to start making love. "I have to ask you a question," she said quietly.

"Shoot," he said.

She took a deep breath, hesitated, and took another breath. "If I—if I told you something about myself . . ." She stopped. What could she say? What could she ask him without giving away more information than she wanted to?

"What is it?" he asked softly.

She shook her head. "No, never mind."

"It's obviously something. Tell me, darling."

"No. I'm sorry, Dennis. Just . . . I'm sorry."

He sighed and stroked her hair. "All right," he said. "I can't force you. And I know you'll tell me when you're ready. But whatever it is, Casey, I'm sure you shouldn't worry about it. Whatever it is, we can work it out."

Lord, please let that be true, she thought. *Please, please let it be true.*

They turned out the light and talked, their voices hushed, their bodies close and warm. And finally, when Dennis asked Casey a question, there was no answer, only slow, gentle breathing. He brushed her hair back from her face, whispered, "Good night, my love," and rested his head against hers.

And before he fell asleep he wished for something he

was sure was impossible, but something he wanted more than anything in the world at that moment. *Please let this work,* he said silently. *I love her so, so much. There are things I've done that she would hate me for; there are sure to be things I'll do in the future that will be equally wrong. She might even know of them now. But let them not count. They're not important. Now matter how it might look now.*
. . .

And he fell into a sleep that flowed into a vivid dream. He was lying by a pool in the sunlight, with Casey at his side. She stood up, dove in, and swam beautifully back and forth, the water catching the sunlight and turning alternately silver and gold. While Casey swam, he wrote, and he felt sure he had never been happier. Then he rose and dove in, wanting to catch her and swim with her. For a while they swam together, slicing the water with strong, clean strokes. And then without warning, without a word, she was gone. He was swimming alone. He stopped, holding on to the side of the pool, and turned. And there was Casey, gleaming in the sunlight, standing next to his chaise and his writing. He thought she was the most beautiful woman in the world at that moment: lithe, athletic, magnificent. He waved, but she seemed not to see him. Then she turned, picked up his script, and walked into the house. He jumped out of the pool and ran along the hard cement toward the house. But the distance had grown, and the more he ran, the farther away the house seemed. His feet hurt as they pounded the wet pavement, and finally he stopped. Inside the house, silhouetted against a back window, stood Casey in the arms of another man.

Dennis awakened with a start. He was sweating, and when he opened his eyes, he didn't know where he was. It was dark and quiet. But then he felt Casey's weight against his shoulder, smelled the faintly flowery scent that was hers and hers alone. He stroked her hair, saying to himself that what had happened in the dream with Casey could never, never happen. There were mysteries about her—she was holding something back from him—but that sort of betrayal could never happen. And if he was ever going to make this work, he'd have to give over his heart in trust, just as he had asked her to do.

When Casey awakened, the morning light was pale gray, just beginning to silhouette the buildings across the street. As she nestled against Dennis's shoulder, she realized she was happier than she had been in ages. Dennis had spent the night with her, cramped in a position that was probably very uncomfortable, happy just to talk softly, hold her gently, and dream. She had tried last night to be honest and had failed because she had no choice. But sometime during her dreams, she had changed. For now, awake and happy, she realized she had been trying to force things, to make everything definite and concrete and sure, and that simply wasn't always possible. It certainly wasn't possible in her situation. She would just have to trust to the wisdom of the future. What other choice did she have?

She had a faint memory of Dennis stroking her hair. Had that just happened, or had that been last night?

And then she looked at her watch: 5:30 A.M.! She had overslept again! "Dennis," she said, shifting so she came untwined from him. And immediately she felt pain, a sharp cramp inside that was like a knife when she moved. "Ohh," she moaned softly, surprised by the severity of it.

"What's the matter?" Dennis asked, instantly awake, gazing at her with deep concern.

"I hadn't—oh, God, that hurts," she said, holding her stomach. "I hadn't realized it would hurt today."

His eyes were velvet with tenderness. "Oh, Casey," he said quietly. "I'm so sorry it hurts you. Here," he said, standing up and stretching. "Come." And he reached down, scooped her into his arms, and carried her into the bedroom.

He laid her down gently on the bed and smiled at her. "You probably need more sleep," he said. "You know, there's no shooting today. I have a script conference at two, but we're not going to do any shooting or rehearsing. Felicia canceled everything yesterday when so many people called in sick."

"She didn't tell me," Casey said.

"I told her I'd tell you," he said.

She didn't even want to think about work.

"Maybe a back rub would help, Case. How does that sound?"

"Great," she said. "But actually I think I should get cleaned up more than anything else. I feel as if I slept in a dumpster."

"Then I'll draw you a bath," he offered.

"That sounds wonderful."

And he went off to run the water.

Though he would never have said a word about this to Casey, he was struck by the almost primitive starkness of her bathroom. There was nothing actually wrong with it, and it had everything it was supposed to have, but Dennis wished that by some magic he could blink and have Casey at his apartment, in a tub that had to be more comfortable and in an atmosphere that was infinitely more relaxing than this. He couldn't bear the fact that she hurt inside, that he hadn't been with her during every moment of her pain.

"Dennis?"

He turned. Casey was standing in the doorway, and he leaped to his feet. "What are you doing standing up?" he demanded. "I would have carried you."

She smiled. "That's okay."

"Well, here, let me help you." And she took off her robe and then held on to him as she slowly lowered herself into

200

the warm water. The moment she was in, she felt better. And when Dennis kneeled and began to soap her, she closed her eyes, reveling in the first comfort she had felt in days. His touch was delicate and gentle as he spread the suds over her shoulders and breasts.

"I don't want to move you too much," he said softly. "We'll have other times, you know."

She opened her eyes and smiled. "I know."

He laughed. "I'm telling myself that, too, Case."

After a while Dennis let the water out and then turned on the hand-held shower and wet Casey's hair.

She couldn't remember the last time anyone had washed her hair, and she loved the feel of it as Dennis lathered with the same gentle movements he had used in the bath, talking softly to her all the while as if that, too, would ease the pain.

And finally, when her hair was rinsed, he helped her out of the tub, wrapped her in a giant towel, and carried her into the bedroom.

Once again he laid her on the bed, looking down at her with such love and caring that it almost brought tears to her eyes.

"Now how does a back rub sound?" he asked.

"Great, but let me get on my stomach and see how it feels." She turned, and though there was pain when she moved, once she was on her stomach she felt utterly drained of energy but not in any pain. And the moment his fingers pulled away the towel and touched her skin, she felt better, as if by magic he could heal her. His touch was light as he trailed his fingers up and down, side to side, over her hips and buttocks and back up to her shoulders. And then his touch grew deeper as he gently worked the muscles, kneading them and leaving them tingling and relaxed.

"I'm glad you're doing it right," she said lightly. "I'm too weak to complain."

"What's right?" he asked teasingly.

"Symmetrically," she said. "I know it's ridiculous, but it drives me crazy when a back rub is uneven—when one hand goes more to one side than the other hand does to the other side. Do you know what I mean?"

He laughed. "I do. Casey." He paused. The question he was about to ask was so—so adolescent, almost. But he had to know. "I'm not asking about men you've made love with. We've all—had brief affairs, things that meant less than we'd like to admit. But this sort of thing—just holding each other, rubbing each other's backs. Have you done that often?"

She slowly, carefully turned so she was facing him. "Dennis, despite the fact that if I move it hurts like hell"— she smiled—"I don't think I've ever felt as content or comfortable as I do now."

"I'm glad," he said, relief obvious in his voice.

"Only I'm very, very sleepy all of a sudden," she said, so tired she could barely talk.

"Then sleep," he whispered, and he climbed over her and then lay down behind her and held her close, entwining a leg between hers and resting his chin on the top of her head. "So we're all right, then," he said quietly. "After last night, I mean."

"We're more than all right," she murmured, and moments later he heard only the soft, rhythmic breathing of his beautiful Casey as she drifted off to sleep.

CHAPTER ELEVEN

When the chimes from the church nearby struck twelve, Dennis gently stirred, trying not to wake Casey. But she opened her eyes and rolled over to face him.

"Time for me to leave," he said regretfully.

"I wish you didn't have to go." She hesitated. "Even though I don't feel so hot, it's really nice to have you here, taking care of me and everything."

He frowned. "I don't have to leave this minute, Casey. Can I get you anything?" He smiled. "My soup offer still stands."

She shook her head. "Thanks, but I can't face anything right now, I don't think. But thank you, Dennis. I really—you've made me feel so much better." And it was true. She remembered times at the end of her marriage when she had been sick, and Steve hadn't lifted a finger to help her. She'd get her own tea, make her own soup (he was "in a big rush—sorry, hon"), lie there with nothing most of the time. And this was just wonderful.

He looked at her with deep tenderness and affection. "You call me if you need anything, all right?"

"I promise. But I really will be fine. I just need to rest."

"Okay. And I'll call you later. I'll come over after the conference, all right?"

"Great."

"You sleep well now." And though the room was

warm, he covered her with a sheet. Then he kissed her, gazed at her again, and left.

After Dennis was gone, Casey slept soundly, not waking up once until she finally opened her eyes and discovered with a start that it was 6:00 P.M. Where was Dennis?

Just then the phone rang, and Casey reached for it quickly, hoping it was he. She felt fine, completely recovered, suddenly hungry, even—and she couldn't wait to tell him and to see him. "Hello?"

"Hi, Casey. Listen, how are you feeling?"

"Much better," she said. "I can't believe it, but I'm really fine. I guess I needed the sleep and the rest. I can't wait to see you."

There was a pause. "Actually," he began. "Actually, Case, let's make it another time, all right?" Her heart began racing, and in the pause she could hear him inhaling on a cigarette. All sorts of images rushed through her mind: Melanie; other women she didn't even know about; a sudden dying of interest because of the overly domestic scene of the morning and the night before. . . .

"I'll see you tomorrow morning, all right?"

"Wait," she interrupted. He had sounded as if he were about to hang up. "That's it? You're not telling me anything other than that?" She winced. She sounded like a fishwife. But if something was wrong, she wanted to know.

"Casey, I'm not doing anything or going anywhere or seeing anyone," he said. "I've had a hell of a rough afternoon with Felicia, and I'm going for a quick swim and then home and straight to bed. I'm sorry if it came out any different, but that's all I'm doing. I can't even face eating, I'm so tired."

"Okay," she said. "And I'm sorry I sounded so naggy. It's just . . ."

"I know," he said understandingly. "So I'll see you early, right?"

"Okay. Have a good swim and sleep well." And she hung up.

Dennis left the town house without even saying a final good night to Felicia. The woman was insane, he had decided, either that or obsessed to such a degree that she might as well be crazy. She was so involved with the show and its "symmetry," as she kept saying, that she simply wasn't ever ready to end a meeting, give the okay to a script, look at the dailies and say, Those are fine. And he just couldn't take it anymore. Hard work was fine—wonderful and rewarding when it had some intrinsic merit. But going over and over and over a script that had been just fine, to the point where you were so sick of it that you barely knew the characters' names anymore, didn't make any sense. And it was doubly frustrating knowing that he could be working just as hard on "The Fortune" if he weren't tied up with this nonsense. He just had to get out of the show.

Dennis realized he was too tired to go swimming, and he began walking down Lexington Avenue toward home in the rush-hour crush, oblivious to the crowds and the traffic. He wondered if he had hurt Casey by not coming over. He had surprised himself, in fact, when he had decided not to. But something was keeping him away from her, something more than fatigue.

When he got home, he found a message from Martina on his tape machine: "Dennis, it's Martina, and it's, um, four. I know you're not there but call me the minute you get back. Please, Den, no matter what you're doing. I really need to talk. I'll be waiting."

He dialed her number, and she answered on the first ring. "Thank God you called," she said. He could hear the clink of ice in a glass in the background, and he realized her voice sounded a little slurred.

"What's the matter?" he asked.

"Everything. Listen. What are you doing tonight?"

"I wasn't planning on anything. In fact, I'm going straight to bed."

"Great. Can I come over? I mean, not to—Dennis, I really have to talk to you."

He hesitated. "I'm beat, Tina."

"Oh, come on," she said. "Some friend, Dennis. I need a shoulder. I'll bring Chinese food."

He laughed. He recognized her forced cheerfulness, the strong Martina trying to make the sad one feel better. "All right," he said. "I'll be here." As she had been for him over the years.

Half an hour later Martina came with two shopping bags in her arms.

"Don't tell me that's all Chinese food!" Dennis cried.

"Almost. You know I have to pig out when I'm depressed. And you're looking at depressed, honey."

"What's the matter?"

She shook her head. "Not yet. I just want to eat, okay? Tell me about *your* problems or something. Can we eat out on the terrace? What's on TV, by the way?"

He grinned. She was like a stream-of-consciousness essay when she was wired up, totally unwilling to look at what was bothering her.

"Hey, isn't your show on tonight?" she asked as they brought food, plates, and silverware out to the terrace.

"No, they switched time slots."

"Why?"

"Oh, they're trying to buoy up some other show's ratings by leading into it with 'The Sinners.' "

"Oh. For a minute I thought you were going to say there was a spinoff they were pairing it with."

Dennis glared at her. "Don't even joke."

"Why haven't you gotten out of that?" Martina asked, pulling cartons out of one of the shopping bags. "I'm really surprised at you, Den. You used to be so resourceful."

"I'm working on it," he said resignedly. "Believe me, I'm working on it." He opened one of the cartons and looked at Martina. "What the hell is *this*?" Inside there was a completely unidentifiable fried-looking mixture unlike anything he had ever seen before.

She shrugged. "Don't ask me. I ordered randomly. I was starved, okay? No criticisms tonight, anyway. I'll burst into tears."

Back at her apartment Casey was pacing the floor. She was itchy, agitated, unsettled. Dennis had sounded so depressed and dispirited. Should she have tried to be more cheerful? she wondered. Should she have suggested something to bring him out of his mood?

The phone rang, and Casey ran down the hall. Maybe Dennis had changed his mind. But it was Tamara, calling from Atlanta and wanting to know how Casey was feeling.

"Oh, fine, physically," Casey said.

"So what's the matter?"

"Oh, I'm just—unsettled. Dennis came over when I was sick, and I got better and we had a fantastic time together, and then I'm not sure what happened. Maybe he turned off. I'm just not sure."

"Why? What happened?" Tamara asked.

"Well, he went to another production meeting today, and we were supposed to get together tonight, but he called and sounded really depressed and really tired and said he just wanted to go home and go to sleep. It didn't sound like the Dennis I know. You know, when he gets in a rotten mood he's angry, not down."

"Then why aren't you with him?" Tamara asked. "Maybe he needs you."

"He said he wanted to be alone," Casey said.

"Yeah, well, haven't you said that when you meant the

207

opposite? When you felt you shouldn't impose your feelings on the other person but secretly hoped he would be perceptive enough to come over with flowers or great food or wine or ice cream? That sort of thing, Case."

"Well, yes," Casey answered, "but I've also said that when I really did want to be alone."

"I don't know, Casey," Tamara said. "I just saw a pretty great movie on the TV in my hotel room, and the woman in the movie went over to the guy's house just when even he thought he was too down and too low to see anyone. And it was beautiful. It meant a lot to him that she had picked up on his nuances and inflections enough to know what he wanted deep down."

"Well, *I've* seen movies—dozens—in which the heroine innocently walks in and finds the lover with another woman. And I hate to say it, but it isn't the most unlikely possibility in the world."

"It's up to you, kid. If you don't trust him or want to help him through a rough time, it's up to you."

"But I'm not a mind reader," Casey said. "I just think that people can ask for whatever it is they want."

"Have *you* always asked?" Tamara asked.

Casey thought of Dennis's tender care of her just the night before. Was it the same?

Tamara moved on to other topics—the trip, her boss, the men at the convention. But Casey's mind was elsewhere. The idea of going to Dennis's was becoming more appealing. He had done the same for her, and he certainly wasn't with Melanie or anyone else—not if last night's talk had meant anything. She tried to shut out the very persistent doubts that kept haranguing her: Wouldn't it be better to call first just to check?

But she told herself she had to learn to trust. Wasn't it time to test that trust, in the interest of doing something for the man she loved?

And so she got dressed and left the house. She would

buy a few things on the way—bread, cheese, wine, fruit—and then surprise him.

Casey went to a couple of stores on Broadway and then caught a cab, and by the time she arrived at Dennis's building, she had once again lost some of her nerve. What if, as she had said to Tamara, Dennis really did want to be alone? What was she doing? Why had she come?

But she chalked up her apprehension to old feelings of mistrust. These were feelings she was trying to shed, not perpetuate. She had decided to free herself of them, and free herself she would. And so she walked into the building with all the confidence she could muster, said good evening with a smile to the doorman, and sailed up in the elevator to the floor marked PH.

When the elevator doors opened, Dennis was standing at the door of his apartment.

"Dennis!" Casey said. "How did you know—oh, the doorman," she finished.

"Yes, the doorman," he repeated. "Casey, why didn't you call?"

She looked at the way he was standing, blocking the doorway; at his unsmiling, disappointed expression; at everything about him that spelled out one thing and one thing alone. Someone else was with him.

She stood there open-mouthed, staring, knowing with horrible certainty that she was right.

"Dennis?" came a female voice from somewhere inside.

Casey looked past him, saw nothing, then looked back to him. "Here," she said hollowly, handing him the sack of groceries and wine. "I think you have more use for these than I do." And she turned and rang for the elevator.

He grabbed her arm, and she turned but couldn't bear to look into his eyes.

"Casey, it isn't what you think."

"How do you know what I think?" she demanded.

"How do you know what's important to me and what's not?"

"Because you've told me," he said.

She shook her head. "You don't know everything about me. And obviously I don't know everything about you."

The elevator door opened, and Casey pulled away from Dennis's grasp and stepped in. "Good night," she said, and the doors slammed shut.

Dennis stood there for a few moments, and suddenly Martina was behind him.

"What happened?" she asked.

He turned and faced her. "That was Casey."

"Where did she go? What happened?"

"What do you think happened?" he asked roughly. "She came over, she knew someone else was here, and naturally she thought the worst."

Martina sighed. "Sorry. Why didn't she call, though?"

He shrugged impatiently. "I don't know. We had just spoken. I had told her I was too tired even to eat. I guess she was just trying to surprise me."

"Well, you can certainly call her up and explain," Martina said. "She *did* act pretty rashly."

"Oh, come on, wouldn't you?" He shook his head. "No, that was the worst thing that could have happened. Casey has a history of involving herself with men who end up cheating on her. And the worst thing I could do would be to call her before she cooled down."

Martina was looking at him curiously.

"What's the matter?" he demanded.

"Let me make a prediction, all right?"

"Go ahead," he said, picking up the bag Casey had left and going back into the apartment. He set the bag down in the foyer and then looked inside, and his heart clutched with pain when he saw what Casey had brought. Damn. He turned to Martina. "Well? I thought you were going

210

to make one of your famous predictions," he said. "And they *are* famous, you know, because they're always negative."

"And ninety percent of them come true," she said.

"You have the odds on your side, Martina. Don't tote it up as insight."

She turned away and began walking toward the living room. "All right, then don't listen," she called.

"Okay, what?" he said as he followed her out onto the terrace.

She sat down on one of the cushioned love seats and put her feet up on the table. She looked beautiful in the moonlight, but there was pain in her eyes. "Give me one of your cigarettes," she said. He lit two and gave her one. She sat back again and spoke slowly, reluctantly. "This isn't another one of my off-the-top-of-the-head predictions, Dennis. You're too good a friend for that. I'm trying to figure this out so I'm sure I'm not just saying something that's to my advantage. But okay—all I really think is that your situation is very clear, and you can go one way or another with it. That woman—Casey—she's probably a lot like me. She sounds like it, anyway."

"I don't think—"

She raised a hand. "Just let me talk. Believe whatever you want, obviously, but hear me out. I think she's like me in terms of what you just told me. She's had some bad experiences with men who walk out on her or cheat on her for one reason or another. Which means, Den, that she's in some way expecting that again. Not necessarily looking for it, although that's a possibility, but expecting it." She took a long sip of wine and then spoke again. "And it's no coincidence that she found you—Mr. Roving Eye himself. And it *doesn't matter* that nothing was going on between us tonight, Den. She won't be able to see it that way—deep down, at least. And that's where you come in."

"I'm glad I come in somewhere," he said dryly. He

211

didn't like what she was saying. She was so damn negative; and he couldn't help feeling that she was in some way infecting his relationship with Casey just by talking about it.

"Don't you see?" Martina asked. "It's no coincidence that this happened. Has anything like this happened before since you've been seeing Casey? Any other women?"

Melanie, he thought. But that was different. "No, no," he said. "Something similar, but it was just a woman— Melanie Kincannon—who needed to see me about something."

"I see," Martina said. "So these two incidents put together don't mean anything to you."

"No, they don't," he said forcefully. "And I don't see what you're driving at, either."

"Just that you've probably found the perfect go-nowhere relationship, something that will stay indefinitely on the right noncommittal level for you because Casey will never trust you, and you'll periodically give her reasons not to trust you. But you'll fool yourself into thinking you're being faithful and true and perfect, and you'll never admit you're driving her away on purpose."

He stared at Martina. She was hastily draining her glass of wine. Her face was flushed, and the moment she put down her empty glass, she lit another cigarette.

"Why don't you tell me what's going on?" he probed.

She looked blank and defensive. "What do you mean?"

"You were nearly in tears when you called me, and you're nearly in tears again. Instead of talking about me and someone you don't even know, why don't you tell me what happened?"

The tears welled up and then fell, coming down her cheeks like rain. "Oh, Den," she said, and he rose from his chair and took her in his arms and held her as she wept.

* * *

Casey felt like a caged animal. Her apartment felt tiny, as if it couldn't possibly hold all the fury and hurt she felt if she let it out. She felt completely alone, completely betrayed, as if no one on earth could help her.

Her brother had called and left a message on the answering machine, wondering how and where she was since he hadn't heard from her in weeks and neither had her parents. But she didn't want to call him or them. She wanted to be alone.

It was past midnight. Casey was now in the living room, half-watching "The Tonight Show," and she could just *feel* that she wouldn't get to sleep.

When the doorbell rang Casey swore and stayed lying down on the couch. Who could it be other than Dennis? And hadn't they been through this before? He would say it wasn't what she thought. He would promise he hadn't meant anything by it, and she would take him back. But how did she know he was telling the truth? The only corroboration of the night he had been with Melanie was Melanie herself. Her behavior the next day had made it pretty clear that she and Dennis hadn't made love or even begun to lead up to that. But was this a pattern? Why was it happening again, damnit?

The doorbell rang again, and Casey swung her legs down off the sofa and padded down the hallway. What was the point in postponing the inevitable?

CHAPTER TWELVE

When Casey opened the door, Dennis looked much as he had when she had seen him at his apartment: sober, serious, concerned.

"I don't know why you came," Casey said flatly. "And why didn't you call, Dennis? How did you know I wouldn't have someone here?"

"I didn't," he answered. "But come on, Casey, that isn't the point." He looked past her. "May I come in?"

She shrugged and turned. "Why not?" she said, walking down the hallway.

He took her by the shoulder and turned her around. "If you don't want me here, I'll leave," he said forcefully. "I asked you a question."

"And I answered," she spat out. "What do you want me to say, Dennis? That I'm thrilled you're here? That I've been holding my breath? What the hell do you expect? If I were smart I probably wouldn't have let you in."

He just looked at her, his mouth set in an angry frown. "Are you ready to listen or not? That's my only question, Case. There's no point otherwise. Your mind is either open or it's closed."

"I don't think you have a right to know the answer to that," she said. "I'm angry at you and I have a damn good right to be, and that's all you have to know."

They stood staring angrily at each other in the narrow

hallway, each looking into eyes that were flashing sparks of rage.

"Come on," she said, backing down, turning in the other direction and walking toward the kitchen. "We might as well have some coffee."

A few moments later Dennis sat at the table while Casey, her back to him, set the water on and put the cups on the counter. As she glanced at the clock on the wall—it said 12:45—she took silent pleasure in the fact that it was so late and Dennis was still up. If he wanted to spend his time with other women, let him suffer!

She set the coffee and milk on the table and then sat down opposite Dennis, pushing a cup toward him without a word. She couldn't bear the situation, the anger that was somehow letting through glimpses of love like a black curtain with worn spots. She was enraged at Dennis, deeply angered. But something about the quiet and the lateness of the hour and Dennis's soft brown eyes kept deflecting the anger from moment to moment.

She took a sip of coffee and then put the cup down, holding it as if for comfort between the palms of her hands. "All I care about," she began, raising her eyes to his, "is that you lied." The moment she spoke, tears of anger began to come from deep inside, and she stopped and took a quick sip of coffee. "That phone call," she said. "That—gets me more than anything else, Dennis, that you made something up—that you lied—instead of just saying, I don't know, something like, Let's not see each other tonight. I want to see someone else. It's the secrecy and the deception more than—"

"Wait a minute," he interrupted. "It doesn't make any sense for you to react to something that didn't happen, Case—"

"Didn't happen? Who the hell called you from inside your apartment?"

215

"That was Martina," he said. "Remember I told you about her? My friend—Tina, I sometimes call her?"

"Oh," Casey said lamely, confused for a moment. "Yes."

"Now if you'll listen to me for just one second, we can see where it is that we stand." He explained what had happened—how he had planned to go to bed, how Martina had called and been desperate to come over, how he hadn't followed Casey because he didn't think she'd be ready to hear him out.

The information was all very new to Casey, and she was happy to hear that the scenarios she had concocted in her mind hadn't borne any relationship to the truth.

"I wish you had told me right then and there," she said.

He shook his head. "It wasn't just that I didn't think you were too angry to listen, Casey. At some level I was angry myself."

"Why?" She frowned.

"Because this is all very new to me—this—this faithfulness and all. It's never worked out for me before, and it seems so fraught with tension. It's so explosive."

"I don't think I really understand what you're saying," she said, taking a sip of her coffee and hoping he wasn't leading into something she didn't want to hear.

"Well, why shouldn't I see my friends or you see yours? Why was what happened tonight so wrong? I shouldn't have to tell you everything I do in advance. I certainly wouldn't want you to do that, Casey. So what happened?"

She sighed and looked down into her coffee. The truth was easy to see and not very cheering. What she wanted was a full relationship in which faithfulness was assumed and not struggled over, and that was possible only if trust was there. And trust—on her side, at least—was missing. She would never really trust him, not fully.

But she would have to try. Wasn't that the only way? She had reacted quickly and rashly because there had been no trust, only fear. And all she could do in the future was try.

"I guess it wasn't really you," she said. "Or what you did. I agree with you. I wouldn't ever, in any relationship, want to have to check before I got together with a friend. I just have to have a little more trust." She looked into his eyes. "But Dennis, there is one thing."

"What's that?" he asked, stroking her hand with his, bringing comfort and warmth back to her little by little, as if she had been out in the cold.

"What would you have done if you had been in my position? If I had said I was going to bed and you came over and there was another man here?"

He thought about it and then grinned. "That's easy. I would have come in and told him to get the hell out, no matter who he was." He shrugged, a mischievous sparkle in his eyes. "But remember, Case, you learned a long time ago that I hold a double standard."

She laughed, and as he stood and came around to the other side of the table, she couldn't help loving the image of him chasing someone out of her apartment. She liked the idea of possessiveness if it worked both ways, if it meant that he went crazy over the thought of her being with someone else, as she had with him.

He held out his hands and she stood, and when she looked up at him, she smiled. "I kind of like that image."

He laughed. "You mean of my chasing another man out of here?"

"Mm."

His eyes darkened. "He wouldn't have a chance, Case. I'd go wild if I found someone here. And tonight I wish I could make up for what happened, how you must have felt. I'm so sorry."

And a few moments later, in the quiet of her bedroom, he determined to show her as tenderly and beautifully as he could how much she meant to him and how sorry he really was.

He undressed her slowly, as always amazed by her beauty, the way she looked more lovely, more lithe, each time he saw her. And more precious than her beauty was her unending responsiveness, the same breathless passion he had found so soon after meeting her.

Casey reached for him as he climbed into bed beside her. There was something very special in his touch tonight, something gentle and wonderful as he had undressed her, as he had drunk her in with his eyes. And she knew he was genuinely sorry about the misunderstanding.

The moment she touched him, letting her hands find his firm chest and her lips the scented pleasure of his neck, his response was swift and strong. There was passion and deep need beneath the gentleness, waiting to be stroked and unleashed.

As Dennis held her close and ran his hands hungrily over the curves of her hips and buttocks, she could feel his hard strength, see the passion in his dark eyes as he looked at her. "I want you to know," he murmured, brushing her hair back from her face. "I want you to know that I'm yours. Don't question it, don't doubt it, just believe it, Casey." He inhaled deeply, and when he spoke again his voice was hoarse. "I don't know what I would do if I knew another man's hands had touched you, pleased you, loved you."

"But I'm yours," she murmured. "I'm yours." And she arched as his fingers quested and captured her pleasure, teasing and then drawing away. "Oh, Dennis, please," she whispered, aching for the touch she had just experienced, writhing as his touch grew deeper and then trailed away. "Dennis," she moaned, grasping at his buttocks and his strong hard thighs, finally making him cry out. And as each touch of her fingers, each grasping stroke blazed and teased, his fingers seared her more deeply, and his lips

218

sank into her neck, covered her lips, parted them with wild passion.

And finally, as she was at the brink, desperate as the fires inside threatened to consume her, she cried out, writhing, whispering, moaning. "Dennis, now," she urged, and she felt the strong grip of his hands at her hips then, felt his breath hot against her cheek. "Dennis, I'm—"

"You're mine," he rasped, and he possessed her then, his hard strength filling her, taking her over the edge and beyond, into a time and place made up only of cries, moans, then rocketing, explosive ecstasy.

Afterward they shifted gently and easily, arms and legs, still wet, entwined. This time there were no words, just deep, sure knowledge of shared pleasure that needed no acknowledgment. And then sleep came quickly, taking each away from the other for only a brief time. For they were together in dreams as well—some to be remembered, some destined to stay forever in that other world.

When the radio alarm came on at 4:30 A.M., Dennis groaned and then laughed. "I don't believe it. I feel as if I just fell asleep an hour ago!"

"That's about what you did." Casey reached over and turned off the radio and switched on the bedside lamp.

When she turned around, Dennis was sitting up and stretching. Casey marveled at his body—the lean yet muscled arms, the broad chest covered with fine, dark hairs and muscles she knew intimately, a scent that was his alone.

He narrowed his eyes at her and shook his head. "I just want you to know something, woman."

"What's that?" she asked, smiling.

"You're the only person in the world who could have gotten me to stay up half the night after the day I had and love it. So don't you forget it."

219

She laughed. "I won't."

"And next time you're exhausted and desperate for sleep," he said, waving an admonitory finger at her, "I'm going to do exactly what you did."

"I think I'm going to be awfully tired *tonight*," she teased. "Desperate for sleep, as a matter of fact." She let the sheet fall to her lap and stretched, and Dennis inhaled deeply as his eyes roved over her.

"I'll be here," he said huskily. "And that's a promise." He smiled and raised a brow. "And it's a fact that we'll never get to work if I don't take a cold shower very, very quickly. And alone."

He stalked off, and Casey laughed, watching with joy as this lean, handsome man left the room.

Casey and Dennis were met with bad news the moment they arrived at the set. Lisa, who had been planning not to renew her contract, had walked out. The food poisoning had been too much for her to take, and her agent was invoking a clause in the contract as her right to leave before the term was officially over.

Felicia's face was flushed with anger as she spoke to Dennis. "This means a total rewrite, Dennis. You know what we had coming up—Veronica Edwards was going to walk in on Steele and—oh lord, I'm blocking her name—"

"Lisa played Sissy," Dennis said.

"Sissy, yes," Felicia said. "Anyway, Dennis, that scene was the basis for scenes for the next three shows. We had written Sissy out, of course, but not until Lisa's contract was up. Veronica's discovery of Steele with Sissy was a crucial turning point to Veronica's leaving Steele for three weeks and considering divorce, to Steele reevaluating his life and his loves, to Steele's setting Sissy up in an apartment uptown and helping along her budding modeling career."

"Well, the budding modeling career was hardly important," Dennis put in, "since Sissy was going to get hit by a bus the next week."

Ted laughed, and Felicia whirled to glare at him. He didn't let his smile fade. "Hit her with a bus today," Ted said. "What's the difference?"

"The difference is in all the scenes that come in between, the scenes I just discussed. They were crucial for Veronica's and Steele's character development, something we've been planning and needing for months."

"I really don't see that it's difficult." Ted shrugged. 'Have Veronica discover Steele with his secretary. He used to fool around with her, didn't he?"

"Well, yes," Felicia said hesitantly.

"So have Veronica walk in on the old buzzard at his office or wherever with—what's her name? Bunny?"

"Muffy," Felicia supplied.

"Muffy, then. Veronica pressures Steele to can her, he refuses, she walks out, Veronica reevaluates her character. Then Steele cans Muffy in a change of heart because she was always a pain anyway, and *he* reevaluates *his* character. Or his life and his loves, if you want. How's that?"

"Bravo!" Dennis cried, and Casey laughed. Morgan was smiling, and even Melanie seemed to appreciate Ted's scenario, despite the fact that there was no mention of Kezia Edwards.

"I could write it up if you'd like," Ted said. "Rush job." Casey was surprised by this suggestion, but not overly so. She hadn't believed Ted when he said he'd never write for the show again.

Felicia's face seemed to be frozen in anger. When she finally spoke, her voice was brittle. "Out of the question," she snapped.

Dennis stepped forward. "Why?" he demanded.

She turned to him with narrowed eyes. "Ted has written one script for us," she said, as if Ted weren't standing two feet away. "That script had to be rewritten half a dozen times. We're three weeks behind, Dennis. We have a team of experienced writers at our disposal who can do the job and do it right. I can't find one good reason to hire someone whose scripts gave us as much trouble as Ted's did."

Dennis's eyes darkened. "You made the script that way, Felicia. You were the one who initially bought it and then sent it through five rewrites. You liked it when you bought it."

"Oh, come now," she said. "You know as well as I that every script has to be adjusted to the needs of a particular episode."

"Exactly," he said. "Which was all that had to be done to Ted's. Now he's come up with some excellent ideas right off the top of his head, and I can't begin to fathom why you won't give him another chance. We massacred one of his scripts. We owe him, I think."

Ted's jaw had been clamped shut as Felicia spoke, but when Dennis finished, Ted's face was lit with hope.

"We owe him nothing!" Felicia muttered, and she turned and stormed into the study.

Dennis followed her and slammed the door, and the rest of the group was left standing there looking confused and shocked. Ted gave Casey an incomprehensible look of apology, and then he turned and walked away. Casey watched as he headed to the stairs that led to the rec and music rooms downstairs, and then she turned away.

"What a bitch that woman is," Morgan said. "A real witch."

Suddenly the door of the study flew open and Dennis stormed out. "Where's Ted?" he demanded of Casey.

She told him, and a moment later Felicia called, "Casey! Get Hank wherever he is and get in here yourself."

Casey went to find the story editor and a few moments later was sitting in the study with Felicia and Hank.

"We're dead," she said. "Shut down for four days while Lou Walsh gives us a rewrite."

Hank Reed frowned. "Lou Walsh? Really?"

"Yes, damnit!" Felicia yelled. "Lou Walsh." Casey took down the details of the script assignment and then left Felicia and Hank alone.

When she came out into the hallway, she ran into Dennis.

"Ted's just quit," he said.

"What?"

"He quit. And I don't blame him. Hell, why should he stay and take that nonsense?"

"Well, none of us is going to stay," Casey said. "At least for the next few days."

"What are you talking about?"

"Production is halted. They're bringing in Lou Walsh, hoping for a rewrite in four days."

Dennis swore and stormed past her into the study, and Casey heard several angry demands from Dennis: "Why didn't you consult with me? Why Lou Walsh?" before the door slammed shut.

Later on, after the cast and crew had been told and sent home for what seemed to Casey like the hundredth time, Dennis took Casey aside in the hallway. "I have to meet with Don and Felicia down at McCann-Fields," he said. He paused. "And Casey, I've just decided. I'm going to California to meet with someone about another project."

"What? I don't—aren't you doing the show? Aren't you continuing with 'The Sinners'?"

He hesitated. "We'll . . . let's just say we'll see," he said. "This break will allow me to talk to some people and see some people I really need to see, and—it's hard to say what will happen. I'm bringing Ted along, too. I'm so damn mad about what happened today I'd like to see what I can do for him out there—at least introduce him to a few agents and producers. Anyway, four days isn't a very long time, and I *will* be working ninety-nine percent of the time, but if you want to come, I'd love to have you with me."

"Thanks," she said, answering quickly so she wouldn't allow herself time to consider the possibility. "But I really couldn't."

He looked at her with a skeptical smile. "Things to take care of?"

"Exactly." She laughed.

"I think I'm beginning to figure you out," he mused. "One small step at a time, right?" He sighed mock-wistfully. "In any case, I know when not to press my luck. But how about staying at my place while I'm gone? I'd like to know my plants are being watered and all that." He smiled. "And I'd like to know where you are, too, Case."

"I'd love to," she said, her face lighting up. The thought of staying at that beautiful apartment for four days with no roommates and no work was absolutely lovely.

"There's only one condition I'm imposing, Case," he said, his voice suddenly subdued. His eyes were dark and serious, and she wondered what he was leading up to that was of such grave concern. He stepped forward and put his hands at her waist, warming her with pleasure. "It's all I insist on."

"What's that?" she asked.

"That you be there when I come back, darling, because I'm going to need you. And I'm going to be desperate for your touch."

"I'll be there," she murmured. "I promise you that, darling."

"And what about later? I'll be tied up in meetings until three, and I'm going to try to catch an early-evening flight, but we could meet at my place beforehand."

She shook her head. She had a meeting with Pete Winter at six. "I can't make it."

He smiled oddly. "Anything special?"

"No, no. Just a meeting with an old friend."

"A meeting?"

"Well, a get-together, a rendezvous. Anyway, something I can't break."

"So I won't see you until I get back," he said softly.

"No, I guess not."

His eyes flashed. "Then remember this," he said, and he leaned down and whispered, "I love you."

When he rose, she looked into his eyes with love.

Then Felicia came rushing out of the study. "I'm on my way," she called. "And I suggest you get on yours, Dennis."

He gave her a look that could kill, made a suggestion that was unprintable, and then turned to Casey. "I'll talk to you," he said gently, and then turned and went out the door after Felicia.

That evening Casey was sitting at a corner table at O'Neal's, across from Lincoln Center, with Pete Winter. He had wanted a briefing on the case. McCann-Fields had requested an official update, and Winter wanted to talk to Casey about some upcoming assignments as well.

"We might as well have a nice dinner on the client," Winter had said, smiling, "if you'd like."

Casey, who felt a deep sense of loss knowing that Dennis was gone, and because she liked Pete Winter anyway, had eagerly said yes. He was a kind, avuncular man in his sixties whose manner to outsiders was as blunt as his Marine-style haircut, but who was infinitely generous and kind to those he knew and liked. He had indeed been in the Marines and had served a brief stint in the FBI. Then, after some trouble Casey wasn't too informed about, he had opened his investigative agency twenty years ago, and he had the dogged intensity of someone who had strived for that many years without quite making it. His business was successful, to be sure. But Casey knew Winter had hoped to be number one, had hoped to retire and move to

Hawaii with his wife. And it didn't look as if this was going to happen.

"So tell me," he said. "You've been real quiet on this one, Casey. That makes me nervous."

She took a sip of her Scotch and looked him in the eye.

"I've fallen in love with our main suspect," she said, surprised she had actually been able to say this.

At first his expression didn't change; not a muscle moved on his granite-edged face. "You're joking," he said finally, his voice gruff.

"I wish I were," she said. "For a lot of reasons."

He drained his drink, hunched over the table, and looked into her eyes. "Maybe you have it wrong, Casey. Tell me about it."

She told him about the case in the quick, organized way he had taught so well over the years, and then asked for another drink. She had avoided thinking about the case at crucial times; she hadn't been doing her best work; she hated the fact that she had let Pete down; and more than anything she wanted him to tell her she was on the wrong track.

He just shook his head and made the clicking sound of regret that was one of his few outward signs of emotion. "Give me the motives," he said.

She sighed. "For Dennis there are lots. He has several things he can't do because of his contractual commitment to the show. Another network just picked up a show he did the pilot for, and they want him to direct but he can't. It's a very, very special project to him. He can't stand 'The Sinners' in general and wouldn't mind one bit if it failed."

"But it's doing well in the ratings," Pete said.

"Very well. But remember, the shows that are on and doing well now were shot several months ago. The ones *I've* seen Dennis work on won't be shown till next season."

Pete nodded. "Okay, so he wants the show to fail and desperately wants to get out of it. How would the acts of sabotage—the accidents and maybe the notes—get him what he wants?"

Casey shrugged. "In lots of different ways, mostly to do with the budget going sky-high. I don't think he would ever purposely fluff his directing. He's too good and too professional—and maybe too vain—to do something like that. But with all the delays the accidents have caused, the show is way, way over budget. That kind of thing can't go on indefinitely. Either McCann-Fields would have to make changes—perhaps hiring a new director—or they'd have to cancel the show. With the legacy of all these directors in Hollywood going millions of dollars over budget and then producing movies that don't even make sense, a certain cautiousness has crept into television production as well. There's only so much they can charge an advertiser to sponsor the show, so much they get for reruns, and that's it. Anyway, what could happen in terms of the accidents and notes has happened—the actors are scared. One actress has already left."

Winter steepled his fingers over the table and let out a deep sigh. "Anybody else, Case? Anybody with that kind of drive to get out?"

"Well, not to get out. Ted Conroy, a guy I went to college with, is an assistant grip on the show, and he's got a lot against it. He just quit today, as a matter of fact."

Winter looked up sharply. "Why's that?"

"He was fed up. He had written an episode of the show that was really messed up. He hated what they did to it, and several times he said things to me like 'they deserve what they get' and 'they deserve to fail.' But he's gone now."

"Where did he go?"

"Well, actually, he went off to California with Dennis. Dennis felt badly about what happened to Ted's script. something kind of similar happened to him years before Anyway, I think he might be trying to make up for it by

227

helping Ted now, introducing him to a few producers and agents out there, things like that."

"So he's helping a guy who might have been dealt a rotten deal by the show."

"Exactly."

Winter raised a brow. "Sounds like a nice guy."

"He is," Casey said.

"Would a nice guy do the kinds of things you've told me about?"

Casey shrugged. "I don't know. With enough motivation wouldn't you do things you normally wouldn't do? You always have to imagine the person as being really hard pressed. To save your career, you'd do X. To save your own life, you'd do Y. To save your child's life, you'd do Z." Winter was smiling. "What's so funny?" Casey asked.

"You," he said. "You've learned well."

"Damn right I have," she said. "And sometimes I wish I hadn't learned quite so well."

"Why's that?"

"Because sometimes—don't you ever get tired of constantly suspecting, distrusting, visualizing people at their worst?"

He looked at her carefully. "Casey, there's a reason we're both in this business. Unfortunately, those things that you just mentioned come naturally to both of us. Why do you think I hired you? You don't feel this way because of the job, kid. You chose the job because those things came naturally to you. That's why you're so good."

Casey said nothing, but as she looked into Winter's eyes and then down into her drink, she knew he had spoken the truth. And she wished he had been wrong.

Unfortunately, even though Casey and Winter spent the rest of the meal discussing suspects and possibilities, Casey came home with no new theories. Winter's "man at his worst" theory, as he called it, fit both Ted and Dennis, but it fit Dennis more logically, Winter had said. "The kid quit," he said, "which says to me he wasn't that bound up emotionally with the show. He could thumb his nose and walk away, get on with his life."

"But that's what Dennis wants to do," she said. And in fact Dennis himself had used the phrase in another context, when she had asked him why he hadn't pursued the Celeste St. Jacques matter. Then, too, he had said he wanted to get on with his life.

"But he hasn't," Winter said. "And that's where you get a trouble spot: someone who's trapped and needs a way out."

As Casey went through her apartment and gathered what she'd need to stay at Dennis's, she thought about Pete Winter and his certainty. What made him so sure?

He had admonished Casey to keep her eyes and ears open "twenty-four hours a day, sixty minutes an hour, sixty seconds a minute," as he had always said. "I'm not saying it's him, Case. For your sake, I damn well hope I'm wrong. But you keep your systems on go and look out, 'cause it seems damn likely."

She had looked at him coldly. "Are you saying you think Dennis would hurt *me*?" she had asked. "That's impossible."

"Do you think it's possible he did any of those things, Casey? Not under the 'man at his worst' theory but in a gut way. Think hard and then tell me." He paused. "When you're with him, do you think those things are possible?" He held up a hand. "Don't answer. Think first."

She thought hard and deep, trying to imagine Dennis— her Dennis—rewiring that mike, poisoning the food, writing the notes, doing any of the other things, even engineering small mishaps that had occurred.

She couldn't picture it, and she had told Pete so, thinking he would then say, "So it can't be."

But instead he had merely picked up his fork, shook his

head, and put the fork down, as if he were so reluctant to say his next words that he couldn't bear to speak. Finally he shook his head again and then sighed. "Then you be extra damn careful," he had warned. "If you can't see this Dennis doing any of those acts you mentioned, you've got a blind spot, Casey. You be damned careful."

She had raised her head in challenge. But she couldn't find any words of defense. Pete wasn't trying to hurt her. He was trying to open her eyes. And if he *was* speaking the truth, that truth had been created not by him but by Dennis.

Now, as she rode across town in a taxi, she felt only irrational resentment toward Pete. He was wrong. He had to be. She was on her way to the apartment of the man she loved. And he was not a criminal, not a liar.

When she got out of the elevator, she had a moment of apprehension. Her heart raced as she remembered the last time she had been here, with Dennis standing guard at the door and at his heart. But now it was different. He loved her.

She opened the door, and the first thing she saw, on the breakfront by the door, was a bouquet of daffodils and tulips. She leaned over and inhaled their deliciously sweet and springy fragrance and then picked up the envelope at the base of the vase. The note inside read: "These reminded me of you. Think of me while I'm gone. I want to make you bloom when I come back." She smiled. How much she loved him.

And as she walked around the apartment, reveling in the quiet, the airy spaciousness, the warm breeze out on the terrace, she gradually put her conversation with Pete Winter out of her mind. *She* knew Dennis; he didn't.

That night, when Casey was in bed, the phone rang and she jumped. The tape machine had picked up the call, and the volume was turned up so that Casey could hear Dennis's voice saying the familiar words ". . . please wait for the tone. Thanks." The tone sounded, and then there was silence, and a dial tone. Whoever had called hadn't wanted to leave a message.

Casey was aware that there was a certain dishonesty in her staying at Dennis's. When she reached over to the machine and turned the volume down so she wouldn't be able to hear Dennis's voice or the messages that were left, she realized she wouldn't have done this if she were just his lover staying at his apartment. She would have been naturally intrigued to hear the calls. He could have turned the volume down himself before leaving, and he hadn't. But she was Casey Fredericks, private investigator, staying at the apartment of a suspect. And because she didn't want to be reminded of this fact, she turned the volume down. She was *not* spying.

But when the phone rang again in the middle of the night, natural instinct took over and Casey turned the volume back up. It was lucky she had, for it was Dennis: "Casey, are you there?" he said.

She smiled and picked up the receiver. "Hi, yes, Dennis. How was the flight?"

"I met the most beautiful stewardess I've ever seen, Casey. She's here with me now." He paused. "Joke. Sorry."

"Skunk," she said with a laugh.

"Case, I'm at the Beverly Wilshire right now. We just got in. And I remembered our pact." He laughed. "I promised I would keep you up all night."

She ran a hand along the smooth sheets of his bed and let his scent waft over her. "I remember," she said softly, memories of their lovemaking flooding her. "It's very easy to remember now that I'm in your bed, missing you," she added.

"I love you," he said quietly. "Casey, it's taken me a long time to say that to you—too long a time. But now that I've said it, I want to say it over and over again." His voice was soft and caressing, and she wished she could reach out for him, touch him, hold him close.

"I love you, too," she answered.

There was a short silence. Then: "How do you like it there? How's the apartment?"

"Oh, it's great. I love it. I miss you, but I could get used to living here by myself. There's so much room."

"I know. Listen, aside from romantic yearnings, there was another reason I called."

"Oh? What was that?" she asked.

"Well, I won't be back as soon as I had thought. Felicia and I had pretty much of a knock-down-drag-out fight this evening, and we agreed—I got her to agree—to my staying out here for another week. That a.d.—Pinkney—is going to direct next week."

"Really?" Casey asked. "But I don't understand. I thought they were so adamant about your being exclusive with them."

"They were," he said. "And they still are. But something set them off—it's hard to say what, exactly. There was a lot of yelling on both sides."

"So . . . you're staying out there?"

"For ten days, yes. Which is great for me. I've already set up a lot of meetings, and ten days gives me much more time."

"Well. I'm happy for you," Casey said, only half-concentrating, for her mind was racing. What did Dennis's not being there mean? If McCann-Fields ended up releasing him from his full contract, what motivation was there for him to sabotage the program? Unless this was evidence that the sabotage had in some way worked.

"Wish me luck," he said. "If all goes right I'll at least be able to line up some interesting work for myself for when my contract *is* up with McCann-Fields."

"Great," Casey said.

"Well, darling, I guess I should let you go back to sleep. But think of me, darling. I know I'll be dreaming of you."

"And I'll be dreaming of you," she said. "Good night, darling."

And as soon as she hung up the phone, the unwelcome words that Pete Winter had said came back to her: "If the show could go on without Dennis, Casey, and there were no more incidents, you'd have a pretty good idea then, wouldn't you?"

She had raised her chin and said, "But that isn't possible, Pete. Shooting has been shut down until Dennis is back. So why think about it?"

Now, when the show would indeed be shot without Dennis, it would in a sense be a test—a test of Dennis and whether his presence made the difference.

Casey reminded herself that the theory also would have to apply to Ted, who would be absent as well. But the thought was cold comfort. She was afraid.

CHAPTER THIRTEEN

When shooting resumed five days later, Casey found herself almost hoping that an accident would occur. But nothing happened. Lou Walsh had turned in a good script —following Ted's suggestions, Casey noticed—and Bruce Pinkney couldn't have been happier in his position as director. Casey guessed he had been yearning for such a chance for years, and he was competent if not inspired.

And Casey had to admit that much of the tension on the

set was gone. Dennis's unhappiness had been contagious, and it was as if each of the cast and crew members had now been unwound.

Shooting went beautifully, and the episode came in on time under the revised schedule and within the budget.

Casey spoke to Dennis on the phone often. He sounded happy and relaxed, filled with enthusiasm for the productive meetings he was having with various agents and producers. Ted was having some success, too, though there was nothing definite yet.

During this time Casey's moods swung wildly. When she was alone in Dennis's apartment, she all but forgot her suspicions of him. He was the man she loved, and she was waiting for him to come back, taking care of home and hearth while he was gone. Living in his apartment added an edge of domesticity that had never been there before, and she viewed herself almost as the wife of a sailor off on a long journey.

And as the days went by, she began to see the shape of his life as she took messages from agents, producers, friends. There were no strange women calling, no more silent calls or hang-ups, and Casey realized that many of her fears about Dennis and his life had been unfounded.

But this sense of security vanished each day when she reported to the set and watched in anguish as nothing unusual happened.

She told herself that it could be Ted just as easily; logically she knew that was true. But an inner voice wouldn't accept this. *Face it*, it said. *Face the fact that now that the man you love is gone, all the accidents have stopped.* And she couldn't bear the thought.

One evening nine days after Dennis had left, Casey was in the bathroom off the master bedroom. It was a magnificent room, the kind she had seen only in magazines up until now. It was almost as big as her bedroom (though she didn't particularly like to dwell on this), with thick plush rust-color carpeting, long, low mirrors, and black-and-white tiles along the walls and ceiling. But the best feature was the sunken tub, which was huge, with beautiful modern brass fixtures and a whirlpool.

Lying in the tub, Casey leaned her head against the wall, delighting in the utter relaxation the warm water could bring, in the total peace and quiet of the room. Since she had come to stay at Dennis's, she had taken plenty of baths, loving the luxury that was absent from her own apartment. And the baths gave her a chance to think, as well.

In the peace and calm of these quiet moments, she realized she could only do as she was doing, that it was pointless and destructive to torment herself. She didn't know about Dennis's guilt or innocence, but she did know that she loved him, that she shared something very deep with him. And though she knew she couldn't go on forever in such an indefinite state, she knew, too, that for now it was her only choice.

Yet at other times her feelings were totally different, and this amazed her, since nothing had changed. In these moments she resented Dennis for her feelings, resented him for the power she felt he held over her. *His* actions—present and past—would ultimately answer her questions; *his* motives had much to do with her mistrust; *his* love had trapped her in a love that was perhaps doomed to unhappiness. And at these times she wished she had never met him, never eagerly said yes when Pete Winter had offered her the job, never breathlessly whispered yes against Dennis's warm lips.

Now as she lay in the tub, the soft music of the stereo as gentle as the scent of the herbal bubble bath she was soaking in, she was filled only with longing for Dennis. She missed him; she loved him; and she wanted him.

And when she heard the front door shut, heard Dennis's wonderful voice call "Casey?" she smiled and called "In here," ready for him.

Dennis reacted physically to the sound of Casey's voice, that voice that always became breathless with passion when he touched her. He had thought of Casey constantly in California, had burned with the need that the mere memory of her aroused in him, and now, knowing she was so near, he was afire with anticipation.

He dropped his suitcases in the foyer and strode into the bedroom, but she wasn't there.

"Casey?" he called.

"I'm in here," she answered. "In the tub."

In a stride he was there, and she rose for him, emerging from the tub dripping wet, a few shining suds clinging here and there, and he sucked in his breath in wonder.

"Casey," he said softly. She was more beautiful than he had even remembered, with glistening skin, long, lithe legs, an unbelievable curve of waist and hips, and firm, full breasts. In the parting of her lips as she looked at him, in the rapid pulse at the ivory base of her long, graceful neck, in the heavy fullness of her breasts, he saw desire dripping with readiness. And as he took her in from head to toe, gazing hungrily, her breathing caught and quickened under his look.

He came forward and took her in his arms and groaned with pleasure at the feel of her wet skin under his hands. "I've been waiting for this for days," he rasped. "But to see you ready like this—oh, Casey."

She drew her head back and drank him in, then came to him again, relishing the scent of his neck, the roughness of his cheek against hers, moaning as his lips covered hers, as hungry hands grasped her buttocks and held her close. Her fingers raked the softness of his hair as the kiss deepened, and the urgent movements of his tongue made her weak with desire.

236

She pulled away and began peeling away his clothes, her fingers working at his shirt as he shed the rest. She let her hungry gaze rove over his body, his male frame that was already fully aroused, ready for love, ready for the urgent joining she ached for. Though her thoughts had been tormented by memories of him and his coaxing touch, she had forgotten his shocking beauty. She hadn't remembered his legs being so sleek, his chest quite that muscled, his desire that potent. And when, wordlessly, she let her gaze travel up to his eyes, she burned under the simmering heat of his obvious passion.

"I think I'll join you," he said huskily, and he stepped over the edge of the tub into the water. Together, their eyes never leaving each other, they lowered themselves into the water, and Casey captured his shoulders as he leaned against the edge. She ran her hands over the beautiful slopes of his chest, found his nipples and made them taut under her touch.

"Casey," he whispered. "My God, how I missed you. I couldn't sleep knowing you were between my sheets, that the woman I love was here without me—"

"Aching for you," she whispered, lowering herself more deeply into the warmth of the water and letting her lips trail through the hair of his chest. Her tongue found the peak of a nipple and she flicked at it, then nibbled as he moaned and reached for her hungrily, his strong hands clasping her hips, promising he'd hold them, take her, bring her with him in a burning blaze of love. And then, with a touch as delicate as his grip had been strong, he cupped each of her breasts, catching her nipples with his thumbs in a double onslaught of delicious pleasure.

"I don't want to wait, darling," she whispered. "I don't want to wait."

In fantasy, as she had relaxed in the tub while Dennis had been gone, she had imagined just this scene—Dennis returning to find her ready and waiting, aching to be enveloped in his strong arms and swept along in the surging pleasure he and he alone could give her. She had become inflamed as she imagined soaping him from head to toe, lingering over his strong chest, his hard thighs, his firm buttocks, his trembling male body. In fantasy she had been able to hold back as he cried out in pleasure and passion, clutched at her with urgent fingers, thrust apart her lips with an eager tongue.

But now she couldn't wait. She was weak, hot, just holding on to him as he made her melt and then melt again, weaving a spell that was endless, making her writhe as her need grew greater and greater. "Dennis, I can't— Oh, Dennis—"

"Do you know how my thoughts of you tormented me while I was away?" he whispered into her ear as he deepened his persistent stroking.

"Dennis, I need you." She reached for him.

With iron will he pulled away. The only touch of hers he wanted tonight was the sweet softness of her desire as he made them one. "Do you know how many times I needed you?" he murmured thickly.

"I need *you*," she cried. "Now, Dennis."

Forgetting himself, he let her hand find him and could wait no more.

She clung as he lifted her out of the water, cried out as moments later he laid her on the bed and possessed her. "I love you," his voice rasped. "I love you so much."

"I love you," she cried, her hands raking his back. And then she was his, utterly his, as she shuddered with wonderment, held him as he burst in consuming passion.

Afterward he held her tightly, and she clung to him, happy he had finally come home.

"I meant every word about missing you. I had never known . . ." he murmured, letting his voice trail off. "I'd like you to stay on here," he said quietly, his breath gentle against her cheek.

She turned so she could face him. "You mean live here with you?"

"That's exactly what I mean. I came to a lot of realizations out in California—realizations and decisions. I wasn't walking a straight line to you, Case. I'd want you and then I'd back off, find some reason not to be with you, find some reason not to trust you." He reached out and stroked her cheek. "I love you, Casey. Being without you made me see how much I need you. I remember that even at the beginning you made me happy on the worst of days, made me feel good no matter what else was going on in my life. And that's true now more than ever."

"I'm glad." She looked into his eyes. At times like this, after lovemaking, she was so comfortable and fulfilled and relaxed that she was filled only with good feelings, only with love. Now he was asking her something that part of her wanted very, very much, and he was telling her something she had dreamed of hearing. He loved her so much he wanted to live with her, to be with her as much as possible.

But there were problems, some that she could tell him, others that would remain secrets perhaps forever, painful only to her and no one else.

"What's the matter?" he asked softly, his brown eyes gentle. "I had thought—"

She shook her head. "It's not you. You know how much I love you, Den. It's—it's me."

He frowned. "But why? Is it trust, Casey? Is it because of the past, with other men? Is it because of that one—or those two nights?"

"No, no," she said. "I can't explain, really."

He was silent.

"I guess it is the past," she said softly. "It's so hard to tell, though. Because once you put a name to something and say okay, I feel this way because of what happened when I was married, it doesn't necessarily help. It doesn't

239

make the fear any less real; so it doesn't really feel right even to say. I can tell you that it's impossible for me to trust you really deep down, in the only way that matters. And I can look back on my life and say okay, I probably feel that way because of Steve. But that doesn't really help. I . . . giving a name to it almost makes it seem less real. It trivializes something very, very deep."

Dennis gazed into her eyes, his own full of concern. "Are you saying you'll never trust me, Casey? Or that you'll never trust any man enough to commit yourself?"

"No," she said. "No, I—I certainly hope that isn't true."

He shook his head. "I don't see how you can say something like that when we share all that we do, when we make love like that. I don't feel you holding back *then.*" He looked at her carefully. "Are you sure it isn't a matter of someone having told you you couldn't commit yourself to a man? Or that you told yourself that and it became a self-fulfilling prophecy?"

"I'm sure," she said, an edge of testiness in her voice. She hated the way it sounded to dissect her feelings as if they were so many specimens on a lab table. Her emotions ran very deep, and while they weren't unfathomable or completely mysterious, she felt that in some way talking about them made them sound less important than they were.

She wondered why she was feeling so self-righteous about her emotions, almost as if they were hers and Dennis couldn't touch them, as if she were back in childhood and she was jealously guarding her toys. And then she realized this was another aspect of her distrust. How could she let Dennis touch her this way, handle her feelings and try to help, when she didn't trust him? She just couldn't get past that point. And when she tried to figure out which was stronger—her distrust of him as a man or her distrust

240

of him as Dennis Mattson, director of "The Sinners," she couldn't even begin to unravel the two.

"But Casey, don't you see?" He hesitated. "Oh, maybe there's no point. I don't believe in trying to convince someone of something like this. That's like trying to talk someone into marriage—not very romantic." He reached out and gently stroked her cheek. "It's just that I had thought we could try. Your living here when I was in California was a bit of a waste from my standpoint. But I guess that's the way these things turn out," he said quietly. "And I guess there's no reason your trust for me should have grown while I was gone."

She propped herself up on an elbow and sat up so she was leaning against the headboard, and he sat up and lit a cigarette. She was suddenly annoyed over Dennis's saying that whatever problems they had were all her doing. He had seemed to need reassurance before, but once she had told him her feelings had nothing to do with him and came from inside, he hadn't bothered to look any deeper. And she knew there was more to the story.

"You know," she said, her voice a little shaky. "It isn't just me. I said that, but it isn't."

"What do you mean?"

"Well, for one thing, I don't believe in living together. I've seen too many of my friends do it and drift off into a formless, indefinite nothingness in which both people just get lazy and don't keep the relationship alive and it peters out, while it might have lasted if there were a commitment. I don't see living together as any kind of commitment at all. It's just something that's convenient. But it holds no promise." She was surprised at how bitter she sounded. Her voice was harsh, and she was sure her face was red. But she was angry.

"Are you saying that commitment is what you want? Casey, I don't see why you're angry or why you would expect me to know that. The only message I've gotten

241

from you since the day we met is 'no commitment, no trust, it can't happen.' You've told me about a marriage that failed and a relationship that didn't work, and every time we've talked about it, you've been very clear about not trusting. Why would I assume you wanted what you're talking about, which seems to be marriage?"

She closed her eyes. She hated the way they were talking, hated the fact that he had used the word *marriage* in such an angry way. "I'm not saying you should have known," she said, opening her eyes and looking at him. He looked as he had sounded—angry and defensive. "I'm just saying that you've presented me with the possibility of something that you assume is great. You think living together is easy and simple and wonderful. I have problems with it as a concept, not to mention as something I'd want to do, and all of a sudden you're acting as if it's all my fault that it couldn't work. All I'm saying, Dennis, is that my reasons don't just come from the past."

He frowned. "You really . . ." He sighed. "You said I think living together would be easy and simple and wonderful. I do, in the sense of having two people live together who love each other and want to be together. But Casey, I don't mean easy in the sense of not being committed, of ignoring problems and letting them slide. Just because that happened with your friends doesn't mean it would happen with us."

"That isn't what I'm talking about," she said. "I just don't like to hear you put all the onus on me, as if everything would be perfect if it weren't for poor, stuck-in-the-past Casey. And what I'm saying is that what you're offering isn't something I'd trust from anybody. Living together: so what? That isn't something anyone should trust. What does it mean?"

He looked into her eyes. "I don't know what it means to you, Casey. I know what it would have meant to me. But there's no point in arguing," he said, his voice ragged.

He took a last drag of his cigarette, stubbed it out in the ashtray, and stood up. He looked down at Casey. "I'm sorry I ever brought it up," he said. And she watched as he walked around the bed, grabbed his robe from a chair, and carried it out.

She closed her eyes and let her head fall back against the headboard. Damn.

She heard the door of the terrace slide open, and she could just picture Dennis standing at the edge, the whole city lit up beyond.

What had just happened? She had been angry, she had said everything she had thought, and now—now he wished he had never even mentioned the subject of living together.

She got out of bed, put her own robe on, and walked out to the terrace. Dennis was standing just as she had imagined. His back was to her, and his tall, strong frame was silhouetted against the lights of the city.

He didn't turn around as she came out onto the terrace, and when she walked up to where he stood, he didn't move.

"Dennis?"

Then he turned. His eyes were shining in the moonlight, and a lock of dark hair hung over his forehead. "I'd appreciate it if you'd gather up your things," he said quietly.

Her mouth dropped open, though she knew she shouldn't have been surprised. "Dennis." She searched his eyes. There was no getting through.

"I told you a long time ago," he said roughly, "that I didn't believe in pursuing someone who didn't want me. I also told you that I was someone who didn't need anyone else, that I'm perfectly happy by myself when I'm not involved with someone. That still holds true, Casey. And I'd appreciate it if you'd leave."

She stared at him, at his brown eyes flashing angrily in the moonlight, at his hard mouth set in stubborn hostility.

No, there was no way she could talk with him, reason with him. She would have to wait until he cooled down, just as he had once done with her.

"All right," she said quietly. "I will." And she turned and walked back into the apartment to pack.

Though Casey didn't know it, Dennis turned and watched her as she walked back through the living room. *Damn,* he thought. *What the hell just happened?* He had thought of her constantly in California, had missed everything from her voice to her laugh to her eyes to her dreams. He had thought of her at the most unexpected moments for the most unexpected reasons. He had dreamed of her, fantasized about her, gone to bed with her image tormenting him. And most important of all, he had come to love the thought of her in his home, of her waiting there for him to return.

And coming home to her had been all that he had hoped for. Casey had looked more enticing than he remembered, had kissed and clung to him more passionately than he could have hoped for. It was all so easy with her; and damnit, that was what she didn't understand. Her view of relationships was so bound to the past that she seemed to be blind to the present. Even when they had disagreements or fights, they were easily resolved. *Everything* was solvable, because he loved her and she loved him. It didn't have to be difficult. It didn't have to be painful. But Casey couldn't see this because she saw everything through the gray light of her past. And what he had discovered in California—that *he* had been so influenced by the past, that he had been doing just what she was doing, more than he had known—he hadn't even had a chance to explain fully to Casey.

And now she was leaving.

He sighed. He had asked her to leave. At that moment the words he had spoken were all he had been capable of.

The only problem was that he had lied. He didn't want

to be alone anymore. He wanted Casey. And he couldn't even say for sure anymore that he didn't want her if she didn't want him. He wanted her, and something in *her* was keeping them apart.

Casey packed quickly, concentrating on what she had done over the past nine days so she wouldn't forget anything. Remembering an evening she had spent reading near the terrace door in a comfortable leather chair, she found a book she had finished and left on the floor. Remembering an article she had begun for *Private Investigating Monthly*, she found a yellow legal pad she definitely would have forgotten on the desk in Dennis's study. She combed the bathroom, the bedroom, and the living room quickly, moving without stopping so she wouldn't have a chance to think about what had happened.

She was through in five minutes, dressed in another two, and when she had her bags packed and by the door and her purse slung over her shoulder, she walked out to the doorway of the terrace.

Dennis turned and looked at her with an expression she couldn't read.

"Well, I guess I'm going," she said.

"The doorman can get you a cab," he said.

She nodded. "I know."

"That's right," he said, and smiled ironically. "I'd already forgotten you were here all this time."

For a few moments they looked into each other's eyes. Had he said "Stay," she would have run into his arms. Had she said she was sorry, he would have forgotten all the words she had hurt him with.

"Well," she said, trying to smile though she knew there was no need. "I guess I'll see you on the set."

He nodded. "Right."

"I'll, uh, leave the keys on the—what do you call that over there?" she asked, her mind suddenly blank.

245

He looked at her questioningly. "Call what?"

"That thing over by the door. That bureau—oh, well, I might as well give them to you." She reached into the outside pocket of her purse and pulled out the keys. "Here."

When she handed them to him, her fingers touched his. She looked into his eyes, but then looked away. It was too painful. "Well, I'll see you on the set." She turned and walked back into the living room.

And then she was gone.

Dennis went back into the apartment and poured himself a drink. Hadn't he gone through another night like this, when he and Casey had fought over Melanie? But that had been different. He hadn't really known how he felt about her then. He hadn't asked her for anything she was unwilling to give.

No, that had been damn different. But it wasn't over yet. He wouldn't let it be over.

He brought his drink into the bedroom and walked to the answering machine, where Casey had left a pad with the messages she had taken in person and collected from the machine. There was a row of familiar names with phone numbers and the times they had called on the right-hand side of the page in a neat column. Nothing unexpected: Parker Claypool ("He'd forgotten you were in Cal.," Casey had written; "will call you there,") and several people he didn't know personally but whose names he knew well.

Casey had done several random drawings on the pad as well, the kind of scribbles he, too, did when he was talking on the phone: geometric patterns, curlicues, arrows, simple drawings. And then, down in the lower right-hand corner of the page, was a name and number. It said, "Pete, 555-7328." There were stars around the writing, with shading and elaborate detail.

Dennis stared. Who was Pete?

The name clearly wasn't meant for him. Casey's list of his messages had been far too organized, the kind that someone who had worked as a secretary would have prepared. No, this Pete number had been Casey's.

And suddenly Dennis had a sickening thought. Casey had never mentioned anyone named Pete, although they had talked of everything from childhood to yesterday, from dreams to failures. Perhaps he was simply an old college friend, someone's brother, a casual acquaintance, her roommate's boyfriend, maybe.

But if he wasn't, wouldn't that explain an awful lot?

CHAPTER FOURTEEN

Dennis stared at the sheet of paper and finished his drink, then looked at it some more, as if it would tell him something new.

Damnit. What was it Casey had said the other night, when she had begun to ask him something and then stopped? She had sounded as if she were going to make a confession of some sort, and he had promised her that whatever the problem was, they could work it out.

He had always had the feeling that there was someone else. Not all the time, not every moment he was with Casey. But from the beginning of the relationship, during the odd moment, or when she would have a certain look in her eyes, a certain withdrawal that seemed to close her off—at those times he had always been suspicious.

And then he had shoved his suspicions aside or, more often, just forgotten them in his enjoyment of Casey.

Hell. During all the conversations they had had about fidelity, the focus had always been on him. He couldn't believe that had been some sort of camouflaging technique. No, he wasn't that paranoid, and he didn't think she was that dishonest.

But still . . .

He didn't fall asleep until three, and then only with a good deal of help from Johnnie Walker Black and a bucket of ice.

Casey felt vile when she walked into her apartment, suitcases in hand, a splitting headache making her dizzy with pain. She felt as if she were returning in defeat, as if she were coming home after some long battle fought hard and lost.

But had she lost? What had happened that evening had happened because of her. True, she had ended up putting some of the onus on Dennis, but basically, had she just said yes, when he had asked her to live with him, things would have looked much rosier than they did at the moment.

No, clearly they had some talking to do, and she had some thinking to do. And while she couldn't seem to unravel her professional distrust of Dennis from her deeper distrust of him as a man, couldn't that be worked out? If she talked to Dennis and just told him she needed to go a bit more slowly, that would surely help. He would surely see what she needed.

And as for the professional distrust, she would have to pray that no more mishaps would occur. For no matter how much she had tried to put the fact out of her mind, the truth remained that when Dennis had left, the accidents and notes had stopped. If they resumed again, it was all over. . . .

* * *

The next morning, when Dennis awakened, he knew
what he would do. Though he felt it was an invasion of
Casey's privacy, though he knew it would be better to just
come out and ask her who Pete was, he was going to call
this Pete and find out exactly who he was and what he was
to Casey. He wanted to know if Casey had been lying to
him, if he could trust her, if the relationship was over.

For he knew now—now that he had a clear head and
some distance from what had happened—that he could
never want her again if she had been lying to him.

Hell, it was the same damn thing as it had been with
Celeste. A jealous woman who turns the tables, a woman
who's been lying all the time—he caught himself. He
didn't know anything yet. Maybe Pete was Casey's cousin.
An old boss. Someone innocuous. There was certainly a
chance.

When Casey saw Dennis first thing that morning, she
smiled and was about to walk up to him but stopped dead
in her tracks. The look in his eyes was unmistakable. He
didn't want to talk; he certainly didn't want to smile; he
merely nodded, said a quiet "Good morning" and turned
and walked away.

Casey swallowed, took a deep breath, and walked on.
He needed more time. *He* didn't know she wanted to talk.
She would have to make that clear when she thought he
was ready.

But as the morning slowly wore on, she began to wonder. He had obviously taken deep offense at her words. He
probably viewed her as some sort of Celeste St. Jacques,
a woman who distrusted him but who in the end had
betrayed him.

Her heart raced at the thought. Thank God he didn't
know the truth. For the circumstances were uncannily
parallel. She had distrusted him just as Celeste had. The

subject of their arguments had always been him—*his* fidelity, whether she should trust him. And she had been lying to him from day one.

And she realized the near-impossibility of ever telling Dennis who she really was. She had never seen the problem so clearly before. She had so often thought of Dennis's guilt that she had ignored her own. Even if they could resolve the differences they had created last night, how would she be able to tell him the rest?

Dennis called a break at ten that morning. He had a violent headache and could barely think. Bruce was underfoot, constantly hovering as if he felt he should be in Dennis's shoes now that he had directed one episode; Felicia was her usual difficult self; and Casey looked too beautiful for words today. Damn.

Dennis shut himself in the study, strode over to the desk, and picked up the phone. Pete's number was burned on his brain, indelibly etched there forever.

He put down the phone, lit a cigarette, and then dialed.

It was answered on the first ring. "Pete Winter Investigations. May I help you?"

Dennis's stomach tightened, and he coughed on the smoke he had just inhaled. "I'm sorry. What?"

"Pete Winter Investigations," the female voice said patiently, without a trace of annoyance over having to repeat the singsong message.

Dennis was completely confused. Investigations? Then Pete Winter was probably a friend of Casey's. Maybe she had done some secretarial work there once. "Uh, I'm sorry—" He stopped. He had to know more. He couldn't leave it like this. On impulse he said, "I'm calling about Casey Fredericks. Do you know her?"

There was a brief pause. Then: "Why yes, but she's out on assignment at the moment, on a case in the field. If you'd like to speak to Mr. Winter about another of our investigators, I'd be glad to—"

"Thank you, no," he said quickly and let the receiver clatter into place.

She's out on assignment, the woman had said. Casey was an investigator, a private investigator. The pieces fell so quickly into place that Dennis was almost shocked that he had never thought of the possibility before. Of course, he told himself, there was no way he could have known. No way. But still, now that he knew, it all made so much sense. McCann-Fields had surely hired her. That bit about Felicia being her aunt—Christ! Why had he believed her?

And then he stopped. Why should he not have? She had deceived him slowly and surely, with the self-confidence that came from years of experience, no doubt. And oh, how he knew she was experienced. He was flooded with images, memories of things she had told him. They had been lies. All those answers to his sincere questions—"I was a secretary and an assistant most of the time"; "Yes, I've always lived in New York except for college"—which ones had been true and which false? Was Steve even real? And what about the absurdly named T. Mark Breckton III?

No, she had done and was still doing a very careful job of investigating the sabotage of "The Sinners." And she was obviously investigating him.

There was a knock at the door, and then it opened. Dennis turned. Bruce was standing in the doorway, looking ruffled.

"What is it?" Dennis demanded.

"It's—it's Felicia. She wants to see you."

"Then why the hell didn't she come in here herself?" Dennis roared.

He stormed out past Bruce and almost ran right into Casey. He walked past her without a glance or a second look. Her perfume—a bit of it, almost like a memory—

had reached him, though, and he was burning with anger by the time he found Felicia, who asked him some trivial nonsense about Lisa's replacement. As usual when Felicia spoke about a person who was standing right there, she talked about Suzette O'Casey as if she weren't there. "Dennis, do you really think her nose is right? I'm beginning to have second thoughts."

Dennis stared at her, glanced at Suzette O'Casey, and then looked at Felicia again. "You know, you're absolutely right," he said. "Her nose *isn't* quite right. Why don't you change it and get back to me when you've finished the job."

"Dennis!" Felicia cried.

He looked at her in helpless confusion. "I don't know what on earth you're talking about," he said. "You get Bruce to call me out of a phone conference to look at this poor girl's *nose*?" He turned to Suzette and shook his head. "You have a beautiful nose, Suzette, and you're a beautiful girl, and please don't worry. Much as Ms. Oates would like, she doesn't have nose approval, so you can get back to Makeup or wherever you were and relax."

Suzette smiled and rushed off, and Dennis turned to Bruce, who had been standing so close behind him that Dennis stepped on his toes when he turned. "Bruce, get everyone ready for the pool scene. I want to get that over with and get this ball rolling." And he walked off without another word to either Bruce, who was already running off, or Felicia.

A few minutes later, as he walked down the hallway, he heard Melanie wailing theatrically from inside the sitting room. "I *can't*," she cried, and she came rushing out to meet Dennis, with her blond mane wild and probably just as she liked it.

"Dennis, why are we doing the pool scene *now*? I thought that was going to be this after*noon*. I—" She paused. "Why are you looking at me like that?" she asked.

"Like what?" he asked.

"Like I'm—like I'm some sort of *bug*!" she said.

He smiled, momentarily distracted by the image, and then shook his head. "Just tell me what the problem is, Melanie. Is there some specific reason you can't do the pool scene now, or is it that you just don't feel like it?"

She opened her mouth to speak and then closed it. She was staring at him. "Dennis, I—"

"What?" he said impatiently.

"I'm scared."

"What of?" he demanded. He could see the hurt and surprise in her eyes. Maybe she had expected his usual dose of tenderness. Well, damnit, today no one was going to get it.

"The *pool*," Melanie said, looking around as people began walking past and heading over to the building next door that housed the health club.

When Morgan came by, Melanie's face lit up. "Morgan, can't you help me explain?"

Morgan came over. "What is it?"

She pouted. "I was telling Dennis I'm afraid. I've been dreading this scene since I read the script. Every single thing Lauren has done to Kezia in the script has come true in real life, and I'm frightened."

Morgan looked confused. "The script doesn't call for anything to happen to you in the pool. The scene is just in so we can get a little cheesecake in the show, Melanie. You're going to have to do it sooner or later. And if Dennis here wants you to do it now, *obviously* you do it now." And he took Melanie's hand and led her off.

By the time Dennis arrived at the pool, Melanie was crying. Dennis could hear her sobs all the way from the other end of the pool area, and the small knot of people gathered around the actress confirmed his fears. Hell. This was all he needed. "Makeup!" he called out, knowing Melanie's cheeks would be streaked with mascara. But

253

when he saw her, he realized it would take more than makeup to fix the situation. She was obviously very, very upset and had apparently been crying since Morgan had led her out of the town house. Her cheeks and eyelids were puffy, her makeup was a mess, her voice was hoarse from crying.

When she saw Dennis, her sobs and wails grew louder, and he realized the only way she would calm down was if he took his old tenderness tack.

And gradually it worked as he put an arm around her shoulder and gently soothed her, talking quietly and steadily. She was totally childlike at times like this and seemed to respond more to the fact that he was talking to her in this way than to the actual words he chose. She seemed simply to need a steady stream of soothing words. But when he drew up and said, "So we can begin now," she burst into another round of tears.

Dennis looked at Morgan, who shrugged and looked mystified.

"All right," Dennis said soothingly. Something caught his eye at the other end of the room, and he looked up just as Casey walked in with Felicia.

He immediately looked away. "All right. Look. I'll tell you what. I'll go in with you. All right?"

The crying stopped, and Melanie looked up at him with swollen eyes. "Will you—will you really, Dennis?"

He nodded. "Get Makeup to fix you up as well as they can, and then get into your suit. I'll get into mine, and we'll go in together, all right?"

She frowned. "You have a suit?"

"I swim here almost every day," he said.

"Oh. Okay," she said, as if she had had to know this.

She seemed completely mollified, with something new to think about plus the pleasure of having been the center of attention again for so long, and she ran off to where the swing girl was waiting with her suit.

Dennis strode off to the changing room without a glance at anyone. He had noticed Casey and Felicia walking down to his end of the pool as he had been talking to Melanie, and he didn't want to look at them.

When he came out a few minutes later, Bruce ran up to him. "Den," he said, airing a habit he had mysteriously acquired while Dennis had been in California. "Den, Melanie's not out yet."

"Fine," Dennis said. "I could use a warm-up anyway. As long as I'm swimming." And he walked past Bruce, ignoring the curious gazes of all who stood near, and dove in.

The water felt good—cool, refreshing, a refuge from all the conflict and dishonesty that was waiting for him above.

He loved swimming. It unwound him, filled him with an exhilaration he felt only when he was working or—damn. Or when he was with someone he loved.

His strokes were rapid and strong, slicing the water cleanly and with a strength that came from constant practice. Dennis swam lap after lap in a long, slow crawl, unwilling to stop or even look up. This was exactly what he needed—a good workout in cool, clean water.

But something was wrong, he realized. The water wasn't as cold as usual; it was just barely cool. His strokes slowed and then stopped as he treaded water and opened his eyes. The water was cloudy. It was murky with—

Dennis swam powerfully to the edge of the pool in two strokes and looked down in disgust one more time before he vaulted himself out of the pool. "There's something wrong with that water," he said loudly to no one and everyone. "There's something very wrong with that water."

And he ran off, sick with the knowledge that he had plunged himself into a murky, warmish brew of God only knew what.

He heard all kinds of cries and questions as he ran down the hall toward the showers. But he didn't have time for any questions. He had to wash off whatever was on him from the pool.

And as he stepped into the tiled shower and turned the water on full blast, he thought bitterly of Casey's investigation. Would she think that what had happened was part of the sabotage? And *was* it?

He thought about Casey, about all the questions she had asked him about his life. Had those all been part of her job?

He knew the answer was no. He knew their lovemaking hadn't held one faked moment, one instant of hypocrisy. But as he stood under the hot needles of water, he was filled only with anger, bitterness, and the conviction that she had lied a thousand times over.

Casey was helping calm Melanie, standing with Morgan and Georgia in a corner by a lifeguard's chair. Melanie was nearly hysterical, screaming that whatever had been done to the pool had been meant for her, and Morgan was gently telling her it wasn't so.

But Casey wasn't nearly so sure as Morgan seemed to be. At this point there seemed to be no reason to assume it hadn't been sabotage. She tried not to think about the fact that Dennis hadn't looked at her once—not once—since they had come to the pool. Did that mean that he had guilty knowledge of what was about to happen? Did it mean that he knew about the pool and went in only to make himself less of a suspect? Or did his not looking at her stem from his anger over last night?

Casey sighed. Whichever it was, she had the horrible feeling that she had been too optimistic up till now. She had assumed that she and Dennis would talk and try to work things out. Of course, this plan didn't address the deception she had been perpetuating or the possibility of

Dennis's guilt. But even so, she had just assumed
. . .

And now Dennis seemed to be giving out only one
message: that it was over. Could that be?

Later on Casey was sitting in the study, talking not to
Dennis but to Felicia, who very annoyingly was sitting in
Dennis's chair. The action made Casey nervous on an
almost visceral level. What was this woman doing? She
had her own production office upstairs, one that she had
picked, according to Ted. And now she was sitting across
from Casey as if the office were her own.

"Anyway," Casey said, checking again to see that the
door was still closed. "I really think it's time to bring in
the police, Felicia. If this was sabotage—"

"Which we don't know," Felicia interrupted.

Casey sighed. "Well, we will soon enough. I wasn't
about to make the mistake I made when the food was
poisoned, Felicia. I took extensive samples of the water
just a few minutes ago."

Felicia raised a brow. "Really? Didn't your fellow crew
and cast wonder why?"

"Oh, they had all gone," Casey said. "The only one left
was the building's pool man, and I told him McCann-
Fields wanted the samples. He didn't seem the least bit
surprised. He *was* surprised by what happened, though.
When he left last night, all the filtration systems were on.
So something obviously happened between last night and
this morning."

"Evidently," Felicia said, though she sounded neither
particularly interested nor concerned. "In any case," she
said, "I doubt that the police would be any more interested
in a cloudy pool than they would have been in spoiled
food. You know that better than I do, Casey. That's why
people like you and Pete Winter can make a living."

You and Pete Winter, Casey thought. Sure, two people

cut from the same mold, two people who couldn't trust, who suspected everyone, who could never really get close. But even Pete Winter was married; he had been for over thirty years. No, this was her problem and her problem alone.

"Anyway, Casey, I wanted to speak with you because I *did* want to let you know," she said. And then she paused, gazing at Casey with a mixture of curiosity and pleasure. "We have released Dennis from his contract. As of today, effective immediately, Dennis is no longer associated with 'The Sinners,' McCann-Fields Productions, or any of its current projects."

"What?" Casey gasped. "How—when did this happen?"

"While you were at the pool," Felicia said. "Just before I sent Bruce up for—".

"I don't understand," Casey cut in. "I thought you wouldn't let him out of his contract."

"Well, it's not for me to go into with you, but—"

"I think it is," Casey interrupted. "Given my involvement in the case, Felicia, it's very much my business, and very much *your* business to tell me."

"Well, I suppose," Felicia said reluctantly. She sighed. "It's actually a matter of cutting our losses, Casey, of limiting our liability, to the extent that that's possible. We received word today that Stacy Woods is suing McCann-Fields for the accident she was involved in before you came. There are threats of other lawsuits I'm not at liberty to discuss." She paused and lit a cigarette, and when she looked at Casey, her eyes were glinting with spirit through the cloud of smoke she exhaled. "Dennis threatened us with the same sort of thing. Not with legal action—I happen to know he's not particularly fond of going to court—but with indirect legal action."

"I don't understand," Casey said.

Felicia took a long drag of smoke and exhaled slowly.

"There is a clause in his contract," she said quietly. "As director, he is not required to undergo certain difficult working conditions. It's a standard clause in that sort of contract and it usually applies to something very, very different. You know, the kind of conditions film directors often encounter on location. In any case, the clause *is* in Dennis's contract, and he marched me in here, absolutely furious over what had happened in the pool, and said he had had enough, that he was walking out, and that if McCann-Fields chose to sue him over the remainder of the contract, we were welcome to, but that he would invoke the conditions clause. And Casey, if he did, he would win."

"Because of all the mishaps?"

"Yes, paired with the fact that we hired *you* without informing him or others on the set of something we perceived as a danger and possible threat. He'd have a very good case."

Casey and Felicia talked a bit more, and finally Casey left in a daze, more confused than ever. If Dennis had a clause in his contract that gave him an out when conditions became dangerous or unacceptable, didn't that point to him now more than ever? Had the sabotage been a perfect means to an end, a way to achieve his goal? Casey remembered the discussion Dennis had had with Lisa and some of the other cast members about ambition and achieving goals at any cost. Had he followed his own advice?

And why was he not speaking to her? Was it the fight, or was it more—guilt, for instance?

Casey went home in a storm of conflicting feelings. Her situation looked worse than ever. For if she hadn't lost Dennis because of the case, she was sure she had lost him because of last night.

CHAPTER FIFTEEN

Dennis swiveled his desk chair around to face the window and laughed. "Right," he said into the phone. "I'm glad, too. I'll see you at one," he said, glancing at his watch. "Good-bye." He hung up, smiling at the thought that this would be the first business lunch he had had in ages in which he could discuss business he'd actually be free to do.

The next few months might be busier than he could even handle. "The Fortune" was his, thank God. And there were half a dozen deals his agent had to wrap up. The freedom was almost unbelievable, better than he had ever let himself imagine.

And as for Casey, he would put her out of his mind. It was as simple as that. She was part of the past—a past that included Celeste St. Jacques and Casey Fredericks—to stay there together forever.

He closed his eyes against memory. He still couldn't believe what he knew to be true. When he had first learned, he had looked back at all the moments they had shared together and had judged them worthless because of her deception.

But they hadn't been worthless. They had been among the best moments of his life, filled with such passion and pleasure and truth—

That always stopped him. How deep did the truth run? Could one lie make all else untrue? Could one deception cancel out a thousand wonderful moments?

Dennis threw down his appointment book and got up from the chair. He didn't have time to ponder unanswerable questions. It was time to get on with his life.

As each day went by and Casey didn't hear from Dennis, her heart grew colder and colder with fear. What had happened? Not knowing was almost as painful as not speaking to him. And not wanting to know was the other side of the coin, the side that put Casey into a no-win situation she felt she'd never get out of.

All she wanted was to have him back, to be able to turn back the clock to a time when there had been no problems.

Of course, there hadn't been any such time. She had always been living a lie. But she had managed. And as the days had gone by, she had begun to see that one *could* love a man who might have lied, a man who might have committed terrible acts. For she loved Dennis deeply.

And as the show continued on its bumbling, stumbling way, Casey resented it and everyone connected with it more and more. There was so much conflict, so much resentment, so much ill will that Casey was beginning to feel everyone deserved whatever he or she got in the way of sabotage. She had lost the most precious moments of her life because of these uncaring people.

The only problem was that no more accidents were occurring.

As before when Dennis had gone away, Casey found that she was wishing things would happen, hoping that whenever Melanie was crying or Bruce was whining, it meant another accident had occurred. But nothing happened.

Tension on the set, however, was higher than ever. Word had come down that McCann-Fields was considering canceling the show after the current contract was up. Despite the show's high spot in the ratings, management felt, having seen the latest episodes, that its popularity

261

wouldn't continue. And with expenditures astronomically over budget, several threatened lawsuits over the mishaps, including one by Melanie, who wanted to take an act to Vegas and wanted out of her contract because of "mental anguish," the rumored feeling was that the show wasn't—or soon wouldn't be—worth the trouble it was creating.

There was an enormous amount of fear on the set. A day after the pool incident, Casey had gotten the results on the water samples she had taken. She had reported these results to Don and Felicia, and one of them had apparently let the cast and crew know. And the results were frightening. High levels of staphylococcus had been found in the pool water, which had almost no chlorine and which had definitely been tampered with. The news made the prospect of shooting almost every scene frightening, especially to people like Melanie. Bruce, who had been directing since Dennis's departure, was not at all equipped to handle Melanie's wild mood swings.

When Casey had found out about the staphylococcus, she had called Dennis immediately. No matter what the problems between them were, it was important that she tell him of the findings. She had called and left a message, and had then waited a day with no answer. She had called again, with no results, and had begun to seriously worry about his health on top of everything else. For Dennis could have been harmed by his swim, infected by the bacteria in dozens of ways. What if something had happened to him? But then she heard Bruce say to Morgan that he had called and spoken to Dennis, and with a pang of relief mixed with sadness, she knew that Dennis was at least not sick.

And the days dragged on, with nothing but more disappointments and more acrimony.

One day, a week after the pool incident, Felicia called Casey into the study, which she had evidently taken over as her own.

262

Casey sat down opposite Felicia, and Felicia gave her a cold smile. "I've just spoken with Pete Winter," she said, "after speaking with McCann-Fields. We've agreed that the contract for your services is terminated as of today."

"What?"

Felicia raised a brow. "As of now, as a matter of fact. We've just received word that 'The Sinners' has been canceled, effective upon expiration of the current contract."

"Really!" Casey said. "But that doesn't—what about the sabotage?"

Felicia hesitated. "As you know, Casey, there have been no incidents of any kind for a week, since that unpleasantness with the pool."

"Yes, but—"

"Let me finish," Felicia said, "if you don't mind. Anyway, in light of that fact and the fact that the show has in any event been canceled, we see less of a need for your rather costly services. In fact, no need at all." She sighed and leaned back in her chair. "You might as well admit, Casey, that the show was garbage anyway. Didn't you think?"

Casey stared, her heart racing. *Garbage.* What an uncharacteristic word for Felicia to use—and the same word that had been used in both notes!

Casey looked into Felicia's gray eyes and for a fleeting moment thought she saw a flicker of surprise and guilt. But it was gone almost instantaneously, and Felicia stood and extended her hand. "But I *would* like to thank you, Casey. It was a difficult assignment, and you did the best you could."

Casey's glance shot back to Felicia's eyes. The thinly veiled insult hadn't gone unnoticed. There were all sorts of things she would have said if Felicia hadn't just insulted her—that she could probably solve the case if she had more time, for one—but as it stood, she didn't want to look as if she were pleading or begging. She wanted to exit gracefully—and give serious, deep thought to her new speculations about Felicia.

Once she got home Casey found it almost impossible to sort her thoughts. Could Felicia have been the saboteur? In which case all her holding back, all her fear with Dennis would not have had to exist, for she blamed her professional distrust of him for exacerbating a deep inner distrust as well. There was no question that each had strengthened the other.

Had it all been unnecessary?

But why? Pete Winter had taught her that motive was everything. What motive could Felicia possibly have?

Casey wanted to call Dennis, and she picked up the phone and hung it up half a dozen times. She had already called him, and he hadn't called her back. But then she decided she had to try one more time. She left a message and hung up, knowing with horrible certainty that he wouldn't call back. Why expect anything else, when he hadn't answered her other message? No, it was time to face facts. Perhaps because he had no longer been able to stand her suspicions, perhaps for reasons she would never know, Dennis had ended the relationship. The most wonderful man she had ever known had walked out of her present and her future, never to return.

She thought of his smiling eyes, the way he brushed the hair back from her face, the way he had held her all night after she had been sick, the way he had made love to her so tenderly and passionately all those wonderful times. And she felt so cheated, for on those nights and so many others, there had always lurked the distrust and suspicion, killing the buds of their relationship each time they tried to bloom.

Dennis sat opposite Martina in the Palm Court at the

Plaza, angrily waiting for her to make up her mind as the waiter stood patiently by. "Tina, come on," he growled.

She shot him an angry look. "Will you relax? It's been about thirty seconds, Den." She flashed a beautiful smile at the waiter, who smiled graciously back. Which only made Dennis angrier. Damnit, didn't he count?

After Martina ordered, she looked at Dennis and shook her head. "This is a fine way to start out the afternoon. If you're going to keep it up, tell me and I'll leave now."

He gave her a black look and took a gulp of his Scotch and winced. Damn. Too early in the damn day.

"All right, come on," she said. "So it's over. Was it so great that you're never going to let it go?"

"I've never said I was planning that," he said hoarsely.

"Well, you have to leave it off sometime," she said. "And Dennis, I really think you're making it into something better than it was. All of a sudden this was your life's great relationship? Isn't that kind of easy to say once it's over? Isn't that easier than making a commitment while it's still going on? And anyway, how can you forget what she did to you? Every moment was a lie."

"I don't believe that," he said.

She stared at him. "Then call her. Call her if you really don't believe that."

He sighed and drained his drink. Hell, he didn't know what he believed. He *knew* every moment hadn't been a lie. He knew she had loved him, but then why hadn't she been able to trust him, to bring him in on what she was doing, to confide in him?

Because she hadn't trusted him. She had never trusted him, which meant he had known only part of her, loved only part of her and been loved back by that same part. But he had never really known the true Casey Fredericks, had never possessed her body and soul.

And so, though he didn't want to admit it, he warned himself that he'd better start following Martina's advice.

Obviously Casey *hadn't* been the love of his life; and his only course was to face that fact, forget the eyes and lips and laugh he loved, and get on with his life.

When Dennis got home that evening he found a message from Casey on his answering machine. He played it once, twice, three times, closing his eyes as he listened to her voice, soaking it up as if it were the sweetest music on earth.

Then he poured himself a drink, erased the tape, and went to bed.

Casey was up all night, wondering about Dennis, Felicia, the whole experience of being with "The Sinners." She would solve the case now no matter how long it took, no matter how many rules she had to break in order to crack it. She didn't care that she was off the case. The instinct that always let her know she had enough to go on told her she had more than enough now. And it also told her Felicia was the one. She was sure of it; instinctively sure. All that mattered was divining the motive. And this she would do no matter how long it took, for the mistake she had made had cost her the most beautiful love of her life.

By daybreak she had thought of a lead, and by lunchtime she was sitting across from him at a restaurant near his Rockefeller Center office. She looked at the sharp blue eyes of Don Atchison as he sat across from her and ordered his drink, and she decided she would be totally honest with him. He looked like an intelligent man, smart and quick. And usually the only way to get something out of this type was to rope them into the mystery, piquing their interest and enlisting their help.

"Thank you for coming," she said after they had ordered. "I need help on the case, and"—she held up a hand when he opened his mouth—"I know I'm not officially on it anymore. Don't worry, that's understood. It's personal at this point, actually." He looked confused, and she went on. "Tell me, if you don't mind, how much you know about Felicia Oates."

He looked taken aback by the question, and when he asked why she wanted to know, she assured him it was for a reason she'd tell him in a moment.

This clearly captured his interest. He began talking with increasing animation as the story went on. And it was an interesting story, one Casey had never, ever thought of.

"And so you see," he was saying, "we had worked together all that time, and suddenly we were—well, we were involved in a pretty serious affair." He hesitated as the waiter set down their drinks. Then he went on: "I shouldn't say pretty serious, Casey. We were engaged."

That was news. "And you were working together," Casey said.

"But no one knew about the engagement."

"Why not?"

He frowned. "I suppose—I suppose I should have taken it as a sign. I had asked her—unfairly, I now feel—to keep the relationship under wraps. Actually she held a higher position than I did at the time, so if it would have been to anyone's disadvantage to make the relationship public, it would have been to hers. But she didn't care about that. She's a number of years older than I am, and—well, she wanted the whole world to know about the relationship. And I said no." He looked into Casey's eyes. "Now I know I should have been more sensitive, but at the time" —he smiled sadly—"I was very selfish, very concerned with my own interests. Anyway, you don't keep something like an engagement secret, Casey, not unless there's a very good reason. And soon I found out what that reason was."

"What was it?" she asked.

"I didn't love her. I didn't want to get married." He hesitated. "And I began seeing another woman."

She shook her head.

He looked a little embarrassed under her gaze. "Anyway," he continued, "it was—very unfortunate that I chose to do things as I had. I didn't give anything very much thought. And it hurt Felicia. I had . . . Well, it all came out very badly, before I had a chance to tell her, and she was very hurt. I've always regretted that."

Casey narrowed her eyes, trying to remember the interaction between Felicia and Don when she had seen them together. It had seemed tight but cordial; yet now she could see how a deep undercurrent of resentment might have been seething beneath the surface of Felicia's calm.

"And now?" she asked. "I don't understand how you two can possibly work together," she said. "Or at least how she could work with you."

He hesitated and took a sip of his drink. "Actually," he said, "I've never really understood it myself. Frankly, I was surprised when she asked me to come in on 'The Sinners.' It was her project initially. But I didn't question it. I loved the concept, loved the show, and figured the rest was water under the bridge. If she was willing to put it behind her, I certainly was."

Casey took a sip of her drink and said, "All right, let me tell you my theory." She told him she suspected Felicia not because of the notes and the word *garbage*, which was too tenuous a clue to mention first. No, she put it together backward, with the help of the time she had spent thinking of the case last night. In every instance of misadventure, Felicia had had the means and the opportunity. Casey had simply never known the motive and had thus missed all kinds of clues. With Stacy and the camera, Melanie and the mike, Dennis—or Melanie as the intended victim—and the pool, with the food poisoning, the small mishaps,

268

the notes—she had always been there. So, too, had Dennis; so had most of the crew members. What had pointed so strongly to Dennis was strong motive. But what pointed now to Felicia was passion. "Don't you see?" she asked. "She's getting back at you."

He blinked. "What?"

"How many other projects are you on?"

"Well, none. I—I haven't been in the business all that long, actually."

"So the sabotage has affected you personally, then. The show is canceled, and—"

"That's true," he said. "My name is linked with accidents, mismanagement, a skyrocketing budget every day of the week." He drained his drink and stared, and Casey could see belief and then rejection of the idea flickering in his eyes. Finally he said, "But I don't believe it." He looked into the distance. "I refuse to believe it," he said quietly. There wasn't very much conviction in his voice, though.

She sighed. "I don't think I'm wrong. But Don, please do keep this quiet. When I'm ready—if ever—to make it public, you'll know."

Half an hour later she left for the town house, burning with determination. She had sounded purposely indefinite to Don, wanting to lessen the urgency of the information she now had. But she knew what she would do. And she would do it today.

Action at the town house was in full swing. Bruce Pinkney was running around looking as unhappy as Dennis had at his worst, Melanie was arguing with Morgan in the sitting room, Suzette O'Casey was laughing charmingly with Hugh.

Casey marched into the study without knocking. Felicia was sitting in Dennis's old chair with her back to the door, talking and laughing on the phone. When she turned and saw Casey, her smile faded instantly. "I'll call you back," she said into the receiver and hung up. "What are you doing here?" she demanded and then apparently caught herself. "Nothing wrong, I hope, in our fee arrangements?"

Casey shook her head and pulled out the chair opposite Felicia.

Felicia forced a smile. "Well, I suppose you can watch the shooting if you'd like. Bruce is coming along quite well, actually, and—"

"I'm not interested," Casey interrupted and paused, knowing that the longer she could maintain this dominance and forcefulness, the better her chances of success were. She held Felicia's gaze and sat forward in her chair as Felicia lit a cigarette. "I know you did it," she said quietly. "I know why. And I know how," she lied.

Felicia blinked and smiled. "Did what, Casey?"

"Stacy. Melanie. Dennis. Morgan. The notes. The food. The pool."

"Are you out of your mind?" Felicia demanded. "Really, Casey. I should call Pete Winter and ask that—"

"I don't work for him, Felicia. I'm a free-lance operative. And I don't work for you, which is too bad for you. Apparently you find it easier to control people when they're in your employ. Or working *with* you," she said slowly.

A flicker of surprise flashed in Felicia's eyes.

"I see I have your interest," Casey said.

Felicia angrily exhaled a cloud of smoke. "You have my amazement, Casey. Where you could possibly have cooked up a—ah," she said. "I see. Wouldn't it be nice if Dennis weren't the one—"

"Dennis *isn't* the one, damnit, and I'll never forgive myself for having—" She stopped. She would ruin everything if she became emotional. Pete always said to be like steel: tensile in white heat, unyielding the rest of the time.

"I only just figured out on my way over here why Dennis was so perfect for your needs. I said to myself, Dennis is a good director, a great one when his heart is in something. If Felicia wanted to ruin the show, why wouldn't she just hire a lousy director? Maybe like your fair-haired boy Pinkney here. And then I realized you had the perfect setup. Don, wanting the show to be as good as possible, naturally wouldn't let Dennis go. And you had your ideal and natural suspect right there. He was so ideal you could even argue against the idea the first time we met: the concept of Dennis as a suspect was that strong."

Felicia stubbed out her cigarette. "I don't even know why I'm bothering to listen to you. You haven't given me one good reason—"

"Why you would do it?" Casey asked. She paused. "Actually I wasn't able to come up with the reason myself. Why would a producer want to ruin her own show?" She hesitated again. "So I should really give credit where credit is due. Don thought of it."

She hadn't expected the response to be so strong or so immediate. Felicia lost all her control, all her composure, as she stared, her knuckles white as she unconsciously clutched the edge of the desk. "Don?" she repeated.

Casey nodded.

And the composure, under Felicia's iron will, returned as swiftly as it had disappeared. "Don is a colleague who has definite limitations as a—"

"Lover," Casey finished, and Felicia's mouth dropped open. "I know the whole story," Casey said. For a moment as she looked into Felicia's eyes and saw real pain there, real fear, she had a wave of sympathy for the woman. Don, charming as he was, had hurt her deeply. Casey knew what that pain felt like. It had affected her entire life. "Just tell me," Casey said quietly.

Felicia leaned back in her chair and closed her eyes, and for a moment Casey wondered if she had lost. With the

271

shock value of what she had said rapidly dissipating, it would be virtually impossible to get Felicia to talk if she didn't do it now.

But when Felicia opened her eyes, Casey knew she had won, for Felicia's eyes were glittering with passion. "How well do you know Don?" she demanded.

She shook her head. "Not very well."

"How much does he know?"

"Almost everything," Casey said. "Unless there are things neither of us knows."

Felicia drew deeply on her cigarette and exhaled with force. "The bastard." She shook her head. "He *isn't* smart, you know. He isn't smart at all. When I first met him, he seemed awfully quick. *Bright,* they used to say, but I thought he was better than that." She smiled. "Willing to be different, willing to be a maverick when that was the best course. We worked beautifully together. I made his career, of course. I made it." She paused, looking off beyond Casey. "And then he just had to prove I had been wrong about him." She angrily stubbed out her half-finished cigarette. "How he ever could have believed—ever—that I would want to help him after what he did to me, I'll never understand."

She drew her brows together. "Do you *know* how easily he fell for it? How vain he must have been to believe I would cut him in on something like 'The Sinners' because of his great talent?" She gave a cynical toss of the head. "Who knows? Maybe he thought I wanted him back again. Bastard." She grinned. "And I waited until the show had hit the top before I pulled it right out from under him. So you see, Casey, I did win in the end." She held out her hands. "Look around. All this will be gone soon. And with it the career of Don Atchison, producer." She shrugged. "I'm not sorry. I won; he lost. That's all I cared about. The fool."

"But what about *you*?" Casey asked. "If he lost, didn't you lose, too?"

Felicia looked confused. "Because of the show, you mean? Hardly. Darling, I've had years to invest, years to put myself into an extremely secure financial position. Whereas Don . . . Don was too vain to ever believe in anything but the rosiest of futures for himself."

"But what about all the people you hurt?" Casey asked. "How could you—it was Don you were after, not Melanie or Stacy. Or Dennis," she finally added.

Felicia's lips tightened. "There are risks in every business," she said quietly. "What actually happened? How seriously was anyone hurt, Casey? Nothing happened that couldn't also have occurred naturally or because of others."

Casey thought back to the accidents, the pool, the food poisoning, and she saw with disbelief that technically Felicia was right, but for her to see it that way was insane.

"How ill were *you*?" Felicia continued, unprompted. "You've been that ill before. Many people I know . . . For instance, in my 'Current Health Issues' show on PBS, we had that staphylococcus around, and many people . . . Stacy's accident is the only one I re—" And then she stopped and looked at Casey as if she were seeing her for the first time. "You're pumping me for information," she hissed. Felicia stood up. "Get out of here. Go back to Don if that's what you want. You'll see he's like all the rest." Her eyes were blazing. "But let's see how long you want him when he has no more money, no more power, no more prestige."

Casey stood up. Felicia's voice was wild, edged with an anger that threatened to burst forth fully at any moment.

"I said get out of here!" she screamed.

Casey didn't wait to be asked again.

The next morning Casey sat in the offices of McCann-

273

Fields Productions, across from Art McCann, a pleasant-looking gray-haired man in his sixties.

"We don't really know at this point," he was saying. "We got a call from Felicia's attorney earlier this morning. He came on strong, gave us a big pitch about her being in some kind of crazy mood yesterday, saying things to you that she didn't mean and could hardly remember." He sighed. "That will really be for the courts to decide one way or the other."

"What about McCann-Fields?" Casey asked. "Are you pressing charges or—or what?"

"We don't know yet, Casey. We're asking for—we'd like to make sure she gets some good psychiatric help. But there are a lot of angry people out there. Stacy Woods is still in the hospital." He paused. "I know it affected you, too."

"Yes. Well." She forced a smile that became genuine when she looked into his eyes and saw the warmth there. "My job is often difficult."

He placed his palms on the desk. "And you did do a good job, Casey. Pete Winter and I have already talked about some future possibilities for you. Not, I hope, that it will be the same sort of case!" He laughed. "But we do have some ideas—here and out at our California offices."

California, she thought. Where Dennis had gone, perhaps where he was now. Of course, it didn't matter. He could be three or three thousand miles away. There was no difference. "Well, thanks," she said. "I'll talk to Pete about it."

"Oh, and by the way," he said. "We've picked up 'The Sinners' again, with Atchison as sole producer." He smiled. "I always liked it. I think America will like it again when we get the knots out."

"I agree." She rose, said good-bye, and left, feeling deflated and not at all fulfilled by the fact that she had finally solved the case.

She wouldn't have solved it at all had it not been for a stray comment Felicia had made. And if she hadn't solved it, would she have spent the rest of her life thinking Dennis was guilty?

Days went by and turned into weeks as Casey went back to the routine of her more usual assignments. She worked mostly around City Hall and the courthouse buildings, a world as different from the world of "The Sinners" as could be. She spent her days surrounded by crumbling last wills and testaments, musty old cabinets, aging documents, once-hopeful litigants walking slope-shouldered with their lawyers. Every case she covered seemed full of unhappiness, disappointment, crushed expectations. And she couldn't stand it anymore.

And so a few weeks later she marched into Pete Winter's office and stood over his desk. "Don't you have any other assignments?" she asked. "I think I need a change. I know I do, actually." She felt close to tears all of a sudden.

He shrugged. "Look, Casey, you know ninety percent of our work is matrimonials. You told me a long time ago you wanted to avoid that if you possibly could. I've helped you avoid it by giving you almost everything else. You want matrimonials, you can have matrimonials." He shrugged. "Personally, I think they're a hell of a lot more interesting than that legal crap we get from Schiller and Crane that you're doing, but you wanted it and I gave it to you."

She sighed. She hated matrimonial work and always had, hated the idea of trailing husbands, wives, girl friends, lovers. It accented her worst fears, trapped her in day-and-night confirmation that love didn't work, that people were jealous, unfaithful, suspicious, unkind. And after seeing what jealousy had done to Felicia . . .

"Pete, I really think I'll pass."

275

He looked at her closely. "What's going on with you and that Dennis fellow, if I may ask?"

She smiled. Pete always got so polite at the strangest of times. But then she remembered the question. "Well, actually, it sort of drifted off."

He narrowed his eyes. "Drifted off? What the hell does that mean? Fizzled out, you mean?"

She shrugged. "I guess. I don't know, really."

"What? What do you mean you don't know? What kind of attitude is that?" He was yelling. "Hell." He lowered his voice. "What's the matter with you, Casey? You really liked him. You were wrong about him. So you can go back to him now."

"I don't know why you think it's that simple," she said. "Pete, I don't even know if I want to stay in this business anymore. I just—I had something, I lost it, and I don't really like what I'm left with."

He sighed. "Then take a vacation," he said. "You've got the money. I know because I sent you a whopper from your 'Sinners' work. So take a few days in the sun, in the mountains, whatever. You could use it." He smiled. "And you know you can believe me when I say the work will be here when you get back, matrimonial or otherwise."

"You know, I think I will take a few days off," she said musingly. "My parents have a house out in Sag Harbor they're not going to be able to get out to till the end of the month. If I went tonight, I could have two weeks by myself if I wanted."

"Sounds good," he said. "Now get out of here and out to the Island, and take a little of my advice when you get there."

"Okay. What's your advice?"

"Mingle," he said. "Get out on the beach, meet a few people, relax. You'll forget about this Dennis guy soon enough. And if you don't, Casey, take some more of my advice—call him."

"We'll see. And thanks for the advice. I'll call you when I get back."

"Right. Have a good time."

That night, as Casey packed, Tamara sat at the edge of her bed.

"So how long are you going for?" Tamara asked.

"A few days. Maybe a week or so."

Tamara shook her head. "You're so lucky to be able to do that."

"I know," Casey answered, stuffing a few pairs of shorts into her suitcase and zipping it up.

"You're not mad at me, are you?" Tamara asked.

"No. Why?"

Her roommate shrugged. "Well, ever since I got back from Atlanta, you've been kind of cool, and I figured you might be annoyed because of the advice I gave you."

"You mean about going to see Dennis that night?"

"Uh-huh."

"Come on," Casey said, swinging the suitcase off the bed. "I'm more than old enough to know what advice I want to take and what advice I should throw out the window. It was my decision."

"But I—"

"Forget it," Casey said, looking her friend in the eye. "I really mean it, Tam. I've done a lot of thinking lately. There are things that happened between me and Dennis that I don't understand. All I've got left is memories, and my own actions and feelings to look back on. And those were mine, not anyone else's. I'm beginning to see a lot. I've never had such a blind spot on a case before. Never. For days after the case was solved, I wanted to blame Felicia, saying to myself, *She put the idea into my head; I was fooled into thinking it was Dennis because of her.* But that's ridiculous. I've never been fooled like that before. I blinded myself, I let my natural distrust of Dennis add

277

to what might otherwise have been very mild professional suspicions. That was my fault, not anyone else's." She sighed. "And the same really does go for that night, Tam. Anyway." She looked at her watch. "I'm going to catch the nine o'clock train, and you have the number, right?"

"Right," Tamara said. "Have a great time."

At least one aspect of Pete's advice was correct. Casey felt renewed and refreshed the moment she got out to the Island. Though it was dark, Casey picked her way along the path to her parents' house with ease after a cab had dropped her off. She had been coming here since she was ten—twenty years of lovely summers, brisk autumns, unbelievably fragrant springs heavy with promise. And the inside of the house, with its homey braided rugs, simple maple furniture, and smell of hickory and cedar even now in June all brought Casey back to a time when problems and joys had been simpler. And she realized she had needed this escape from the city more than she had known.

The days went by quickly. Casey rose early, naturally, by the light of the summer sun slanting in her bedroom window. She ran along the water's edge on some mornings, lazed on the front lawn on others, bicycled to the beach with a book and blanket almost every day.

She grew tan slowly, and she added a few streaks to her hair to augment the sun's natural effects. Maybe she'd turn into a California Girl yet, she thought, even if this *was* Sag Harbor. For she surprised herself every time she looked into the mirror. Her skin was glowing, her eyes shone with health, her hair was glossy and thick.

But inside she was still hurting in a way she was sure no one could ever understand. Pete and Tamara had given her friendly advice, but what did they know? Only that she had had an affair that had ended. But how could anyone know the deep pain that stemmed from all the mistakes

278

she had made, the love she felt she had been cheated out of? She had known even then how deeply she loved Dennis. Despite all her suspicions, her distrust, her fears, she had loved him, embraced him with body and soul as they had shared bliss, deep pleasure, wondrous intimacy. But even so, she had been living with a profound misunderstanding—loving him in *spite* of his possible guilt, in spite of her distrust. And that had all been unnecessary. She could have loved him simply, deeply, without question.

Sometimes when she saw a couple walking hand in hand along the beach, gazing at each other across a table in a restaurant, embracing on a street, she wondered whether she was fooling herself. Was she blaming the circumstances of their love for feelings she would never be able to shake? *Would* she ever be able to trust? Would it ultimately have been any different if she had met Dennis under other circumstances?

And then she would always come back to the fact she put out of her mind over and over and over again. He had broken off the relationship, and she didn't even know why. And what she didn't want to face, deep down, was the thought that he was yet another man she shouldn't have trusted. She had been wrong about him professionally. Had she been right about him personally? She would never know.

All she knew each day as she rose with the sun and went out into the just-warm June breeze was that someday her feelings would pass. Someday she would forget Dennis. And until then it was time to do what he had always said. It was time to get on with her life.

Ten days after Casey arrived, there was a knock at the door. It was midday, the sun was shining brightly, and Casey had just stepped into the cool darkness of the house to make lunch. She wiped her hands on a towel and

279

walked to the door, curious. She had spoken to virtually no one since she had arrived.

When she got to the hallway, she stared. Dennis was standing in the open doorway. He looked wonderful in white pants and a pale yellow short-sleeve shirt. He was tan, though not as deep a shade as she, and oh lord, those brown eyes were as beautiful and clear as ever.

Before she could think, before logic and reason could rule her, before she had a chance to say a word, Dennis swept her into his arms, enveloping her in the warm strength she had missed so deeply. He held her tight against his chest, resting his head against hers, holding her as if he'd never let go, as if he wanted never to let her go.

And then he cupped her face in his hands, and she saw love in his eyes, and sorrow, and pain. In moments his lips were on hers in a tender kiss that grew instantly deep, earthshaking, a kiss that reached the core of her being. When his tongue touched hers, she was reeling with pleasure, steadied only by his strong hands now at her hips, holding her as if in steel.

She heard a cry of deep longing escape from inside her, and then she froze as she realized what was happening. Tearing her mouth from his, she looked up into dark eyes that were now fired with an emotion she was unable to divine. "Dennis, I can't," she said.

He inhaled deeply. "I'm sorry," he said. "I forgot myself. Just seeing you . . ." His voice trailed off, and he looked beyond her for a moment. The closeness of his handsome jaw, his high cheekbones and sandy cheeks made her look away. But she couldn't pull away from the hands that held her so tightly in their grip, not from this man who was a mystery all over again. "Are you alone?" he asked.

"Yes," she said and bit her tongue against further comment, for it was all coming back. He had asked her that once before, and—

"We have to talk," he said, his voice so quiet it was edged with a huskiness she remembered well. "Casey, we have to talk."

She looked at him for a long moment. "How did you find me?" she asked. Her voice sounded flat. But she was trying desperately hard to keep her feelings in check, to keep herself from trembling as her body used to tremble beneath his touch.

"I went to see Pete Winter," he said, following as she turned and led him into the kitchen.

"What?" She whirled to face him.

He nodded, silent.

"But how do you know who Pete Winter is? Then you know—" She stopped as he nodded again, guided her into a chair and sat beside her, covering a hand with his. It was an immensely distracting gesture. "I don't understand," she said.

He sighed, looking into her eyes with infinite regret. "Everyone knows who you are," he said quietly. "*Now,* that is, with all that's happened. But I found out that you were investigating on the set the day after I came back from California. After I asked you to live with me and we fought." His voice was hoarse with emotion. How well she remembered that awful night.

"But how?" she asked. "I still don't understand."

He sighed again, as if reluctant to continue. "You had written the name *Pete,* with a phone number, on the pad by my bed. I—I found it after our fight. I thought you were seeing someone else."

She stared at him, understanding washing over her as he spoke.

"I called the number," he continued. "After all our fights about fidelity, all the times I had asked myself—and asked you—whether you could possibly be seeing anyone else, I had to know. Casey, I was—I can't begin to tell you how I felt: cheated, outraged, angry, hurt. But I didn't know for sure. And I had to know one way or the other."

"Why didn't you ask me?"

He looked at her carefully. "What would you have said?"

Her mouth opened, but no words came out.

"Even if you had said he was an old boss, a friend, whatever, you would have lied, wouldn't you?" He sighed. "Anyway, I didn't ask. I couldn't stand the thought, after what had just happened between us. Maybe I didn't even want to give you the satisfaction." He sighed. "Anyway, I did call, in the morning, from the studio. I didn't know what to think when I heard the words *Pete Winter Investigations.*"

"Then how did you connect it with *me?*"

"Chance, almost. Something made me ask. And the woman who answered the phone was very forthcoming."

Casey closed her eyes. She swore softly, and when she opened her eyes, Dennis's gaze was soft, tender, less pained. "Casey, not a night has gone by in which you haven't come to me in my dreams. Not a day goes by that I don't think of you a hundred times. I realize I made some mistakes. I think we both did." He shook his head. "Over and over again I asked you to trust me. But I was asking you to do something I hadn't yet done myself. I *didn't* trust you. That was why the news that you had deceived me was so hard to take. It was just confirmation that I was right—that a woman can't be trusted. Especially a woman I loved."

"Oh, Dennis." She sighed, filled with happiness over what he was saying, pain over the pain he had suffered. But she couldn't forget her own pain. "Do you know how difficult it was?" she asked quietly, holding his clear dark gaze with hers. "Do you know how difficult it was to be torn, to be unsure of my feelings almost every moment of the day?" She hesitated. "I want you to know I didn't use you, Dennis. At some deep, primal level, when we were making love, I trusted you. That trust never wavered at those times. But at the other times, it was so, so difficult. And when I heard you talk about Celeste St. Jacques, I kept thinking, *Oh, God, if he ever finds out, will he think I'm like her?* I promise you I wasn't."

"I know," he said positively. "I know. I suppose I always expected the worst once I acknowledged that I loved you." He smiled. "Do you remember the night we made love after the bet? Each of us trying to wrest power from the other?"

"I've never forgotten a single time," she murmured.

"Well, I needed things like that—the bet, the distance I sometimes created, little things I did to show myself I didn't need you, that you didn't have any power over me. But darling, I was yours. I think I was yours the moment I met you."

She smiled, loving his words. "What about your—idea that men need other women?" she asked.

"Other men need other women. I need *you*, Casey. I couldn't admit that because I didn't trust you." He paused. "That last evening was the turning point for me. Finding out about Pete Winter was just confirmation of the worst."

"But why? I don't understand. I never understood what happened that night, except that somehow I lost you. We were both so angry."

"I remember why you were angry, and it infuriated me. You were angry because stupid me had asked you to live with me, when what I should have done was . . ." His voice trailed off, and he looked into her eyes with love shining clearly. "It was a rotten offer," he said musingly, shaking his head. "Rotten from your standpoint, a completely cowardly thing to do from mine. Because, Casey, what I really *wanted* to do that night—wanted to but didn't know

283

it—was ask you to marry me," he said softly. "Will you marry me, Casey?"

"Oh, Dennis," she whispered, tears rising from deep inside.

"Say yes," he breathed, his face close to hers, his eyes capturing hers. "Say yes, Casey."

And he rose, drew her up, gathered her into his arms. And when he was holding her tight, so tight she knew deeply and without question that he wanted her forever, she whispered yes with soaring joy.

And he swept her up into his arms as she whispered, "Love me now, Dennis. I've missed you so much."

And he loved her deeply, urgently, bringing them together in a passion greater than any she had ever known. At every moment, with every breath, every kiss, every caress, her whole being knew one thing—that he wanted her forever—and she soared with pleasure, clung with need, cried out with profound and everlasting love for this man she had always loved so much. He seemed possessed by fierce hunger that culminated in an earth-shattering, trembling release, making each for a time unconscious of anything but an overwhelming, endless love.

Afterward, drenched in sweat, unwilling to separate, they kissed again, embraced again, with smiles and tears and gentle sighs of pleasure.

But then as the glow began to ebb, Casey was shadowed by a fear that made her cold outside, hollow and deeply apprehensive inside.

Dennis sensed it immediately and drew her more tightly into his arms. "What's the matter?" he asked. "What's wrong, darling?"

"I'm afraid," she whispered, knowing suddenly what it was. "Dennis, how do I know—how do I know the same thing won't happen with us?"

"What same thing?" he asked.

"I'm sorry," she said, realizing she wasn't being clear.

284

But she was so afraid. She turned and looked into his eyes. "I told you about my marriage. I told you the way I felt so soon afterward, with the man I thought I loved. I didn't—I didn't even want to make love with him," she said haltingly.

He stroked her hair, gazed gently into her eyes. "You were afraid," he said softly. "And that made you withdraw. You were afraid, feeling as if he held all the power, that he could withdraw his love at any minute, and that that would hurt you deeply because you loved him. And so you protected yourself, closing yourself off instead." He paused, then kissed her gently, lovingly on the lips. "Casey, I know because that's what I've done, too. Up until you, I wasn't willing to give of myself that way. I thought I would be hurt, that I would lose. And I was constantly trying to show myself it didn't matter. I had other women, so it didn't matter. And at the first sign of what I saw as betrayal, I would rush to the conclusion I had been right all along. But Casey, with us it's different. I didn't realize it at first. But when you were gone and I was alone, I had so much time to think of what you had done, to analyze what I had thought of as your betrayal." He smiled. "I should have listened to some of my own speeches, the kind I used to give to some of the actors on the set. You were doing a job in the best way you knew how, and I should have known"—he shook his head— "damnit, I should have known you couldn't have done it any differently."

"I'm so sorry," she whispered. "It was such an awful situation. And it was awful for me because I did suspect you, Dennis. You kept moving back into first place, and it was so difficult to unravel one kind of distrust from the other." She frowned. "And by the way, now I can ask you, because there's still one thing I don't understand."

"What's that?" he asked softly.

"One day—one of the first days I was on the set—you

found me kind of lurking in the hallway after you had made a phone call. And that phone call sounded so suspicious, Den. You said, 'How obvious do you want to get?' and it was right after that thing with Melanie had happened. Almost as if you were in league with someone . . ." Her voice trailed off. It was almost silly to ask, but it was the one loose end she had wondered about.

Dennis smiled. "Now I know why you looked so stricken when I found you. You were sheet-white. I remember that call. It was to my agent, and we were talking about a very, very delicate negotiation for a movie I might do next year." His gaze deepened in intensity. "But you know what? Now that I'm with you, darling, so many of the things that seemed so incredibly important and earthshaking just seem—not unimportant, exactly, but like nothing compared to being with you."

"I think I know what you mean," she said lovingly. "Before I came out here I thought I was going to lose my mind because of work. It had never bothered me in quite that way before. I was even thinking of quitting. But it doesn't matter now; not the way I thought."

For a while they just looked into each other's eyes, drinking in the pleasure of finally being together, knowing it was forever, knowing their love ran as deep as the oceans. And then Dennis drew her into a loving kiss, drew her into his loving arms, and whispered, "Don't ever worry, darling, about our love not lasting." He inhaled deeply, his eyes dark with satisfaction. "We came through because we were meant for each other, because that miracle of love, of being together, making paradise anywhere and anytime—once you've found it and you *know* you've found it, you never give it up. I didn't know what we had until I lost it. And neither of us ever had it before, Case, neither of us, until we found each other. Now it's ours to keep, forever, a beautiful gift no one can ever take away. It will carry us along, just as it brought us through that